Elsie and the Raymonds

The Original Elsie Classics

Elsie Dinsmore
Elsie's Holidays at Roselands
Elsie's Girlhood
Elsie's Womanhood
Elsie's Motherhood
Elsie's Children
Elsie's Widowhood
Grandmother Elsie
Elsie's New Relations
Elsie at Nantucket
The Two Elsies
Elsie's Kith and Kin
Elsie's Friends at Woodburn
Christmas with Grandma Elsie
Elsie and the Raymonds
Elsie Yachting with the Raymonds
Elsie's Vacation
Elsie at Viamede
Elsie at Ion
Elsie at the World's Fair
Elsie's Journey on Inland Waters
Elsie at Home
Elsie on the Hudson
Elsie in the South
Elsie's Young Folks
Elsie's Winter Trip
Elsie and Her Loved Ones
Elsie and Her Namesakes

Elsie and the Raymonds

Book Fifteen of
The Original Elsie Classics

Martha Finley

CUMBERLAND HOUSE
NASHVILLE, TENNESSEE

Elsie and the Raymonds
by Martha Finley

Any unique characteristics of this edition:
Copyright © 2000 by Cumberland House Publishing, Inc.

Published by Cumberland House Publishing, Inc.,
431 Harding Industrial Drive, Nashville, Tennessee 37211.

Cover design by Bruce Gore, Gore Studios, Inc.
Photography by Dean Dixon Photography
Hair and Makeup by Calene Rader
Text design by Heather Armstrong

Printed in the United States of America
1 2 3 4 5 6 7 8 — 04 03 02 01 00

CHAPTER FIRST

"Excuse me, Miss, but do you know of any lady who wants a seamstress?" asked a timid, hesitating voice.

Lulu Raymond was the person addressed. She and Max had just alighted from the Woodburn family carriage—having been given permission to do a little shopping together. She had paused upon the pavement for a moment to look after it as it rolled away down the street with her father, who had some business matters to attend to in the city that afternoon. He had appointed a time and place for picking the children up again to carry them home.

Tastefully attired, rosy and bright with health and happiness, Lulu's appearance was in strange contrast to that of the shabbily dressed girl with pale, pinched features that wore an expression of patient suffering who stood by her side.

"Were you speaking to me?" Lulu asked, turning quickly at the sound of the voice and regarding the shrinking figure with pitying eyes.

"Yes, Miss, if you'll excuse the liberty. I thought you looked kind and that maybe your mother might want someone to do plain sewing."

"I hardly think she does, but I'll ask her when I go home," replied Lulu. "Are you the person who wants the work?"

"Yes, Miss. I'd try to give satisfaction. I've been brought up to use my needle and the sewing machine, too. And—and—" in a choking voice, "I need work badly. Mother's sick, and we've only what I can earn to depend on for food and clothes and doctors and medicine and to pay the rent."

"Oh, how dreadful!" cried Lulu, hastily taking out her purse.

"You are very kind, Miss, but I'm not asking for charity," the girl quickly replied, shrinking back, blushing and shamefaced.

"Of course not, you don't look like a beggar," returned Lulu with warmth. "But I'd be glad to help you in some suitable way. Where do you live?"

At this instant Max, whose attention had been drawn for a moment to some article in the show window of a store near at hand, joined his sister, and with her listened to the girl's reply.

"Just down the alley yonder, number five," she said. "It's but a poor place we have, a little bare attic room, but—but we try to be content with it because it's the best we can do."

"What does she want?" Max asked in an aside.

"Sewing. I'm going to ask Mamma Vi and Grandma Elsie if they can find some for her. But we'll have to know where she can be found. Shall we go with her to her home?"

"No, papa would not approve, I think. But I'll write down the address, and I'm sure papa will see that they're relieved, if they need help."

Turning to the girl again as he took notebook and pencil from his pocket, "What is the name of the alley?" he asked.

"Rose," she answered, adding with a melancholy smile. "Though there's nothing rosy about it except the name. It's narrow and dirty, and the people are poor, many of them beggars, drunken, and quarrelsome."

"How dreadful to have to live in such a place!" exclaimed Lulu, looking compassionately at the speaker.

"Rose Alley," murmured Max, jotting it down in his book. "Just out of State Street. What number?"

"Number five, sir, between Fourth and Fifth."

"Oh, yes, I'll put that down, too, and I'm sure the place can be found without any difficulty. But what is your name? We will need to know whom to inquire for."

"Susan Allen, sir."

The girl was turning away, but Lulu stopped her.

"Wait a moment. You said your mother was sick, and I'd like to send her something good to eat. I dare say she needs delicacies to tempt her appetite. Come with me to that fruit stand on the corner," hurrying toward it as she spoke, the girl following at a distance.

"That was a good and kind thought, Lu," Max remarked, stepping close to his sister's side as she paused before the fruit stand, eagerly scanning its tempting display of fruits and confections.

"You don't doubt papa's approval of this?" she returned, giving him an arch look and smile.

"No, not a bit of it. He always likes to see us generous and ready to relieve distress. I must have a share in the good work."

"Then they'll have all the more, for I shan't give any less because you're going to give, too. Oh, what delicious looking strawberries!"

"And every bit as good as they look, Miss," said the keeper of the stand.

"What's the price?"

"Dollar a box, Miss. They always come high the first o' the season, you know. They were a dollar ten only yesterday."

"Do you think your sick mother would enjoy them?" Lulu asked, turning to Susan, who was looking aghast at the price named.

"Oh, yes, indeed, Miss, but—but it's too much for you to give. We have hardly so much as that to spend on a week's victuals."

"Then I'm sure you ought to have a few luxuries for once," said Lulu. "I'll take a box for her," addressing the man and taking out her purse as she spoke.

"A dozen of those oranges, too, a pound of your nicest crackers, and one pound of sugar to eat with the berries," said Max, producing his wallet.

They saw the articles put up, paid for them, put them into Susan's hands, and hurried on their way, followed by her grateful looks.

In trembling, tearful tones she had tried to thank them, but they would not stay to listen.

"How glad she was," said Lulu. "And no wonder, for she looked half-starved. And, oh, Max, just think, if we hadn't a father to take care of and provide for us we might be as poor and distressed as she is!"

"That's so," returned Max. "We've hardly a thing worth having that hasn't come to us through my father."

"My father, sir," asserted Lulu, giving him a laughing glance.

"Yes, our father, but he was mine before he was yours," laughed her brother.

"Well, here we are at Blake's, where you have an errand — at least, so you said, I think."

They passed into the store, finding so many customers there that all the clerks were engaged. While waiting till someone could attend to their wants, they amused themselves in scrutinizing the contents of shelves, counters, and showcases. Some picture frames, brackets, and other articles of carved wood attracted their attention.

"Some of those are quite pretty, Max," Lulu remarked in an undertone. "But I think you have made prettier ones."

"So have you, and see," pointing to the prices attached, "they pay quite well for them. No, I'm not sure of that, but they ask good prices from their customers. Perhaps we could make a tolerable support at the business, if we had to take care of ourselves," he added in a half-jesting tone.

"Earn enough to buy bread and butter, maybe, but not half the good things papa buys for all of us," said Lulu.

"Has anyone waited upon the two of you?" asked the proprietor of the store, drawing near.

"No, sir, they all seem to be busy," answered Lulu politely.

"Yes, what can I show you? Some of this carved work? We have sold a good deal of it, and I'm sorry to say that the young lady who supplied it has decided to give up the business — and go into matrimony," he added with a laugh.

A thought seemed to strike Lulu, and she asked, coloring slightly as she spoke, "Does it pay well?"

The merchant named the prices he had given for several of the articles and asked in his turn if she knew of anyone who would like to earn money in that way.

"I—I'm not quite sure," she answered. "I know a boy, and a girl, too, who are fond of doing such work, and I think can do even a little better than this, but—"

"You doubt if they would care to make a business of it, eh?" he said inquiringly, as she paused, leaving her sentence unfinished.

"Yes, sir. I'm not sure they would want to, or that their parents would be willing to have them do so. If you please, I should like to look at materials for fancy work."

"Yes, Miss. This way, if you please. We have them in great variety and of the best quality."

Captain Raymond expected a friend on an incoming train and had directed the children to be at the depot a few minutes before it was due. Punctuality was one of the minor virtues he insisted upon, and while interested in their shopping, they were not forgetful of the necessity for keeping their appointment with him. Their watches were consulted frequently and ample time allowed for their walk from the last store visited to the depot.

"We are here first. Our carriage isn't in sight yet," remarked Lulu with satisfaction, as they reached the outer door of the building.

"Yes," said Max, "but papa will be along presently for it wants but ten minutes of the time when the train is due."

"And he's never a minute late," added Lulu.

Max led the way to the ladies' room, seated his sister comfortably in an armchair and asked if there was anything he could get or do for her—treating her with as much gallantry as if she had been the sister of somebody else.

"Thank you, Maxie. I'm really comfortable and in want of nothing," she replied. "I'll be glad if that gentleman doesn't come," she went on. "It's so much nicer to have papa all to ourselves driving home."

"Yes, and afterward, too. But, Lu, we mustn't be selfish, and perhaps he would be disappointed if his friend shouldn't come."

"Oh, I hadn't thought of that! And if papa would rather have him come, I hope he will."

"Of course you do. Ah, here comes papa now," as a tall, remarkably fine looking man of decidedly military bearing entered the room and came smiling toward them.

"Good, punctual children," he said. "I hope you have been enjoying yourselves since we parted?"

"Oh, yes, papa," they answered, speaking both at once. "We did all our errands and are ready to go home."

"The train is just due," he said, consulting his watch. "Ah, here it comes," as its rush and roar smote upon their ears.

Lulu sprang up hastily.

"Wait a little, daughter," the captain said, laying a gently detaining hand on her shoulder. "We need not be in haste as we are not going on the train."

"Everybody else seems to be hurrying out, papa," she said.

"Yes, they are probably passengers. Ah, the train has arrived and come to a standstill, so we will go now. Max, you may help your sister into the carriage, while I look about for our expected guest."

The captain scanned narrowly the living stream pouring from the cars, but without finding him of whom he was in quest. He turned away in some disappointment and was about to step into his carriage when a not unfamiliar voice hailed him.

"Good evening, Captain Raymond. Will you aid a fellow creature in distress? It seems that by some mistake my carriage has failed to meet me, though I thought they understood that I would return home by this train. If you will give me a lift as far as your own gate I can easily walk the rest of the way to Brairwood."

"It will afford me pleasure to do so, Mr. Clark, or to take you quite to Briarwood," responded the captain heartily. "We have abundance of room. Step in and I will follow."

This unexpected addition to their party gave Lulu some slight feeling of vexation and disappointment, but her father's proud look and smile as he said, "My son Max and daughter Lulu, Mr. Clark," and the affectionate manner in which, on taking his seat at her side, he put his arm about her waist and drew her close to him, went far to restore her to her wonted good humor.

Mr. Clark said, "How do you do, my dears?" then engaged the captain in conversation, taking no further notice of the children.

But they were intelligent, well-instructed, and when the talk presently turned upon one of the political questions of the day they were interested, for their father had taken pains to give them no little information on that and kindred topics. He did not encourage their reading of the daily secular papers — indeed, forbade it, because he would not have their pure minds sullied by the sickening details of crime or love of the horrible cultivated by minute descriptions of its punishment in the execution of murderers. But he examined the paper himself and culled from it such articles, to be read aloud to the family, as he deemed suitable and instructive or entertaining. Or he would relate incidents and give instruction and explanations in his own words, which the children generally preferred to the reading.

The gentlemen were deep in the midst of their conversation when the great gates leading into the avenue at Woodburn were almost reached, and Mr. Clark caught sight of his own carriage approaching from the opposite direction.

He called and beckoned to his coachman, and with a hasty good-bye and hearty thanks to Captain Raymond, transferred himself to his own conveyance, which at once faced about and whirled away toward Briarwood, while the Woodburn family carriage turned into the avenue and drove up to the house.

Violet and the three children were on the veranda, waiting for its coming, and ready with a joyful welcome to its occupants.

"Papa! Papa!" shouted little Elsie, as they alighted. "Max and Lulu, too! Oh, I'se so glad you all tum back adain!"

"Are you, papa's sweet dear?" returned the captain, taking her in his arms with a tender caress.

Then he kissed his wife and the lovely babe cooing in her arms. Reaching out his chubby ones to be taken by his father, he seemed evidently as much rejoiced as Elsie at his return.

"In a moment, Ned," laughed the captain, stooping to give a hug and kiss to Gracie waiting at his side.

Then taking possession of an easy chair with a pleasant, "Thank you, my dears," to Max and Lulu, who had hastened to draw it forward for him, he took a baby on each knee, while the three older children clustered about him, and Violet, sitting near, watched with laughing eyes the merry scene that followed.

"Gracie and Elsie may search papa's pockets now and see what they can find," said the captain.

Promptly and with eager delight they availed themselves of the permission.

Gracie drew forth a small, gilt-edged, handsomely bound volume.

"That is for your mamma," her father said. "You may hand it to her, and perhaps, if you look farther, you may find something for yourself."

Violet received the gift with a pleased smile and a hearty, "Thank you, Gracie. Thank you, my dear. I shall be sure to prize it for the sake of the giver, whatever the contents may be."

But the words were half drowned in Elsie's shouts of delight over a pretty toy and a tiny box of bonbons.

"Hand the candy 'round, dear, to mamma first," her father said.

"May Elsie eat some, too, papa?" she asked coaxingly as she got down from his knee to obey his order.

"Yes, a little tonight and some more tomorrow."

Gracie had dived into another pocket. "Oh! Is this for me, papa?" she asked, drawing out a small paper parcel.

"Open it and see," was his smiling rejoinder.

With eager fingers she untied the string and opened the paper.

"Three lovely silver fruit knives!" she exclaimed. "Names on 'em, too. Lu, this is yours, for it has your name on it. And this is mine, and the other Maxie's," handing them to the owners as she spoke. "Thank you, papa, oh, thank you very much for mine!" holding up her face for a kiss.

Bestowing it very heartily, "You are all very welcome, my darlings," he said, for Max and Lulu were saying thank you, too.

And now they too hastened to display their purchases of the afternoon and present some little gifts to Gracie and Elsie.

These were received with thanks and many expressions of pleasure, and Lulu was in the midst of an animated account of her shopping experiences when her father, glancing at his watch, reminded her that she would have barely time to make herself neat for the tea table if she repaired to her room at once.

"Max and I, too, must pay some attention to freshening up," he added, giving the babe to his nurse who had just appeared upon the scene.

"Now, papa, let's run a race and see who'll be done first," proposed Lulu laughingly, as she went skipping and dancing along the hall just ahead of him.

"Very well, and I'll give you a dollar if you are first and there are no signs of haste or negligence in your appearance."

"And is the offer open to me too, papa?" asked Max, coming up behind.

"Yes, I shall not be partial," answered the captain, suddenly lifting Lulu off her feet and starting up the stairs with her in his arms.

"Oh, papa, you'll tire yourself all out!" she exclaimed with a merry laugh. "I'm so big and heavy now."

"Not a bit," he said. "I'm so big and strong, you see. There, now for our race," as he set her down in the upper hall.

"It's so nice to have such a big, strong papa!" she said, lifting a flushed, happy face to his and reaching up to give him a hug and kiss.

"I'm glad my little daughter thinks so," he returned, smiling down on her and laying his hand tenderly on her head for an instant.

The captain and Lulu met in the hall just as the tea bell rang, and at the same instant, Max came down the stairs from the third story almost at a bound.

A merry peal of laughter from all three and then the captain said, "So nobody is first. We shall all reach the tea room together."

"And you won't have any dollar to pay, papa," said Lulu, her face bright and no disappointment in her tone. She was clinging to her father's hand as they went down the stairs, Max close behind them.

"But I don't care to save it," was the reply. "So what shall be done with it? Suppose I divide it between you and Max?"

"And yourself, papa," added Max laughingly.

His father smiled. "Perhaps a better plan would be to put it into the missionary box," he said.

"Oh, yes, sir!" exclaimed both children. "That would be the best thing that could be done with it."

They had taken their seats at the table and all were quiet while the captain asked a blessing on their food.

CHAPTER SECOND

"I HAVE SOMETHING to tell you, my dear," Violet began, giving her husband a bright smile from behind the coffee urn as she filled his cup.

"Ah?" he said, returning the smile. "I am all attention. No doubt it is something worth hearing."

"Perhaps you will remember that mamma's fiftieth birthday will come early next month," Violet resumed.

"No, not the fiftieth surely!" exclaimed the captain. "Really I think that, judging from her looks alone, no one would take her to be over forty."

"So we all think, and everybody says she has a remarkably young face. But it will be her fiftieth birthday, and we, her children, want to do her unusual honor. Of course, as you know, my dear, we always remember the day, and each of us has some little gift for her, but this, being her semi-centennial, we think should be observed in some special manner."

"I agree with you, and what do you propose doing in order to celebrate it appropriately?"

"We have not fully decided that question, and we would be glad of suggestions and advice from you, if you will kindly give them."

"I am sensible of the honor you do me, but must take a little time to reflect," was his pleasant rejoinder.

"Papa, how old are you?" asked Gracie with sudden animation, as if the question had just occurred to her.

"About twenty-four years older than Max," replied the captain, turning upon is firstborn a look of fatherly pride and affection.

"And I'm almost fifteen," added Max.

"That makes papa thirty-nine," remarked Lulu. "You'll be forty next birthday, won't you, papa?"

"Yes, daughter."

"Then Grandma Elsie is only about ten years older than you, not nearly enough older to be your real mother."

"Quite true," he said with a humorous look. "But I feel it not at all unpleasant to have so young and beautiful a mother—a lady so lovely in character, as well as in form and feature, that I should greatly rejoice to know that my daughters will grow up to resemble her in all respects."

"I'd like to be exactly like her, except—" But there Gracie paused, leaving her sentence unfinished.

"Except in being fifty years old?" her father asked, regarding her with laughing eyes.

"Yes, sir, I'd rather be a little girl for a good while yet—your little girl, papa, who can sit on your knee whenever she wants to."

"That's right," he said heartily. "I am by no means ready to part with my little Gracie yet."

"I feel just as Gracie does about it," said Lulu. "I want to be a little girl for a while longer, then a young lady. But when I get to be fifty years old, I'd like to be as nearly like Grandma Elsie as possible."

"I hope not to be," remarked Max facetiously. "But I know a gentleman I would like to resemble so much when I am forty, that people would say to me, 'He's just a chip of the old block,'" and with the last words the lad turned a proud, admiring, and affectionate look upon his father.

The captain's countenance expressed pleasure, and Violet, looking pleased also, said, "I hope you will have your wish, Max, and I think there is every prospect of it."

"What plans are thought of for the coming celebration, dear?" asked the captain.

"We talked of a garden or lawn party, if the weather is fine — all the relatives to be invited, and perhaps a few intimate friends beside. Certainly our minister and his wife."

"I don't think I could suggest anything better," the captain said.

"But you may be able to give some useful hints in regard to plans for the entertainment of the guests and suitable gifts for mamma."

"Possibly. You must help me decide upon my gift."

"I shall be only too glad," she answered with a bright, pleased look.

"We children may give something nice to Grandma Elsie, too, mayn't we, papa?" they asked, all three speaking at once.

"Most assuredly," he replied. "The very nicest thing, or things, you can think of that will come within the limits of your financial ability."

"Papa," remarked Gracie doubtfully, "I don't believe I know exactly what that means."

"You understand the meaning of ability, surely?" returned her father.

"Yes, sir, but that other word — fi — finan —"

"Financial? As I used it then, it means the amount of money you children may have at your disposal at the time of making your purchases."

"Oh, I'm glad I have some money saved up!" she remarked with satisfaction.

"How much?" he asked.

"A good deal, papa, about five dollars, I think."

"Ah, so much as that? Quite a fortune," he said with a look of amusement.

"I suppose, wife, your mother is to be consulted in regard to the manner of the proposed celebration—about the party, the guests to be invited, and so forth?"

"Oh, yes, sir—about everything but the gifts she is to receive."

❄ ❄ ❄ ❄ ❄

The babies had had their evening romp with papa and been carried off to the nursery with Gracie going along at Elsie's urgent request. She was all the more willing because she had heard her father say he must write a letter immediately, that it might be in time to go in the next mail, so she knew that for the present she and Max and Lulu must do without their usual bit of chat with him.

Lulu was particularly desirous for an opportunity for a talk with him, for she had a scheme in her head about which she wished to ask his advice and permission. She would not have minded broaching the subject before Max and Gracie, but thought it would be still more enjoyable to talk it over with papa alone.

"I'll not go far away," she said to herself. "And when papa has finished his writing maybe I'll get a chance to talk a little with him before anybody else comes."

She took a book and seated herself on the veranda, but she did not read. The captain, stepping to the door presently, saw her sitting with the book lying unopened in her lap, her attitude and expression denoting profound thought. She did not seem aware even of his approach as he drew near her side, but she started and looked up in surprise as he laid his hand gently on her head, saying, "A penny for my little girl's thoughts! She looks as if she had the affairs of the nation on her shoulders."

"I'm sure they're not worth a penny, papa, but you are welcome to them for nothing," she returned laughingly. "If you have time to let me talk to you."

She rose as she spoke, and taking the chair, he drew her to his knee.

"Plenty of time now that that my letter has been dispatched," he said. "But are you to do all the talking?"

"Oh, no, indeed, papa. I hope you'll do most of it, but I suppose I must begin by telling you my thoughts on several subjects."

"Yes."

"I was thinking about a poor girl that spoke to me in the street today and asked for sewing to do to earn money to support herself and her sick mother.

"I told her I would try to get some work for her. Afterward Max and I went into a store where we saw brackets and picture frames and other things carved out of wood as we do it, only they were not so pretty as some we have made—at least we both thought so. We wondered how much was paid for such work. The price they were asking for them was on them, and Max thought it was a good one. We were talking together about it when the merchant came up and asked if we wanted to buy any of those things.

"He said he had sold a good many and was sorry the lady who had carved them for him was going to give up doing it. I asked if it paid well, and he told me how much he gave. Then he asked if I knew anybody who would like to earn money in that way."

"And what answer did you make to that?"

"I said I wasn't sure and that I knew a boy and a girl who were fond of that kind of work, and I thought could do it a little better than those were done, but I didn't know whether they would want to do it for pay, or whether their parents would be willing to let them."

"And the boy and girl you referred to were Max and yourself?"

"Yes, sir. Would you let us do it if we wanted to?"

"That would depend upon circumstances. It is a question to be considered."

"Well, papa, this is what I was thinking of when you spoke to me. You know I spend some of my spare time sewing for the poor, and you know that I don't like to sew—I mean I don't enjoy doing it—and I do enjoy carving. That poor girl wants sewing to do, because she needs to earn her living, and that's her way of doing it. I was trying to decide whether or not it would be right for me to give her the sewing to do and pay her for doing it with money I earn by carving? Would it be right, papa? And will you let me do it?"

"I say yes to both questions. I think it a good idea, for you will be doing good in two ways—helping the poor to whom the garments go, and the poor girl who wants employment—and that without indulging yourself in laziness."

"Oh, I am so glad you approve, papa!" Lulu exclaimed in delight. "I was afraid you would not. I was afraid that perhaps I ought to do the sewing myself if only because I dislike it so."

"No, my child, there is nothing praiseworthy in doing a thing merely because it is unpleasant to us. If another is needing help which we can give in that way and no other, duty bids us to perform the unpleasant task, but in this case it seems you can do more good by allowing the young sewing-girl to act as your substitute, helping her at the same time that you help those to whom the garments will go.

"But the sewing you can give her will not really be enough to keep even one seamstress busy."

"Oh, no, sir. But I am going to tell Mamma Vi and Grandma Elsie about her, and I think they will find her work and recommend her to the other ladies who want sewing done, if they find that she does it well."

"Did you learn her name and where she lives?"

"Yes, sir. And I wanted to go and see the place, but Max said you would not approve, so I didn't go."

"Max was quite right. You must never venture into strange places about the city without my knowledge and consent, unless with Grandma Elsie or some other equally wise and trustworthy person."

"I will not, dear papa," she answered, smiling lovingly into his eyes. "I do hope I shall never again disobey you in anything."

"I hope not, indeed," he said, smoothing her hair caressingly. "So far as I know, you have been good and obedient for the last six months or more."

Just then Violet and Gracie joined them, followed almost immediately by Max, and as he stepped from the doorway the Ion family carriage was seen coming up the drive.

It brought Violet's grandparents, mother, and young brother and sister—Rosie and Walter. They spent the evening. The proposed birthday celebration was under discussion for some time, several questions in regard to it were settled, and then Lulu found an opportunity to tell of Susan Allen and her needs.

Grandma Elsie, always ready for every good work, said, "If you will accompany me, Captain, I will hunt them up tomorrow and inquire into their needs, should nothing unforeseen happen to prevent."

"I shall be at your service, mother, then, or at any other time," returned the captain gallantly. "And we will take Lulu with us, if you have no objection," he added, as he caught an entreating look from her.

"Not the slightest," replied Mrs. Travilla, smiling kindly upon the little girl.

"Oh, thank you, Grandma Elsie! Thank you, papa. I should like to go very much indeed!" exclaimed Lulu joyously.

ऊँ ऊँ ऊँ ऊँ ऊँ

While Lulu had talked with Susan Allen in the street that afternoon, the girl's mother lay on a bed of straw in the small attic room they called home—a very forlorn specimen of home it was, though everything in and about it was scrupulously neat and clean. The floor was bare, save a strip of carpet beside the bed. There were three unpainted wooden chairs, a little table to match, and a tiny stove. Their few changes of raiment hung on hooks along the wall back of the bed, and a few cheap dishes and cooking utensils were ranged in an orderly manner on some shelves in one corner.

The one window was shaded by a paper blind and short white curtain, both bearing evidence of careful mending, as did the nightdress worn by the invalid, the sheets, and pillowcases of her bed.

She was certainly not an old woman. Susan was but sixteen, and her mother, who had married very young, little more than twice that age. But toil and privation had broken her health and aged her before her time, so that she looked full forty. There were perceptible lines in her forehead, and the dark hair was streaked with gray. Yet it was a pleasant face to look upon—so full of sweet patience and resignation.

A well-worn Bible lay beside her, and one hand rested upon the open page. But her eyes were closed and tears trickled down her wasted cheek, while her lips moved as if in prayer.

One standing very near might have heard the low, murmured words, but they reached only the ear of Him who has said, "Call upon Me in the day of trouble; I will deliver thee and thou shalt glorify Me."

It was that promise she was pleading.

"Lord," her pale lips whispered, "I believe Thy word and obey Thy kind command: it is the day of trouble with me and my beloved child. We are in sore straits; the last cent is gone, the last crust eaten. We have neither barn nor storehouses, yet I know Thou wilt feed us as Thou dost the sparrows, for Thou hast said, 'Your heavenly Father knoweth that ye have need of all these things.' Lord, increase my faith and let me never for one moment doubt Thy word—Thy promise to deliver those who call upon Thee in the day of trouble, and never to leave or forsake any who put their trust in Thee. Oh, blessed be Thy holy name, for all the great and precious promises Thou hast given Thy people, and upon which Thou hast taught me to lean in every time of trouble!"

She was still pouring out her soul in prayer and praise when Susan's light step came up the stairs. The door was hastily thrown open, and she entered with flushed, beaming face, and arms full of bundles, half-breathless with excitement and exertion.

"Mother, dear mother!" she cried, as she hastened to deposit her burdens on the table. "I know you have been praying for help, and God has sent it. See here! The very luxury I have been longing to get you, but without the least hope of being able to do so—great, lovely, luscious strawberries!" she said, gently pouring them from the paper bag in which she had carried them onto a plate. "I'll put some of the finest on a saucer for you. Here is sugar for them, too, and delicate crackers to eat with them. And here are oranges—the finest in the market! Oh, mother, eat and grow strong!" she added, tears springing to her eyes, as she put a saucer of berries into her mother's hand and laid a fine orange by her side. "I won't keep you waiting till I can stem the berries, but just give you some sugar on another saucer to dip them into. Oh, if I only had some of the rich cream for you that we used to have before we left the farm!"

"Oh, child, our Father has sent us so much, so much. Don't let us fret after anything more!" cried the mother at length, recovering the power of speech, of which surprise and joy had robbed her ever since her daughter's entrance so richly laden.

"No, mother, no indeed! Only I should love to give you every comfort and luxury to make you well. You are so thin and weak! There, do lie back on your pillows and let me feed you. Isn't that delicious?" putting a berry into her mouth.

"Oh, very, very! But let me thank God, and then do you eat with me."

They were very hungry, having scarcely tasted food that day, but when the edge of their appetite had been taken off, Mrs. Allen remarked with an inquiring look at her daughter, "But you haven't told me yet where you got all these good things."

"No, mother, but I'll do it now. You know I went out in search of work. I can't beg, but I am willing to ask for employment. I asked at some private houses and two or three stores, but no one seemed to care to risk trying me.

"Then I saw a carriage—a very handsome one it was with matched horses—stop at a street crossing, and a boy and girl stepped out on the pavement. A tall, fine-looking gentleman handed the little girl out, then stepped back into the carriage and it drove off.

"You can't think how pretty and beautifully dressed the little girl was. She had bright, dark eyes, rosy cheeks, and a smiling mouth, and as the gentleman set her down, they gave each other such a loving look! I felt sure she had a kind heart, so I stepped up to her, as she stood looking after the carriage as it drove away down the street. So I asked her if she knew of anybody wanting a seamstress.

"She turned around quickly and answered in a very pleasant tone. She promised to tell her mother about me when she went home and see if she could get me work to do. She opened her purse—such a lovely one with gold clasps—as if she meant to give me some money, and I felt my face grow hot at being taken for a beggar. I said it wasn't charity I was asking for, but work.

"Then she said in the kindest tone, 'Of course not; you don't look like a beggar. But I'd be glad to help you in some suitable way,' and then she asked where I lived.

"While I was telling her the boy came up and stood beside her listening. He asked me questions, too, and took out a notebook and wrote down my name and address. He was as nice and kind-looking as his sister—as I suppose she is, for they resemble each other strongly—the gentleman, too, that helped them out of the carriage. I think he must be their father.

"They called each other Max and Lu and talked between themselves about what would please or displease papa.

"I had told her that you were sick, and we'd nothing to depend on but what I could earn, and as I was turning to go after her brother had taken down my address and promised that somebody would hunt us up soon, she told me to wait a moment and go with her to a fruit stand. She wanted to get something nice for my sick mother to eat.

"And there they bought all these things—she, the berries at a dollar a box, mother! Only think of it! And he bought the oranges and crackers and sugar.

"Oh, I remember I saw her slip something into the bag with the oranges. I wonder what it was. I must look!" she exclaimed, turning hastily to the table where she had deposited the bag.

She took the oranges out one by one till the bag was empty. Then catching sight of something shining in the bottom, she made a dive for it and drew it out with a little cry of joy.

"Oh, it's half a dollar! Now, mother, you shall have some tea and a bit of broiled steak or a lamb chop. I'll run out to the nearest provision store now and get them."

She began putting on her hat as she spoke.

"Child, you must buy for yourself, too," her mother said with tears shining in her eyes.

"Oh, no, mother! I shall do quite nicely without meat, but you are so weak you must have it to strengthen you."

She stepped to the side of the bed again, bent over her mother, and kissed her tenderly.

"Dear child, I cannot enjoy it unless you share it with me. You need nourishing food quite as much as I," returned the mother, gazing fondly into the eyes looking so lovingly into hers. "The Lord has sent us money enough to buy what we need for today, and we will trust Him for tomorrow. A text—a precious promise—has been running in my mind ever since you came in laden with so many good things. 'Before they call I will answer, and while they are yet speaking I will hear.' I had been asking Him very earnestly to send us help in our sore extremity, and while I was yet speaking it came.

"Oh, daughter, let us ever stay our hearts on Him, never for a moment doubting His loving kindness and faithfulness to His promises, no matter how dark and threatening the cloud may be."

"I'll try, mother. Ah, I wish I had your faith. Now I must go, but I'll be back again in five or ten minutes. But I'll put some more berries in your saucer, first, and I don't want to find a single one in it when I come back," she added with playful merriment. "Aren't they making you feel a little better already, you dear, patient mother?"

"Yes, dear, they are very refreshing. But you are giving me more than my fair share."

"No, indeed, mamma, they were all given to you, and I have eaten a good many. I want you to finish the rest, for I do hope they will do more for you than any medicine could. Now, I'm off. Don't be lonesome while I'm gone," and she hurried away with a light, free step, tears of joy and thankfulness shining in her eyes.

Not many minutes had passed ere she returned with the materials for what was to them a feast indeed.

"See, mother," she said, displaying her purchases. "See how extravagant I have been! There are two nice lamb chops, two fresh eggs, a loaf of bread, half a dozen potatoes, a quarter of a pound of tea, and five cents' worth of butter. Oh, but we shall have a feast! I'll broil the chops, bake the potatoes, toast a few slices of the bread, and make you a cup of tea. I'd have bought a few cents' worth of milk, but I remembered that you like your tea quite as well without."

"But you don't drink tea, dear, and should have bought some milk for yourself."

"No, no, mother. I'm very fond of cold water and fortunately a very good article in that line can be had for the going after, no farther than to the hydrant in front of the street door," she answered with a merry look and smile.

As she talked she was moving about with light, quick step between table and stove, performing her tasks with the ease and dexterity of a practiced hand, and without noise or bustle, her mother's eyes following her with loving glances.

"You are very bright and cheery tonight, dear child," she said.

"Yes, mother, I haven't been in such spirits for weeks. I do believe better days are dawning for us, mother dear, and all in answer to your prayers."

She paused at the bedside to bend lovingly over the dear parent and touch her lips to the pale cheek.

"Yes, my Susie, and yours, too. The Bible tells us that God is the hearer and answerer of prayer, and many times I have proved it in my own experience. But He is no respecter of persons, but ready to hear and help any, however humble and unworthy, who come in the name of Jesus and pleading His merits."

"Yes, mother, I know it. I have been praying for help, and I'm sure He sent it. And while I feel grateful to that dear little girl and boy, I'm thanking God with all my heart for these good things, for they were only His messengers, and the gifts were more from Him than from them even—the dear, kind children!"

CHAPTER THIRD

THE SUN WAS HALF an hour high when Susan Allen opened her eyes the next morning.

Her mother greeted her with a smile and a cheery, "Good morning, my child. You have slept sweetly ever since I have been awake to watch you. And I have had the best night's rest I have known for weeks."

"Oh, I am so glad to hear that, mother!" Susan exclaimed, raising herself on her elbow to give the invalid a searching look, "And you feel better and stronger, don't you?"

"Yes, indeed, almost as if I could sit up and sew a little, if we had any work on hand."

"Oh, no, I should not think of letting you do that yet!" the girl answered. "Not if we had any quantity, and as we have none at all, you can surely lie still quite contentedly. I'll get up now and have breakfast ready in a few minutes.

"It is only to make a few slices of toast, boil the eggs, and draw the tea. Then I'll tidy the room and you and myself, and we'll be all ready to receive our hoped-for visitors."

"Yes, we need not expect them for two or three hours, at the very earliest," Mrs. Allen said in reply. "Even if they lived in town they wouldn't be likely to come before the middle of the forenoon, and probably their home is in the country, as you saw them getting out of a carriage."

Events proved her conjectures correct. It was near the middle of the afternoon when in answer to a rap on the door Susan answered it to find a lady and gentleman there, accompanied by her little girl acquaintance of the day before.

"Oh, yes, papa, it's the right place!" exclaimed Lulu in a very pleased tone. "Susan, I've brought my grandma and father to see you."

"You are all very kind to come," said Susan, blushing vividly. "Will you please walk in and take some seats?"

She made haste to bring forward the chairs as she spoke, but with a word of thanks, Mrs. Travilla and the captain turned toward the invalid, asking, "Is this the sick mother Lulu has been telling about?"

"Yes, ma'am. Yes, sir," said Susan, Mrs. Allen adding with a grateful look from them to Lulu, "But better already for the kind gifts of the little girl and boy. I thank them from the bottom of my heart. I am sure God sent them to our relief in answer to prayer. But, dear lady, won't you be seated? And you, too, sir?" addressing the captain. "It is extremely kind of you to call on us—strangers and living in this poor and unpleasant locality."

"It is nothing—it is a privilege, if in so doing we bring succor to one of God's dear children," Grandma Elsie replied, taking the wasted hand in hers and seating herself close by the bedside. "How glad I am to learn that you are one of His. I had heard only that you were ill and in want."

"And you, too, are His, dear lady? Ah, one look into your face would tell us that."

"It is the joy of my heart to be numbered among His followers, and to own Him as my Lord and Master," returned Mrs. Travilla, the light of joy and love shining in her eyes.

"As it is mine," said the captain. "We belong to one family, we own one Lord and King, and it is His command that we love one another and that we do good to all men as we have opportunity, 'especially to them who are of the household of faith!'"

A conversation followed, in which, by questions put with delicacy and kindness, Grandma Elsie and her son-in-law contrived to draw from Mrs. Allen the story of the trials and struggles with poverty and privation which had reduced her to her present state of feebleness and distress.

Her husband had been an intelligent, industrious farmer, and working and saving together, they were looking forward with hope to getting their land clear of encumbrance and finding themselves in comfortable circumstances by the time they should reach middle life. But sickness entered the house, child after child was taken away, till Susan was the only one left. Then, Mr. Allen sickened and died, and the foreclosure of a mortgage robbed the widow and her daughter of their home.

They came to the city seeking employment by which to earn their daily bread, but found it scarce and ill paid. They had been growing poorer and poorer, till, but for the precious promises of God's Word, they would have been in utter despair.

Her listeners seemed deeply interested, tears rolled down Grandma Elsie and Lulu's cheeks more than once during the course of the narrative, and Captain Raymond was evidently deeply moved.

It was he who broke the momentary silence that fell upon the little company at the conclusion of the tale.

"This close, filthy alley is no place for one brought up in the pure air of the country. I have not the least doubt that the tainted air you breathe here is largely responsible for your feeble condition. We must get you out of it as speedily as possible. I own a little cottage on the outskirts of Union—a village some two or three miles from us. It is at present without a tenant, and you and your daughter may take possession today if you wish and feel strong enough for the necessary exertion."

"Oh, sir, how kind, how wonderfully kind you are!" exclaimed Mrs. Allen, as soon as astonishment would let her speak, tears of joy and thankfulness coursing freely down her cheeks. "Country air is what I have been longing for more than words can express.

"But you are far too generous in offering us a whole house. One room will hold us and our few belongings."

"But will not hold all that we hope to see in your possession before very long," he replied with a benevolent smile. "Your daughter—and you also when you are well enough to desire it—shall be provided with an abundance of employment, at remunerative prices, and so will soon be able to gather about you many more comforts than I see here," sending a sweeping glance about the room.

"And it shall be my care, my great pleasure, to anticipate somewhat the time when you will be able to provide such things for yourselves," Mrs. Travilla said, rising to go, taking the poor woman's hand in hers and holding it for a moment in a kindly pressure. "You must be made as comfortable as possible without delay."

Mrs. Allen tried to speak her thanks but was too much overcome by emotion.

"I shall send a conveyance for you and your goods day after tomorrow," the captain said, as he also rose to take his departure. "And I trust you will be well enough to bear the short journey. But, if you are not, you must not hesitate to say so, and the opportunity shall be given you again, whenever you send me word that you are ready."

"We brought you some work, Susan," Lulu said, giving her hand to the girl in parting. "It is down in the carriage."

"And shall be sent up at once," added the captain.

"Oh, thank you, sir!" returned the girl. "But—" looking from Lulu to Mrs. Travilla, "Will I not need some instruction to how you want it done?"

"I think not," said Mrs. Travilla. "The garments are all cut and basted, and written directions given with them. If you want more work when they are done, you have only to ask for it. But do not over-work yourself in the effort to accomplish more than your strength is equal to."

With kindly good-byes the visitors went, refusing to allow Susan to accompany them to the outer door of the house, saying that doubtless she had to climb these steep flights of stairs far too often for her good.

In a few minutes a rap called Susan to the door again, to find there a large covered basket. No one was with it, but she heard the retreating footsteps of its bearer hurrying down the stairs.

She lifted it inside and closed the door, then began with eager, trembling hands to unpack it and examine the contents.

There was the promised roll of work with a note pinned to it, on opening which she found, not only the promised directions, but liberal pay in advance.

She read the note aloud in tones faltering with emotion and eyes dimmed with tears so that she could scarcely see.

"Mother," she cried, "did you ever hear of such kind, generous people?"

"It is because they are Christians. They do it for the dear Master's sake," responded Mrs. Allen, her own voice quivering with feeling.

"I'm sure of it, mother, and that He sent them to help us in our sore need. Just look! Just look!" as she took out one article after another from the basket and laid it upon the table. "How we shall feast for the next few days! Here are tea, coffee, sugar, a cold chicken, delicious-looking bread and rolls, fresh-laid eggs—I am sure they're that from their appearance, and a pot of currant jelly. It's wonderful how many things they have thought of! I shall try very hard to do the work to please them.

"What a lovely, beautiful lady Mrs. Travilla is! I don't know how to believe she's really grandmother to Miss Lulu."

"Perhaps a step-grandmother," suggested Mrs. Allen. "She can't be the captain's mother, though I noticed he called her that."

"What a noble-looking man he is! And the little girl—weren't you pleased with her, mother?"

"Yes, with both her looks and her behavior."

The palatable, nourishing food and the cheering prospect for the future opened up before her by these new and kind friends had so beneficial an effect upon Mrs. Allen that when the captain's promised conveyance came she was up, dressed, and ready for her journey.

Great was her surprise and gratitude when she learned that he had sent his own luxurious family carriage to take her and Susan to their destination, while a wagon was to convey their effects.

It was a lovely day, and their drive took them through a beautiful country, diversified by hill and valley, meadow and woodland, all clothed in the charming verdure of spring. Now they crossed a dancing streamlet, now flew past a lordly dwelling with its lawn of emerald green and avenue or grove of noble trees and its cultivated fields spreading far on either hand, now traversed pine woods or skirted the banks of a flowing river, and anon from some slight eminence caught a distinct view of the ever-restless sea.

The easy motion of the smoothly running carriage, the soft sweet air, bringing gratefully to their nostrils the mingled spicy odor of the pines and the refreshing saltiness of the sea, the beautiful sights and sounds that greeted eye and ear, were all so intensely enjoyable to the mother and daughter, after their long sojourn in the stifling atmosphere of the close and filthy alley they were leaving behind, that even the invalid was scarcely sensible of fatigue until they had reached their destination and found themselves in the new home, which, though small and humble, seemed to them almost an earthly paradise.

It was a four-roomed cottage with a trim little flower garden and grass plat in front and on each side, fruit trees, currant and gooseberry bushes, and space for raising vegetables at the back. Porches, richly festooned with flowering vines and two giant oaks that cast shadows from the front gate to the porch, made the house seem from the outside a bower of beauty and gave promise of the delightful shelter from the too fervid rays of the sun when the sultry summer heats should come.

"This surely cannot be the place!" exclaimed Mrs. Allen, as the carriage drew up at the gate.

"No, hardly," said Susan. "Haven't you made a mistake?" addressing the coachman.

"I reckon I habn't, Miss. Dis un gin'rally knows what he's 'bout," laughed the man. "Dar's Miss Elsie a-settin' on de poach, an' hyar comes de cap'n fo' to help you light."

Captain Raymond was there, sure enough, hurrying down the path.

"Welcome to your new home," he said with a benevolent smile, as he threw open the carriage door. "Mrs. Allen, you must be very weary, though you are looking much brighter than when I saw you the other day. Let me help you into the house."

"You are so kind, sir," she returned with feeling, as he lifted her out. "And, oh, what a paradise you have provided for us here! I can hardly believe it is really to be our home. I feel that it is far beyond our deserts. The flowers, the vines, the grand old trees, and the green grass—how lovely they all are!"

"Yes," he returned pleasantly, "as someone has said, 'God made the country, and man made the town,' and I for one have no desire to make my home in the man-made city."

Max and Lulu came racing down the path after their father, bringing up the rear with Susan in tow.

"How do you like it?" Lulu was asking eagerly. "Is it an improvement upon Rose Alley?"

"Oh, Miss Lulu, it's too sweet and beautiful for anything!" exclaimed Susan, clasping her hands in an ecstasy of delight. "What lovely flowers, what a delicious perfume from them! Oh, I think myself the happiest girl alive to be going to live here! I never dreamed of anything half so delightful!"

"And Grandma Elsie has made it nearly, if not quite, as inviting indoors as out," remarked Max.

"What a kind, kind lady!" said Susan in tones tremulous with grateful emotion. "She is the kindest and most generous I ever saw."

Grandma Elsie was at that moment standing at the entrance to the porch with hand outstretched in friendly greeting to Mrs. Allen and to assist her up the steps.

"Welcome home," she said with her own sweet smile. "I hope you will find it a happy home."

"Dear madam, it seems to me a paradise upon earth," returned the poor woman, tears of joy and gratitude coursing down her wasted cheeks.

Her strength seemed giving way and the captain half carried her in and laid her down on a lounge which was so placed that it commanded a partial view of each of the four rooms.

Parlor, living room, and bedroom were all simply and inexpensively, yet tastefully, furnished with every comfort, including a luxurious easy chair provided for the invalid. White curtains at the windows and vases of flowers set here and there lent an air of elegance to the otherwise unpretending and modest apartments.

In the neat little kitchen a tidy, pleasant-faced colored woman was moving briskly about, evidently preparing the evening meal, while in the living room a table was laid for two.

It was a delight to Lulu to lead Susan from room to room, calling her attention to all the beauties and conveniences and explaining that Grandma Elsie had provided this, papa or Mamma Vi that.

"Mamma Vi," repeated Susan inquiringly. "Is it your mother, you mean?"

"No—yes, my second mother, but not old enough to really be my mamma. That's why Max and I put the Vi to it."

"Come, daughter," the captain said to Lulu as she and Susan reentered the parlor, where they had left the others. "Put on your hat. We are going home now."

"Yes, it is time," Mrs. Travilla said, taking Mrs. Allen's hand in farewell. "We will leave you to rest, my good woman, for you look sadly in need of it. Sally has your supper nearly ready. I hope you will both enjoy it, and she will stay to wash the dishes and set everything to rights, so that you will have no occasion for exertion till tomorrow."

"I think they are very happy," Lulu remarked, as the carriage rolled away toward Woodburn. "And how delightful it is to be able to make other folks happy!"

"Yes," said her father, "'it is more blessed to give than to receive.' We should be very thankful that we are in circumstances to be givers—stewards of God's bounty. He has given largely to us in order that we may distribute to others. He never intended that we should spend all on ourselves."

CHAPTER FOURTH

GRANDMA ELSIE TOOK tea at Woodburn but drove home to Ion directly after. Edward, her eldest son, met her on the veranda with a face full of pleasurable excitement.

"It is over, mamma," he said. "Most happily over!"

"Ah, how thankful I am!" she exclaimed. "Can I see her?"

"Yes, oh, yes! She is sleeping though, the influence of the ether having not yet passed off."

"It is a surprise," she said. "I should have hastened home if I had the least idea of what was going on."

"It was sudden and unexpected, rather quickly over, too, or you should have been sent for. Fortunately Cousin Arthur happened in just as I was about to summon him."

"Which is it?"

"Both," he returned with a joyous laugh.

"Indeed! That too is a surprise. But none the less delightful, I should say."

He was leading the way to the suite of apartments occupied by himself and his wife, his mother following close behind.

They passed into the bedroom where Zoe lay extended on her couch in placid slumber. They drew near and stood looking down at her, each face a trifle anxious.

She stirred and opened her eyes sleepily. "Mamma," she murmured. "Edward—"

"Yes, love, we are both here," he answered in tender tones. Then bending over her and pressing a tender kiss upon her cheek, "Do you know how rich you are, my darling?"

"Rich?" she repeated with a bewildered look up into his face, still only half-awake.

"Yes, both you and I. We have more than doubled our wealth since you went to sleep two hours ago."

"Oh!" rousing to full consciousness. "Is it all over? Which is it? Show it to me, do, dear."

"It's both," he said with a low, gleeful laugh.

"Look! They are close beside you," folding back the covers of the bed and bringing into view a pair of tiny forms and faces. "Your son and daughter, young Mrs. Travilla."

She raised herself slightly to get a better view. "Oh, the darlings, the lovely darlings! Indeed we are rich! You may have the girl, but the boy's mine," she added with a silvery laugh. "But they're like as two peas. If they were both boys or girls, I should never be able to tell them apart. So it's a blessing they're one of each."

"There, lie down now," he said. "They're great treasures, but both together worth less to me than their mother. And I can't have her running any risks. Mamma, dear, what do you think of your new grandchildren?"

"Just what the new-made parents do," she answered, bending over them from the other side of the bed. "Welcome, welcome, little strangers! There is plenty of room in grandma's heart for you both."

"Our birthday gift to you, mamma," said Zoe.

"What, giving them away already, my dear?" queried Edward playfully. "And that without even consulting me!"

"Only as grandchildren," she answered in the same tone. "You and I are papa and mamma. Ah, how delightfully odd it seems! Poor little dears, to have such a silly young thing for their mother," she added sorrowfully, reaching out a hand and softly touching the tiny faces with the tips of her fingers. "But then they have a good papa, and such a dear, wise grandma. Are you pleased? Will you take them for your birthday gift from me, mamma?" lifting loving, entreating eyes to the sweet face of her mother-in-law.

"Indeed, I will, dear child. You could have given me nothing more acceptable," bending down to touch her lips softly to the velvet cheek of first one and then the other. "Which is the boy and which the girl, Ned?"

"I really don't know, mamma," he said, laughing. "For, as their mother says, they are as like as two peas."

"We'll have to put some sort of mark on them," said Zoe, gloating over her new treasures. "Or one may be blamed for the other's faults. Ah, I wonder whether they will be wise and good like their father or silly like their mother."

"You are slandering their mother, and I can't allow it," Edward said, frowning in mock indignation. "But you weren't to talk. You must be quiet or I'll have to run away."

"We'll have use of both of our names, Ned," remarked Zoe, smiling up into her husband's face the next time he came to her bedside.

"Yes," he said with a glance of pride and pleasure from her to the little ones.

Then turning to his mother, "Please understand, mamma, that we had selected a suitable name for the expected little stranger, whether it should prove to belong to the one sex or the other. Of course we desired to name for you or my father, but there are already so many Elsies and Neds in the family connection that we decided to add another name, as you did in my case, to avoid confusion—that if a boy, he should be named Edward Lawrence, for both Zoe's father and mine, and commonly called Laurie, but if a girl, she should be Lily, for the dear little sister who went to heaven so many years ago."

"I entirely approve your choice," said his mother, her eyes shining through tears of mingled joy and sorrow, as her thoughts were carried back to a husband and child whose loved presence would cheer her earthly pilgrimage no more. "Laurie and Lily— the two names go nicely together. It will be sweet to have a Lily in the family again, and I trust she and her brother may be spared to their parents, even to be the stay and staff of their old age."

❧ ❧ ❧ ❧ ❧

"How cunningly you have managed to catch up with Elsie and me in the matter of providing mamma with grandchildren," was Violet's jesting remark to Zoe when she came for the first time to look at the new arrivals.

"Yes, haven't I?" laughed Zoe. "We have two apiece now, making six in all. Mamma says she is growing rich in grandchildren."

"Six of her own, and four others who address her by that title, though it has always seemed ridiculous to me, considering how young my darling mother looks."

"Yes, to me, too. But these darlings are her very own and—Vi, don't you think they're the sweetest things that ever were made?"

"Oh, Zoe, don't ask quite so much as that of me!" returned Violet with playful look and smile. "I do really think them as sweet as they can be, but my own two no less so!"

"Oh, of course!" laughed Zoe. "It was just like my silliness to ask such a question. I tell mamma they are Ned's and my birthday gift to her, though they came three weeks before the time."

"They'll not be less worth having for being three weeks old," remarked Violet.

"No, they develop new beauties every day. Mamma herself says so. And I am glad there is time for me to recover sufficiently to enjoy the festivities of the occasion."

Zoe, hovering over her babies, made a pretty picture to look upon. She would scarcely let them out of her sight. She rejoiced over them with singing and laughter, full of mirth and gladness, as though the veriest child herself. Yet at times her mood changed, her face wore a pensive expression akin to sadness, and caressing them with exceeding tenderness, she would murmur softly, "My wee bit darlings, my precious treasures, what trials and sufferings may be yours before you reach the end of life's long journey! Ah, if your mother might but bear all your pains and troubles for you, how gladly she would do it."

"Dear daughter," Grandma Elsie said one day, on overhearing the words, "that is one of the cares we are privileged to cast on Jesus. He dearly loves the little ones, and He has all power in heaven and in earth. 'I will be a God to thee, and to thy seed after thee,' is one of the great and precious promises of His Word. 'Train up a child in the way he should go, and when he is old he will not depart from it.' Seek wisdom for that work by prayer and the study of God's word."

"I will, mamma," Zoe answered thoughtfully. "I am quite sure Edward will make a good father, and I shall try very hard to be a good mother. I shall take you, dear mamma, as my pattern, for there couldn't be a better mother than you are, and always have been."

"I have tried to be—tried in the very way I have recommended to you—but I sometimes made mistakes. I would have you follow me only in so far as I have followed Christ and the teachings of His Word," Grandma Elsie answered, in sincere humility.

"Mamma," said Zoe, "I do not believe it possible for any frail human creature to follow more closely in the Master's footsteps than you do."

The Ion twins were objects of great interest to all the children of the connection, and from the first news of their arrival they were eager to see them. It was not allowed, however, till the proud young mother was able to exhibit them herself.

Rosie and Walter had of course a look at them on the day of their birth, but they were nearly two weeks old before the others were admitted to Zoe's room, where she insisted on keeping her precious treasures all the time.

The Woodburn children were anxious for their turn, and at last it came. Lulu and Gracie rode over to Ion one pleasant afternoon on their ponies, Fairy and Elf, the captain and Max accompanying them on their larger steeds.

The little girls did not know when they started that Ion was their destination and on arriving were still in doubt whether they were to see the babies. But the greetings were scarcely over when they asked if they might.

"Yes, Zoe is feeling well today, and I think it will do her no harm to see you all for a few moments," replied Grandma Elsie, leading the way. "You may come, too, captain. Zoe is always delighted with an opportunity to exhibit her treasures."

"Thank you, mother. I accept your invitation with pleasure," he answered, following with his children.

Zoe, lying on a couch with a dainty crib close beside her, greeted her visitors with smiles and words of welcome.

"It seems an age since I last saw your very pleasant countenance, captain," she said, as he took her hand.

"You could hardly miss me with such fine companionship as you have here," he returned playfully, as he bent over the crib and took a scrutinizing look at its tiny occupants. "They are really worth showing, little mother."

"I should say they were," she responded, laughing a low, gleeful, silvery laugh.

Grandma Elsie had led Lulu and Gracie to the other side of the crib. "Oh, Aunt Zoe, what lovely little darlings!" they both exclaimed. "And it's such a pretty sight, two babies just the same size and exactly alike!"

"So it is," said the captain, but added playfully. "Both together, though, would hardly make one of our Ned, so Aunt Zoe need not propose to swap."

"Aunt Zoe has not the remotest idea of making such a proposition," she returned merrily. "No, indeed, mother's darlings," raising herself on one elbow that she might have a good look at each tiny face. "You needn't fret," for one stirred in its sleep and gave a faint little cry. "No one could persuade your mamma to give even one of you for the biggest baby in the land."

"Was that Laurie or Lily, Aunt Zoe?" asked Lulu. "Such pretty names you have given them!"

"Yes, I think so. It was Laurie that cried out. He's not so quiet as Lily, but one must expect a boy to make more noise in the world than a girl."

"But how can you tell which is which, Aunt Zoe," queried Gracie. "They look exactly alike to me."

"To me, too, but see, we have put a gold chain round Lily's neck, and Laurie has none."

"Ah, no wonder he cries out at such favoritism," remarked the captain sportively.

"Sure enough!" exclaimed Zoe. "Strange I had not thought of it before. But he shall have that excuse no longer. He shall wear that lovely necklace of coral beads Ned gave me on my last birthday. Lu, if you will go to my jewel case and get it, I'll be much obliged."

"I will, Aunt Zoe. I'm delighted with the errand," exclaimed Lulu, hurrying into the adjoining dressing room.

She had been there often enough to know where to find what she had been sent for, and she was back again in a moment with it in her hand.

"Thank you, Lu. Hand it to mamma, please," said Zoe. "She will put it on him. I'd like to do it myself, but presume I wouldn't be allowed. They are all so exceedingly—I'd almost say absurdly—careful of me."

"It would be better for you not to make the effort, my dear," Grandma Elsie said, taking the necklace from Lulu's hand.

All eyes were upon her as she gently raised the tiny head just enough to enable her to slip it under and around the child's neck, then fastened the clasp in front.

"I don't know," she remarked in a doubtful tone, "that he will be quite as comfortable with as without it, and I'm positively certain he will not appreciate the honor."

The babe was fast asleep and did not rouse himself to give his opinion.

Rosie had come softly into the room, and she was standing beside the crib with the others.

"Aren't they the loveliest, darlingest, wee dears that ever were seen?" she exclaimed. "I think it would be delightful to have one baby in the house—really belonging here—but to have two such pretty ones is doubly delightful."

"Yes, but I think you'll find it better still when they're grown as ours and can run about and talk," said Lulu. "They do say such smart things sometimes."

"Yes, what fun it will be when these two begin to talk!" Zoe exclaimed with a low, gleeful, happy laugh, touching each tiny face caressingly.

CHAPTER FIFTH

The planned celebration of Grandma Elsie's approaching semi-centennial was now the most important event in the near future, the principal theme of conversation in the connection, and grand preparations for it were going forward.

By her express wish, all of the poor of the neighborhood were invited to spend a large part of the day on the plantation, amusing themselves with outdoor games and enjoying a bountiful feast spread for them in the shade of the wood in which Mr. Leland, the uncle of the present occupant of Fairview, had once concealed himself when attacked by the Ku Klux.

Another party, consisting of all the relatives, close connections, and intimate friends residing in the vicinity, would be given the freedom of the house and grounds to enjoy themselves as they should please.

Circumstances were auspicious. All of the party preparations had been thoroughly well attended to. The day dawned bright and beautiful and found everyone in high health and spirits.

She, whom all were seeking to honor and make the happiest of the happy, awoke with a heart full of love and gratitude for the unnumbered mercies and blessings of her lot in life. Her first act was to rise from her bed, and, kneeling beside it, pour out her thanksgivings and praises, mingled with her confession of sins, petitions for herself and others, and a renewal of her oft-repeated consecration to His service.

She had scarce completed her dressing, singing the while in low, sweet strains a song of praise, when a light tap at the door was followed by her father's entrance.

He folded her in his arms, and holding her close to his heart, wished her, in moved tones, many happy returns of the day.

"I know not how to believe that you have seen fifty years," he said, holding her off a little to gaze searchingly into her face—still as sweet and well-nigh as fair and smooth as it had been thirty years before. "There are no silver threads in your hair, no lines on your forehead or about your eyes or mouth. You are no less beautiful than you were in your early girlhood. My darling's charms have only matured, not lessened."

"Ah, papa," she returned, shaking her head with an incredulous smile. "You always did see me through rose-colored glasses. I dare say any eyes but yours—so blinded by love—can readily perceive many traces left by the passing years.

"Yet, dear father, why should we regret it? Why care that we are both growing old, since each day as it passes brings us a step nearer to our dear heavenly home."

"That is a delightful thought," he responded with a smile and a sigh. "A thought that more than reconciles me to the inevitable in my own case."

"And surely in mine, too, papa, for you would not want to be in heaven without me," she said, creeping closer into his embrace and hiding her face on his chest.

"No," he replied with emotion, tightening the clasp of his arm about her waist and pressing his lips again and again to her cheek and brow. "Not for long, but in the course of nature I shall probably be called away first, and for your children's sake, I hope you may yet live many years, and that those years may be for you as free as possible from the infirmities of age."

"And it is that I wish for you, dear father, for your children's sake, my own especially," she returned, gazing lovingly into his eyes.

Another tap at the door, and Edward and Zoe entered, each carrying a baby.

"Here we come, mamma, with your birthday gifts," cried Zoe merrily. "And wishing you many, many happy returns of the day."

"Thank you, my dears. But, oh, Zoe, this is too much exertion for you! You should not have done it, child!" Elsie answered, stepping hastily forward and taking little Laurie from his young mother's arms, while Zoe sank into an easy chair, panting a little, the color coming and going in her cheeks.

"The nurse carried him to the very door, mamma," she said. "And I thought I was stronger than I am."

"It is my fault. I should not have allowed it," said Edward, looking anxiously at Zoe.

"Don't be alarmed, my dear, I am not injured in the least," she responded, smiling up into his face as he stood over her, forgetting everything else in concern for her. "You haven't presented your half of the gift to mamma, nor any good wishes either."

"As if both halves didn't belong to both of us," he responded with an amused smile. "Mamma, I wish you many, many happy returns of the day and beg to present you with what I consider a priceless treasure—my little daughter, your youngest granddaughter," laying the babe in the arms she held out to receive it, having already resigned the other to its great-grandsire.

"They are indeed priceless treasures and very dear to their grandmamma's heart," she said, cuddling her close in her arms and pressing kisses on the tiny velvet cheek.

"Now, mamma, it's Laurie's turn," remarked the young mother laughingly. "You didn't take time to kiss him in your concern for me, and it will never do to be partial."

"No, most certainly not," Grandma Elsie said, exchanging babies with her father. "But they are so exactly alike in looks that one will have to be a little careful to make sure of avoiding such a mistake."

Now came Mrs. Dinsmore, Rosie, and Walter with their congratulations and good wishes.

The scene was a lively one for a little while. Then the old people and Zoe and Edward with their babies withdrew, leaving Grandma Elsie alone with the youngest two of her flock.

They spent a short time together in the usual way, then the breakfast bell rang, and at the same moment the family carriage drove up to the door bringing her college boys, who had arrived in the village by the early train which the carriage had been sent to meet.

Each in turn held his mother in a long, tender embrace, then greetings with the others were exchanged, questions were asked and answered on both sides. So it was some time before any attention was paid to the summons to the breakfast table. And when they did gather about the board, the flow of talk was such as to seriously interfere with the business of eating, so that the meal was prolonged to twice its ordinary length.

Zoe, down for the first time since the advent of the twins, was smiling, happy and eager to show her darlings to the young uncles.

They had already given congratulations by letter to her and Edward, and they had not been many minutes in their company before renewing them.

"I am quite in haste to see my new niece and nephew," said Harold. "I presume, Zoe, they are the prettiest, brightest, sweetest wee mortals that ever were seen. Isn't it so?"

"Of course, they are to their mother," she answered laughingly. "But she doesn't expect anybody else, except papa," with an arch look at Edward, "to see the darlings through the same rose-colored glasses. You and Herbert shall judge for yourselves presently though. They will be on exhibition as soon as prayers are over."

"We may judge for ourselves, you say, Zoe, but dare we express our opinions freely, should they not coincide with that of the parents?" queried Herbert, in a bantering tone.

"At a safe distance I think you may venture," returned Zoe demurely.

"But Zoe won't be the only one to take part with Laurie and Lily should anybody have the bad taste to utter a word in depreciation of them," remarked Rosie warningly.

"And yet this is called a free country!" exclaimed Harold with an expressive shrug of his shoulders.

"Ion's to be a monarchy today," remarked Walter. "Mamma's to be crowned queen of it in the arbor."

"Indeed!" exclaimed his mother in surprise and amusement. "It is the first hint I have had that such doings were in contemplation."

"Yes, mamma," said Rosie. "We have been keeping it a secret from you, and Walter's communication is a little premature. But it really doesn't signify, for you would have had to know very soon."

"Yes, I suppose so, for some of our guests—the nearest relations at least—will soon begin to arrive. But when is this important ceremony to take place?"

"I suppose as soon as the guests are all here, mamma dear."

"The other ceremony—the presentation of the babies to their newly arrived uncles—will be gone through with first, doubtless?" Harold remarked in an inquiring tone.

"Oh, yes, of course," answered several voices, as they all rose from the table and withdrew to the library to unite in the usual morning worship.

The babies' dainty crib had been brought down to an adjoining room for the day, and there they lay sweetly sleeping.

As soon as the short service had come to an end, Zoe, motioning to Harold and Herbert to follow, led the way to the side of the crib, and laying back the cover, brought two tiny forms to view lying side by side, the little plump faces turned toward each other—round, rosy, and dimpled.

"There, aren't they beauties, boys?" exclaimed Zoe, bending over her treasures in a perfect rapture of mother-love and admiration. "Did you ever see anything half so sweet?"

"Well, really, they are quite passable, considering their extreme youth," returned Harold sportively. "I say, Ned, what would you take for them?"

"They are not on the market, sir," replied the young father, regarding them with pride and admiration. "Though you should offer every dollar you possess it would be utterly refused."

"Ah, 'tis just as well, Ned, for I should not know what to do with such tender, delicate little morsels of humanity if I had them."

"You don't half appreciate them," said Zoe, half jestingly, half in earnest. "You don't deserve the honor of being their uncle."

"We'll enjoy and appreciate them more a year or two hence, when they can be romped and played with," remarked Herbert. "But, really, Zoe, they're as pretty as any young baby I ever saw."

Rosie looked in at the door with the announcement, "The Woodburn carriage is coming up the avenue." The three brothers hurried out to greet its occupants. They were the whole Raymond family, from the captain down to baby Ned, and scarcely had greetings been exchanged with them when the Lelands from Fairview arrived, and Grandma Elsie had all her children about her.

She was the center of attraction. Everybody had an embrace, good wishes, and a gift for her, and all were most graciously received.

But her daughters presently hurried her away to her private apartment where they busied themselves in attiring her for the day in such manner as suited their own ideas of what would be most fitting and becoming. She smilingly submitted to their will.

"You must wear white, mamma," said Violet. "Nothing but white could be more suitable to the weather or more becoming to you. Do you not say so, Elsie?"

"Yes," replied Mrs. Leland, opening her mother's wardrobe and glancing over the dresses hanging there. "And it will please grandpa better than anything else. There," taking down a nun's veiling, "this is just the thing."

"My dears, remember how many years have flown over your mother's head and don't dress me too youthfully," Grandma Elsie said with an amused look and smile.

"Never fear, mamma," returned Violet in her sprightly way. "How can you fear for a moment that your daughters would do such discredit to the training of so good and wise a mother as theirs?"

"What ornaments shall mamma wear?" asked Rosie.

"Only flowers—natural flowers," returned her sisters, both speaking at once.

"Oh, yes, and they must be roses and lilies—a knot of them at her throat and another at her waist. I'll go and get them myself," exclaimed Rosie, hurrying from the room.

In one of the lower apartments of the mansion she found Zoe, Edward, Captain Raymond and his children, all busy with flowers from conservatories, gardens, fields, and woods, which were piled in fragrant heaps upon tables and in baskets, making them into bouquets, wreaths, garlands, and arranging them in vases.

With deft fingers Zoe was weaving an extremely beautiful wreath.

"Oh, Zoe, how lovely!" exclaimed Rosie. "It is to be mamma's crown, isn't it?"

"Yes, and everything in it has a meaning. These laurel leaves are to say to mamma, and everybody, that she is the glory of this house. The calla lily says that she is beautiful—though, of course, no one who looks at her can help seeing that without being told. This sweet alyssum means that she has worth beyond beauty; this white jasmine, that she is amiability itself; and the yellow, that she has grace and elegance. This china rose means the same; this moss rose, superior merit; and this myrtle, that we all love her dearly, dearly!"

"Oh, what a nice story they tell!" exclaimed Rosie. "The wreath has my entire approval," she added with a merry laugh.

"What a relief to my mind!" said Zoe, joining in the laugh. "We are going to make a perfect bower of the dining room, the only room in the house that will be much used by the company today.

"That's a nice idea. We must have flowers everywhere today in mamma's honor. I have come to select some for the adornment of her person.

"This is for that very purpose," said Zoe, holding up her nearly completed wreath and regarding it with satisfaction.

"Yes, I know, but I want a knot of flowers for her throat and another for her belt—roses, lilies, and heliotrope.

"Grandma Elsie is versed in the language of flowers, isn't she?" asked Evelyn.

"Yes, indeed!" answered Rosie.

"Oh, then, wouldn't it be a nice idea for each of us to select a few flowers expressing our feelings of love, admiration, and so forth. Then, after grandpa

Dinsmore has put the crown on her head, go one at a time, kneel before her on one knee, kiss her hand, and present the little floral offering?"

"Capital!" "Quite a bright thought, Eva!" "Just the thing!" exclaimed several voices in response to the suggestion.

"Oh, let's do it!" said Lulu. "I think it would be ever so nice!"

"All in favor say 'aye,'" said Harold.

A chorus of "Ayes" came in response.

"Contrary, no!"

There was a dead silence.

"The ayes have it," he announced. "But, of course, everybody is at liberty to do exactly as he or she pleases."

"I don't know anything about the language of flowers," remarked Gracie shyly.

"And my memory needs some refreshing on the subject," Herbert said, smiling pleasantly at the little girl. "So I'll bring a book from the library that will tell us what we want to know."

"Will it be objectionable if several of us choose the same flower?" asked Lulu.

"Oh, no, not at all," replied Harold. "I shall take some of these beautiful pinks. This one means pure affection; this clove pink, dignity; this double red, pure, ardent love; this white one, 'You are fair.' I should like to say all that to mamma."

"So should I," said Gracie. "May I take some of the same flowers, Uncle Harold?"

"Surely, dear child," he returned, selecting them for her.

"A bit of myrtle, too, please," she said. "Because I do love Grandma Elsie dearly."

"I want a bit of that, too," Lulu said. "And all the kinds of lilies and roses that mean something nice. I do think they are the loveliest flowers!"

"I'll have heliotrope, 'I love you'; pansy, 'Think of me'; purple heartsease, some of the myrtle, and honeysuckle, 'bond of love,'" Evelyn said, after consulting the book Herbert had brought and culling them from the fragrant heaps as she spoke.

In the meantime, Rosie had made up the two bouquets she had come for. "See!" she said, holding them up to view. "Aren't these roses and lilies just the perfection of beauty? They'll put the finishing touch to mamma's attire, and I'll be back presently to select some others as my offering to the queen of the day."

So saying, she tripped merrily away.

"There, the crown is done!" said Zoe, turning it about in her hands and viewing it with quite a satisfied smile.

The others pronounced it beautiful.

"Now I'll help with the wreaths for the rooms."

"No, no, my dear, you have exerted yourself quite enough for one day," said her husband. "Just lie back in that easy chair and give as many directions as you please."

"Nonsense!" she exclaimed, laughing. "You are as careful of me as if I were made of china or glass."

"A great deal more so," he returned with a look that spoke volumes of loving appreciation. Bending over her to bring his lips close to her ear, "Your price is above rubies, my darling," he added, in a low aside.

"Dear Ned, you are so good to me!" she responded, lifting to his eyes as full of love as his own.

"The queen of the day! The queen of all our hearts!" announced Rosie, preceding her mother and sisters into the room.

"We are all ready to do her homage," said the captain, stepping forward and saluting his mother-in-law with much respect and affection.

The others were prompt to follow his example, all crowding about her with expressions of both love and admiration.

"You are too good to me, my dear children and grandchildren," she said, glad tears springing to her eyes. "I am quite sensible that I am by no means the beautiful and admirable person your affectionate appreciation leads me to imagine."

"Oh, mamma!" exclaimed Zoe. "There's not a single bit imagination about it! Girls, you have shown great taste in arraying her for the occasion. It only needs the addition of my floral crown to make her dress quite perfect."

But carriages were driving up the avenue, and near friends and relatives came pouring in with their congratulations and gifts, which last were received with grateful thanks and bestowed, for the present, in a small reception room set apart for the purpose.

When the last of the guests had arrived, all repaired to the grounds, wending their way toward the arbor where the heroine of the day was seated on an extemporized throne garlanded with flowers. Her father made a neat little speech and placed the floral crown on her head, then, dropping on one knee at her feet, kissed her hand and presented a bouquet of calla lilies, pinks, and roses.

It was altogether a surprise to her, and a vivid blush mantled her cheek.

"My dear father," she said, low and tenderly, looking up into his face with eyes half filled with tears, as he rose and stood by her side, "you should never have knelt to me—your own child."

"Only in sport, dearest," he said, bending down and imprinting a kiss upon her lips. "You know young lads like myself must be allowed to indulge in a trifle of that kind occasionally."

He stepped aside, and amid jesting and mirth, the others followed his example till the throne and its occupant were half hidden in the fragrant heaps of floral offerings.

But father and sons, coming to the rescue, extricated her without damage to person or attire, and she went about among her guests doing the honors of the place with a sweet and gentle dignity all her own.

There were no strangers among them, however, and everybody felt at home and free to follow his or her own inclinations—to sit and converse in the grateful shade of the fine old trees, wander about the lawn, shrubbery, and gardens, or take part in the active sports with which the children and youth of the company were delighting themselves.

But it was not in the kind heart of Grandma Elsie to neglect her poorer guests. Her father, sons, and a few others accompanying her, she paid a short visit to each assembly, went about among them with kindly inquiries concerning their health and welfare—no air of condescension marring their enjoyment of her sweet looks and words—and distributing gifts from a large basket carried by two men-servants. There were articles of food and clothing as she knew would be acceptable. Forever like her Master, going about doing good, she was a frequent visitor in their dwellings and well acquainted with their needs.

And they looked upon her as a kind, powerful friend from whom they might ever expect with confidence, sympathy, and help in their trials and struggles with life's hard problems.

The birthday feast at the mansion was served somewhat later in the day. It was a banquet not only of such things as would appease the hunger of the physical man, but also "a feast of reason and a flow of soul."

The celebration of Grandma Elsie's semi-centennial was pronounced by everyone so fortunate as to have a share in it to have been from beginning to end a most decided success.

CHAPTER SIXTH

MAX AND LULU were on the veranda at Woodburn—its only occupants. The western sky was all aglow with the gorgeous hues of a brilliant sunset. Rich masses of purple, gold, amber, pale green, and delicate rose color were piled from the horizon half way up to the zenith, while flecks, patches, and long streaks of flame, changing every moment. Here spreading and deepening and there contracting and fading to paler tints, it stretched above and beyond on every side.

It was a grand scene and Max, who was whittling a bit of soft wood, paused for several minutes to gaze upon it with admiration and delight.

"What a splendid sunset!" he exclaimed, turning toward his sister.

But she was absorbed in a story book, holding it in a way to catch the last beams of the fading light and reading on in eager haste and utterly oblivious to the glories of the sunset sky and the beauties of the grounds arrayed in all the verdure of June.

"Lu, you're straining your eyes, reading by this fading light," said Max. "If papa were here he would certainly tell you to stop at once."

Lulu made no reply, but continued to read as if she had not heard the remark.

Max waited a moment, then began again, "Lu—"

"Oh, Max, do be quiet!" she exclaimed impatiently, without moving her eyes from the page.

Max gazed at her for another minute without speaking, an odd sort of smile in his eyes and playing about the corners of his mouth.

"Yes, I'll do it," he muttered under his breath. "Now's as good a time as any for the experiment."

At that instant their father's voice was heard in grave, slightly reproving accents, coming apparently from the hall. "Lulu!"

"Sir," she answered promptly, dropping her book while a vivid color suffused her cheek.

"Don't read any longer. You will injure your eyes. Lay aside the book and come here to me."

She obeyed at once, hurrying into the hall, Max looking after her with a gleam of mingled fun and triumph in his eyes.

"Why, papa, where are you?" he heard her ask the next moment. Then she came rushing back with a face full of astonishment and perplexity. "Max, where can papa be? Didn't you hear him call me? I was sure he was in the hall, but he isn't. And I can't find him in any of the rooms. Oh, now I remember, he drove away with Mamma Vi not half an hour ago, and they were going to the Oaks. He can't possibly be back by this time, even if they didn't stop there long enough to get out of the carriage. Besides, we would have seen it drive up from the gate."

"Couldn't they have come back through the wood, as you and I do sometimes?"

"Yes, so they could, but even then we should have seen and heard them, and—no, they can't have come back. Papa can't be at home, and yet I heard him call me as plainly as ever I did in my life. Oh!" And she dropped into a chair with a look of dread and alarm that frightened her brother.

"Max," she went on in low, tremulous tones, "I—I—do believe it means that I'm going to die."

"Why, Lu!" he exclaimed. "I should never have thought you would be so silly! What on earth can have put that notion into your head?"

"I've heard stories of people hearing themselves called in that mysterious way and dying very soon afterward," she answered, looking rather ashamed.

"Well, that's all nonsense," he returned with an air of superior wisdom. "I'm perfectly sure papa would tell you so."

"Maybe you wouldn't care if you thought it did mean that?" she said half interrogatively.

"Oh, of course not. You don't suppose I care anything about you, do you?"

"Yes, I know you do. And if you didn't, you know papa loves me and would be grieved to lose me, and you love him well enough to be sorry on his account."

"Well, maybe so, though I hadn't thought it out. But you're very healthy, and I've a notion are going to outlive all the rest of us."

"Dear me, how awful that would be!" she cried. "To be left all alone, after seeing you all dead and buried. I believe I'd rather go first."

"But not very soon?"

"No, I—think I'd like to live a little longer. We do have such good times nowadays—in our own home with papa. But—Max, who could have called me like that?" she queried with a look of anxious perplexity. "You heard it, too, didn't you?"

"Yes."

"But why do you laugh and look so pleased and amused? I should think you'd be troubled by the mysteriousness of it, same as I am."

"No, I'm not," he answered. "Because it isn't really very mysterious to me. Lu, to save you from worrying, I'll explain."

She looked at him in wide-eyed surprise.

"Then you know who it was?"

"Yes, it was I—myself."

"You? Why how—what do you mean, Max?"

"That I've found out I'm a ventriloquist, like Cousin Ronald."

"Oh, Maxie! Is it so? Oh, how nice!"

"Yes. I wondered if I could do it, and I asked him to tell me exactly how he did it and if people could learn how if they tried very hard. He said it depended upon practice and dexterity and explained and showed me as nearly as he could. And I tried and would go off into the wood yonder, when I could get a chance without anybody noticing, and practice. Tonight I thought I'd try it on you, and I'm just delighted that I succeeded so well."

"Indeed you did!" she exclaimed. "I don't believe Cousin Ronald himself could have done it any better. Oh, Max, I think it's ever so nice! What fun we shall have! Try it on papa when he comes home; do! He wouldn't be vexed. Papa enjoys fun just as much as we do, and he is never angry, even if the joke is at his expense."

"No, indeed! And I never had a boy friend that was better company, or even as good, going gunning or fishing, or in a game of baseball, or anything else."

"And I never enjoy our parlor games half so much when he doesn't take part."

"No, but he always does, unless he's too busy or has company to entertain. I tell you, Lu, it's just splendid to have a father you can talk to just as freely as if he was a boy like yourself—tell him all you think and feel, and see that he's interested, and know that if your thoughts and feelings aren't right he'll show you it's so without being angry or stern or making you feel that he considers you a simpleton or a fool. I like to be reasoned with as if I had some sense, and that's the way papa does with me. And sometimes he asks my opinion, as if he thought it was worth something."

"Yes, I know he does and mine, too, and I'm younger than you and not nearly so far along in my studies. But, oh, Max, let's be thinking of the tricks you can play with your ventriloquism. What will you do tonight to astonish papa and Mamma Vi?"

"I don't know. Have you any suggestions to make?"

She had several and was very eager to see one or more of her plans tried. Max had some of his own, too, and they made themselves very merry talking them over.

The sunset had faded from the sky, but the moon had risen and was flooding the beautiful grounds with silvery light. Suddenly a mocking bird in a tree close at hand began to pour forth a perfect flood of melody. The children ceased talking to listen to its song.

"Oh, isn't that delicious music?" cried Lulu, as the bird paused for a moment. "Max, you couldn't do that, could you?"

"No, indeed," laughed Max. "I'd give a great deal if I could. But hark, he's beginning again."

"It sounds as if he's praising God," Lulu remarked, at the next pause. "He sings as if his little heart is so full of joy and thankfulness that he doesn't know how to express it."

"Yes," said Gracie's voice, close at her side. "I think he's rejoicing in the beautiful moonlight, Lu, and isn't it lovely? It makes a rainbow in the spray of the fountain, and I can see the dewdrops glitter in the grass. And look at the fireflies dancing in and out among the trees and bushes."

"Some of them soaring away above the treetops," put in Max.

"And maybe birdie is rejoicing in the sweet scent of the roses and honeysuckle, the mignonette, the moon flowers, and others too numerous to mention," said Lulu. "But where have you been all this time, Gracie?"

"With Elsie and baby Ned. Mamma put them to bed as usual before she and papa went, but she couldn't stay till Elsie went to sleep, and I offered to stay beside Elsie and sing to her and tell her stories, and mamma said I might, and she should be very much obliged to me for it."

"That was good of you, Gracie," Lulu said, pulling Gracie down into her lap and putting her arm round her. "I suppose it was my place to do it, really, as the oldest, but I never thought of it. But you are always such a dear, kind, unselfish girl."

"And so you are," said Max and Gracie, speaking together, Max adding, "Who was it was so brave the night the burglars got into the strong room, and so unselfish as to prefer to risk her own life, locking them in there rather than have papa risk his?"

"Lulu, of course," said a voice that sounded like Evelyn Leland's, speaking near at hand, on the other side of the little girls. "For who else would have done it?"

Even Lulu was startled enough to turn her head, half expecting to see her friend standing there, while Gracie sprang up and turned in the direction of the sound, exclaiming, "Why, Eva, when did you come? I didn't know you were here! Oh, she isn't there! How quickly she got away—into the hall, I suppose," running toward the door. "Eva, Eva," she called, "where can you have gone so fast?"

Max and Lulu looked after her with a low and gleeful laugh.

"Another success for you, Max." Lulu said.

"Oh, I hope Gracie won't be frightened!" he exclaimed in sudden fear of the effect of his experiment upon his timid, nervous, little sister, and just then Gracie came hurrying back, looking a little alarmed and very perplexed.

"Why," she said, "where could Eva have gone to? I've looked all about and can't find her."

"Shall I tell her, Max?" asked Lulu.

"Yes," he answered and Lulu went on. "Max has learned to be a kind of Cousin Ronald, Gracie, and we shall have lots of fun because of it, don't you think so?"

"A ventriloquist, do you mean?" asked Gracie in astonishment. "Why, how can he?"

"Because he is so smart, I suppose," laughed Lulu. "Aren't you proud of being the sister of such a genius? I am."

"Yes," returned Gracie promptly. "I always was proud of Maxie. But this astonished me very much indeed. Oh, I'm ever so glad of it! I'm sure he can make a great deal of fun for himself and us. Does papa know?"

"No," said Max. "And you mustn't tell him. When he comes home we'll see if we can't have some fun out of him. He'll enjoy it as much as we will."

"Of course, and be as proud of you, Maxie, as Lu and I are."

Just then they saw the carriage, bringing their parents, turn in at the great gates leading from the highway into the Woodburn grounds and come rapidly up the drive.

It drew up before the entrance, and the captain alighted and handed out his wife.

The children, always delighted to see them return after even a short absence, sprang up and ran forward with eager, joyous greetings.

"I hope you have not been lonely, dears," said Violet, bending down to receive and return an ardent kiss from Gracie. "But I must hurry up to the nursery to see how the babies are doing."

"Papa, sit down here in this easy chair, please," said Lulu.

"And let me take your hat and hang it on the rack," added Max.

"And may I get you a glass of ice water?" "And a fan?" asked Lulu and Gracie.

"Thank you, my darlings, I do not feel the need of either," he answered, seating himself and drawing Gracie to his knee, Lulu to his side, and putting an arm affectionately around each.

Max drew up a chair close to his father's side. "Had you a pleasant time, papa?" he asked.

"Very; we happened upon quite a number of the relatives—Dr. Conly and his brother Calhoun from Roselands, the Fairview family, Grandpa and Grandma Dinsmore, and Grandma Elsie. Some of them were spending the day, while others, like ourselves, had just dropped in for a call."

At the sound of the carriage wheels upon the driveway, Prince, Max's big Newfoundland dog, had come rushing round from the back of the house with a joyous welcoming bark. He was devotedly attached to every member of the family, but to no one of them more than to the captain. He had followed Max into the hall and out again and stood close beside him now, evidently considering himself to make one of the little group — pushing himself a little farther in among them, he laid his head on Gracie's lap, wagging his tail in pleased expectancy and looking wistfully into the captain's face.

"Good Prince! Good dog!" the captain said kindly, stroking and patting the dog's head. "How are you tonight, old fellow?"

"Wide awake and glad to see you home, sir," were the words that seemed to come from Prince's own mouth in reply.

"What!" exclaimed the captain, hastily putting Gracie off his knee to rise and turn around toward the open hall door. "Cousin Ronald here? Children, why didn't you tell me he had come?"

He was moving quickly in the direction of the doorway as he spoke, the children exchanging amused glances and finding some difficulty in suppressing an inclination to laugh aloud.

The captain glanced within the hall, saw no one, though it was brilliantly lighted, then turning toward the group, "Max," he asked, "where is Mr. Lilburn?"

"I don't know, papa. Not here. At least, I have not seen or heard anything of him."

"Strange!" said his father with a look of perplexity. "Ah, I see you are all laughing. Come, if you can explain Prince's sudden power of speech, do so at once."

Captain Raymond's tones were perfectly pleasant. Evidently he was not at all angry at the liberty taken with him.

He sat down again, and they crowded round him, Max answering, "Yes, sir."

The little girls said, "Max can tell you, papa," generously resigning to him the pleasure of revealing the secret.

The captain began to have an inkling of the truth. "Out with it, Max," he said, pretending to be very stern. "So you've been playing tricks on your father, have you? I never expected such disrespectful treatment from you."

Max had dropped his eyes and did not see the twinkle of fun in his father's.

Coloring deeply, "Papa," he said in a remorseful tone, "I—I wouldn't for anything have been disrespectful to you. I didn't mean it. There's nobody else I so sincerely respect as I do you. Please forgive me, and—"

"My boy, don't you see that I am only in jest?" the captain asked, taking his hand and holding it in a kindly pressure. "But come," he added sportively, "make a clean slate of it now, and let me judge whether you have sinned beyond forgiveness."

Max answered with a full confession and complete explanation, making them as brief as possible, and his sisters gave a mirthful account of the exhibitions of his powers that he had given them.

"Well, son," the captain said, "this newly discovered talent may be made a source of innocent amusement to yourself and others, but I trust you will never use it to injure or annoy — unless the victim of a slight annoyance is to be more than recompensed for it by the after results," he added in a playful tone, laying his hand affectionately on the boy's head.

Max heaved a sigh of relief. "I'll try not to, papa," he said with an arch look and smile up into his father's face. "You'll forgive me for tricking you, won't you?"

"Yes, taking into consideration the extenuating circumstances of its being the first offense."

"Thank you, sir. But I hope you don't forbid me to try it on Mamma Vi one of these times," returned Max insinuatingly and with another arch look and smile.

"No, I shall not, as I incline to the opinion that she would rather enjoy it," laughed his father.

"Oh, Max, when will you do it?" cried Lulu. "Gracie and I will want to be there to see and hear it all, for you know it's only once you can play the trick on any one person. At least, if you try it again, they're very apt to think immediately that it's you doing it."

"I'll take some time when you two girls are by," said Max. "Papa, also. But perhaps," with an inquiring glance at his father, "I'd better not try any more of it tonight."

"No, it is time for our prayers," the captain answered. "We will go in, and, Max, you may ring for the servants."

They all repaired to the library, where Violet and the servants presently came also, and the short service was held.

At its conclusion, as the children were bidding goodnight, Violet noticed a large doll sitting in state in its own tiny chair. She picked it up, saying, "Ah, Elsie has forgotten her favorite Fatima and will probably be crying out for her before morning."

Max's eyes twinkled, and he sent a questioning, wishful glance in his father's direction.

The captain smiled and gave a nod of acquiescence.

"Where's my little mamma?" asked a tiny voice that seemed to issue from Fatima's lips. "Please take me to my little mamma."

Violet started and opened her eyes wide in great astonishment then glanced quickly around the room. "Cousin Ronald!" she exclaimed. "But where is he?"

No answer but a half-suppressed giggle from the little girls and an exchange of amused glances between them, their father, and Max.

"Captain, is Cousin Ronald here? Have you seen him? What does it all mean?" Violet asked, piling one question upon another.

"No, my dear, but it seems he has left his own representative behind him," returned her husband pleasantly, laying a hand on Max's shoulder, and giving him a little playful shake.

"Max!" she cried in fresh astonishment. "Is it possible that you can imitate his powers as a ventriloquist so well, Maxie?"

Max modestly repeated the explanation already made to his father and sisters. They gave a laughing account of his exploits witnessed by them, then the captain bade Lulu and Gracie say goodnight and seek their nests.

"But you, Max, my son," he added, "may stay a little longer. I have something to say to you."

CHAPTER SEVENTH

THE CAPTAIN OPENED his secretary, took a letter from one of the pigeon holes, glanced over the contents, restored the missive to its place, then turned to Max, who stood patiently waiting by his side.

"We will go out on the veranda and have our little talk there, my boy," he said, leading the way, Max following. "The air is so much more pleasant there than within doors this warm evening."

"Yes, sir, perfectly delightful, I think, papa. I don't know where a lovelier, happier home than ours can be found."

"Ah, I am very glad you appreciate it, my dear boy," the captain said with a pleasant look, beginning to pace the length of the veranda to and fro, Max keeping close at his side. "And I shall miss my eldest son sadly when the time comes for him to leave the home nest. Have you made up your mind yet as to what calling you would like best to pursue?"

"I have been thinking a great deal about it of late, papa, and if you are willing and there is an opening for me, I want to go into the navy."

"I willing? Entirely so. I have not lost my old love for the service, and I shall not grudge my son to it."

"Perhaps I inherit my love for it from you, papa," remarked Max. "Anyway, I know that your having been in it, and hearing you speak so highly of it, has had a good deal to do with my desire to go into it. And your son could hardly fail to be patriotic and full of love for the old flag. Then you have furnished me with so much interesting reading about the doings of our navy in the Revolutionary War, the War of 1812, and the Civil War, that it's no wonder I feel a strong desire to help in its work if we ever have another one."

"No, I suppose I have only myself to blame," his father said pleasantly. "Yet I am not at all sure that I should act otherwise if I could go back to the time of your babyhood and begin over again.

"Well, Max, today's mail brought me the offer of an appointment to a naval cadetship for my son, if I desired it. My boy, shall I accept for you?"

"If you think best, papa, I'll be delighted to have you do it," Max said in a joyous tone. "But am I old enough to go this year?"

"Just the right age," answered his father slowly, half-sighing at the thought of the separation the acceptance of the offered appointment must involve. "But, Max, I fear I may have shown you the pleasant side of the life too exclusively. I must discourse to you of its hardships before allowing you to decide for or against it."

"I hope, papa, you don't think me such a milksop or coward that I'd be frightened at the thought of a little hardship?" Max said with heightened color. "I'm sure I ought to be willing to stand as much such things as my father did."

"No, my boy, I should not be the proud and happy father I am if I were compelled to entertain so mean an opinion of you," returned the captain, looking down at the boy with a smile of fatherly pride and affection. "Perhaps love blinds me to the faults of my first-born, but to me he seems a son that any man might be proud to call his own, and if ever tempted to an unworthy act, let the remembrance that it would go nigh to break your father's heart to hear of it restrain you from yielding to the temptation."

He paused in his walk and laid an affectionate hand on the lad's shoulder.

"Papa," returned Max with emotion, "I think no punishment could be too bad for a boy that could grieve such a father as mine. I—I think I'd rather die than know I had hurt you so!"

"I believe it, my son," responded the captain with feeling. "I have not the least doubt that you have a very strong affection for me, and would be very loath to cause me pain. I hope, too, that you are quite as anxious to please and honor your heavenly Father—much more so, indeed.

"But let us sit down here while I tell you of the hardening process a naval cadet must pass through, and the trials of his after-life as an officer in the service if he be so fortunate as to secure a permanent place in it."

"Yes, sir, I'll be glad to hear anything you can tell me about both. I suppose I'm not quite sure of getting into the academy, even if I do accept this offer, am I?"

"No, not quite. There is an examination to pass through, as to both your physical and educational qualifications. To be accepted, a boy must be physically sound and of robust constitution—both of which you are, so far as I can judge. You have never been seriously ill in your life.

"Beside, the applicant must have a sufficient knowledge of reading, writing, spelling, geography,

English grammar, United States history, arithmetic and algebra. You are well grounded in all these, and must review during your summer vacation under the tutor who has had charge of you for some time past," he added with a playful look and tone.

"Papa," Max said a little tremulously, "shall I ever have such another so kind, so patient, and always so ready to take any amount of trouble to explain things and make them clear to me?"

"It is not at all impossible that you may find one or more who will be all that, my boy," the captain responded. "But certainly none that can have the same affection for you or the same fatherly joy and pride in seeing your progress. It would not be natural for any other than your own parent."

"No, sir, I know that. And of course I couldn't feel the same toward any other teacher."

"I shouldn't want you to, Max," laughed the captain. "I must acknowledge that I couldn't be quite willing to have my son loving any other man with the same filial affection that he gives me.

"But to return to the subject at hand—you will have to resign many of the luxuries you enjoy at home. You will not be allowed a room to yourself. You must share it with another cadet, and with him take turns in keeping it in the most perfect order—sweeping, dusting, and arranging its contents every morning for inspection. Every article will have a place and must be found there when not in use.

"Your furniture will be severely plain—an iron bedstead, a wooden chair, a washstand, looking glass, wardrobe, rug, and a table which you will share with your roommate. You can have no curtains at your windows, no maps or pictures to adorn your walls."

"I shouldn't expect the government to provide such things," remarked Max. "But can't I take some from home?"

"No, it is not allowed."

"That seems odd, papa. What harm could it do for a boy to have such things if his father could afford to provide them?"

"It is because some of the lads may come from very poor families, and the government chooses — very wisely, I think — that all shall fare alike while students in that national college."

"Yes, to be sure," returned Max thoughtfully. "I think that's just as it ought to be, and it will be a trifling hardship to have to do without such things while I'm there."

"The discipline is very strict," the captain went on. "But my boy has learned to obey one naval officer, and perhaps will in consequence find it at comparatively easy to obey others."

"Yes, sir, I hope so."

"Your academic standing, number of demerits, and so forth, will be reported to me once a month and will gratify or distress me according to what they are. I am sure the thought of that will be a restraint upon any inclination my boy may have to idleness or breaches of discipline."

"I ought to be called an ungrateful wretch if it doesn't, papa. How long is the course?"

"If appointed, you will have to take an oath to serve for eight years, including the probationary period. After graduating two years are spent at sea, then there is another examination, and if passed successfully and there is a vacancy to be filled, there will be an appointment to the line and to the marine or the engineer corps of the navy."

"But if there is no vacancy, papa?"

"The candidate is, in that case, given an honorable discharge, a certificate of graduation, and one year's pay."

"I hope I'll get through it all right and that there'll be a vacancy ready for me to fill," said Max.

"I hope so, my son, if that is your desire, but don't forget that there are hardships in a seafaring life that do not fall to the lot of landsmen. There will be many and long separations from their families, exposure to danger from disasters at sea or on foreign shores, and others too numerous to mention at present. Yet, it is a life that has many and great attractions for me. But those I have often told you of."

"Yes, sir, and all you have told me tonight does not frighten me out of my wish. Life is very easy here at home, and perhaps it may be good for me to go through some rougher experiences. Don't you think so, papa?"

"Yes, I rather agree with you in that. A life of both luxury and ease is not the best for the development of a strong, manly, self-reliant character."

"Then you will write and accept for me, will you, sir?"

"Yes."

"How soon do I go to the academy, papa?"

"In September. And I have a plan for you in the meantime with which you will be pleased, I think.

"I find I must pay a visit to some property that I own in the far West, and I want my son's companionship on the trip, supposing he fancies taking it with me."

The captain looked smilingly into the lad's eyes as he spoke.

"Oh, papa, how delightful!" cried Max. "Will you really take me with you?"

"Such is certainly my intention, if nothing happens to prevent," the captain replied, smiling to see how pleased the boy was with the prospect.

"Mamma Vi can hardly be going along on such a trip, I suppose?" Max said inquiringly. "Oh, no! We could not take the babies along, and she would not be willing to leave them."

"Then are you and I to be the whole party, sir?"

"I have some thought of inviting Lulu to go with us," replied his father. "Do you think she would like it, and that we two could take proper care of her?"

Max laughed. "I shouldn't be a bit afraid to trust anybody to your care, sir," he said. "And I'd do anything I could to help. Beside, I don't believe Lu's the sort of girl to give much trouble on such a journey, and I'm sure she'll be fairly wild with delight when you tell her about it and that she is to go along."

"I am of the same opinion, and I am enjoying the prospect of witnessing her pleasure on hearing the news.

"Well, my son, our talk has been a long one, and it is late. Time for a growing boy, such as you, to be in bed. Bid me goodnight and go."

They both had risen to their feet. Captain Raymond held out his hand as he spoke. Max promptly put his into it, saying with a bright, happy, affectionate look up into his father's face, "Thank you so very much, papa, for all your kind plans for me. Is Lu to hear about the journey tonight?"

"I think not," was the reply. "She is so excitable that I fear such surprising news might keep her awake. I dare say, though, she is already in bed and asleep."

To make sure of that, he went softly into her room on his way to his own. He rarely failed to look in upon his little girls after they had gone to their rooms for the night, and when he did fail it was a sore disappointment to them.

Lulu was in bed and had fallen into a doze, but she woke at his approach, albeit he moved with a very quiet step, and started up to a sitting posture.

"Papa!" she exclaimed in an undertone, mindful not to rouse Gracie from her slumbers in the adjoining room. "Oh, I'm so glad you came!" throwing her arms round his neck as he reached the bedside and bent down to give her a kiss. "You must have talked a long time to Maxie. I was really growing jealous," she added with a laugh.

"Were you?" he asked, seating himself on the edge of the bed and drawing her into his arms. "Isn't Maxie entitled to a fair share of his papa's attentions as well as of his love?"

"Oh, yes, indeed! And I wouldn't want to rob him of a bit of either, but I do so love the little bedtime chat with you that I think I'd rather miss 'most anything else."

"Well, dear child, perhaps we can have an unusually long talk in the morning to comfort you for the loss tonight. So go to sleep as fast as you can, that you may be ready for an early waking," he said. Then with another kiss and a fervent, "Goodnight, my darling, and may He who neither slumbers nor sleeps have you in His kind care and keeping," he left her.

CHAPTER EIGHTH

LULU'S FIRST WAKING thought was of her father's promise.

"Perhaps he is going to tell me what he and Maxie were talking about last night," she said to herself. "Likely it was something of importance to keep them so long. I wonder what? Maybe about going to the seashore, or somewhere, for the hot months, as we always do."

She slipped out of bed and began a brisk dressing, determined to be quite ready to receive her father whenever he might come.

She and Gracie were together in their own little sitting room looking over their tasks for the day, when hearing his approaching footsteps they hastily laid aside their books and ran to meet him.

"Good morning, my darlings. You look well and bright," he said, bending down and opening his arms to receive them.

"Good morning, dear papa," they answered, running into them and putting theirs about his neck. "Yes, we are well, and hope you are, too," hugging and kissing him with ardent affection. "Now, papa, won't you give me that long talk you said I should have this morning?" pleaded Lulu.

"Yes, don't I always keep my promises?" he asked, taking possession of an easy chair and allowing them to seat themselves one upon each knee.

"Yes, indeed you do, papa—sometimes when I'd rather you wouldn't," returned Lulu laughingly.

"Would you be willing to lose faith in your father's word, dear child?" he asked with a sincere and sudden gravity.

"No, papa, no indeed!" she answered earnestly. "That would be worse than being punished when I deserve it, for naughtiness that you've said you'd have to punish me for."

"I trust there will never again be any call for me to keep such promises," he said caressing her. "You have been very good for some time past and intend to keep on doing so, do you not?"

"Yes, sir, but I'm afraid the badness that I still feel inside sometimes will crop out again one of these days," she said half sadly, half jestingly.

"The same danger threatens your father, too," he said. "And the only safety for either of us lies in constant watching and prayer."

"But, papa, how can we be praying all the time?"

"The Bible," he replied, "bids us 'Pray without ceasing,' not meaning that we are to live on our knees, or with words of prayer always on our lips, for that would be impossible without neglecting other duties enjoined in God's Word—such, for example, as 'Six days shalt thou labor and do all thy work,' 'Distributing to the necessity of saints,' and so forth—but that we are to live near to God and with so much of the spirit of prayer in our hearts that they will be often sending up swift, silent petitions, or songs of praise and thankfulness.

"Well, Lulu, I know you are curious to hear what Max and I were conversing about last night."

"Oh, yes, sir, indeed! If you are willing I should know," she responded eagerly.

"Quite willing," he said. "It was of his choice of a business or profession. I had received a letter offering an appointment for my son as a naval cadet. So, as I wish Max to choose for himself, it was necessary for him to decide and to do so promptly, whether he would accept that offer or decline it."

"Oh, which did he choose, papa?"

"He said he had quite made up his mind to go into the navy and asked me to write an acceptance for him, which I did before I went to bed."

"You are always so prompt, papa," remarked Lulu, putting her arm round his neck and gazing with loving admiration into his face.

"Yes," he said, "I must try to be all I would have my children, for 'example is better than precept.'"

"And Maxie will have to go away and not be in school with us anymore?" Gracie said, inquiringly, tears filling her eyes.

"Yes, daughter," her father answered with a slight sigh. "But boys can't always be kept at home. But I hope to keep my girls a long while yet," he added, drawing them into a close embrace as he spoke.

"Dear, dear! How we will miss Max!" exclaimed Lulu. "But then how nice it will be when he comes home for his vacations!"

"So it will," said the captain. "But now I have something else to tell you, something that concerns you, Lulu, a little more nearly."

"I hope it isn't that I'm to go away! You can't make a cadet out of me, though Aunt Beulah called me a tomboy when I was with her," Lulu remarked.

"No, but there are other places more suitable for girls," her father replied with a grave look and tone that she was at a loss to interpret.

"Oh, papa, you can't mean that really I—I'm going away, too?"

"Perhaps some better instructor than your present one might be found for you," he began rather meditatively, then paused as if considering the matter.

"Oh, no, no, no!" she cried. "There couldn't be a better one, I'm sure, and I just love to be taught by you and couldn't bear to have anybody else teach me—'specially if I had to go away from you. And wouldn't you miss me a little, papa?" she asked with tears in her voice and hiding her face on his shoulder.

"Yes, a great deal more than a little should I miss the darling daughter always so ready, even eager, to run papa's errands and wait upon him lovingly," he said, pressing his lips again and again to her cheek. "In fact, her companionship is so sweet to me that, having to go upon a long journey, I would prefer to take her with me.

"But I shall not force her inclination. If you would rather stay at home with Mamma Vi and the little ones, you may do so."

"Oh, papa, what ever do you mean?" she asked, looking up in joyful surprise, not unmixed with perplexity. "Won't you please explain?"

"Yes, I am going out to the far West on a business trip, shall take Max with me and you, too, if you care to go."

"Care to go? Wouldn't I!" she cried, clapping her hands in delight and smothering him with caresses. "Oh, I think I never dreamed of anything so, so, so delightful! Papa, you are such a dear, dear father! You are so, so good and kind to me! Oh, I ought to be the best girl that ever was made! And if I'm not it shan't be for want of trying!"

But tears were rolling down Gracie's cheeks and with a little sob she drew out her handkerchief to wipe them away.

"Oh, Gracie, dear, I wish you could go, too!" exclaimed Lulu.

"If she were only strong enough," her father said, caressing her with great tenderness. "She, too, should have her choice of going or staying, but I know the fatigue of the journey would be more than she could endure."

"I don't want to have a journey," sobbed Gracie. "But how can I do without papa? Without Maxie? And without Lulu? All gone at once?"

"But mamma and the babies will be left, and you love them dearly, I know."

"Yes, papa, but I love Max, and Lu, and oh, I love you better than anybody else in all the world!" she cried, clinging about his neck and laying her wet little cheek to his.

"Sweet words for papa to hear from your lips, darling," he returned, holding her close and kissing her many times. "And papa's love for you is more than tongue can tell."

"Then why will you go away and leave me?"

"Because business makes it necessary for me to go, darling, and you are not strong enough to go with me. But cheer up. It will be very pleasant at home with mamma and the babies. Grandma Elsie and the others will come over from Ion and Fairview very often, and after a while, you will all be going to some nice seaside resort where I hope to join you with Max and Lulu before it is time to come home again."

"That will be very nice, papa," she said a little more cheerfully.

"And how would you like to get a letter from papa now and then? And from Max and Lulu, too? And to answer them? You can write very nicely now, and a talk on paper to your father will be better than none at all, won't it?"

"Oh, I'd enjoy it ever so much, if you'll excuse the mistakes, papa!" she exclaimed with animation.

"Indeed, I will, Gracie" he said, and just then the breakfast bell rang.

Violet's face as she met them in the breakfast room was not quite so sunny as husband and children were accustomed to see it. She was feeling very much as Gracie did about the captain's contemplated absence from home. Also, it was a sad thought to her that Max was not likely to be a permanent resident of his father's house. He would be at home now and then for vacation, but that, probably, would be all, for after graduating he would go out into the world to make a career for himself. It would seem hard to give him up, for she was fond of the lad, her husband's son, and he was like a dear younger brother to her. She noted the traces of tears on Gracie's cheeks with a fellow-feeling for the child's distress.

"So papa has been telling you, dear?" she said, bending down to kiss the little girl. "Well, we won't fret. We'll try to just keep thinking of the joyful time we shall have when they come back to us."

"Oh, that will be nice, won't it?" exclaimed Lulu. "I'm just wild with delight at the prospect of going, but I know I'll be ever so glad to get back, for this is such a dear, sweet home."

"And papa will be in it again when you get back. You'll have him all the time going and coming. I'm glad for you, Lu," Gracie said, smiling affectionately on her sister, through her tears.

But they had taken their places at the table, and all were quiet for a moment while the captain prayed a blessing on their food.

Lulu asked a question the instant she was free to do so. "Papa, when will we start on our journey?"

"In about a week. Can you get ready in that time, Lulu?"

"Oh, yes, indeed, sir! I don't believe I have anything to do but pack my trunk. I have plenty of nice clothes and pretty things ready to wear!"

"Yes, plenty of them, such as they are, but you will need something plainer and more durable than the dresses you wear at home for the traveling."

"Shall I, papa?" she asked in surprise and dismay. "Surely, papa, you won't want me to look shabby, and I've heard that people dress quite as handsomely and fashionably away out West as they do here or anywhere else."

"That may be so, daughter," he said. "But sensible people dress according to circumstances—suitably for time, place, and occupation. For instance, a sensible lady wouldn't put on a ball gown in the morning and when she is engaged in domestic duties any more than she would wear a calico wrapper to a ball."

"No, I wouldn't think of doing either of those things, papa," she returned. "But you don't expect to set me to doing housework out there, do you?"

"Perhaps we are to live in a tent and have you for our housekeeper, Lu," suggested Max.

"Oh, is that it?" she exclaimed, with a look of delight. "Oh, that would be fun! Papa, are we to do so?"

"I have no such scheme in contemplation," he said, smiling kindly into her excited face.

"I rather think we will find a place to board, and that it will not be one where you will find occasion for much fine dressing. Besides, I shall not care to take anyone decked out in laces and ribbons with me to climb mountains, roam through forests, go down into mines, or to ride an Indian or Mexican pony, or a mule over rough roads—and that not always in fine weather.'

"Oh, papa, are you going to let me do such things as that?" she cried, laying down knife and fork to clap her hands in glee and feeling a strong inclination to jump up and dance about the floor.

"Some, or possibly all of them, if I can have you in suitable attire," he answered. "But certainly not otherwise, young lady."

"What additions to her wardrobe do you wish made, my dear?" asked Violet.

"Two or three dresses of some material not easily torn or soiled—flannel perhaps—and they must be plainly and strongly made—no flounces, furbe-lows, or trimming of a kind that would be liable to catch on twigs or bushes or points of rock."

"I shall look a fright, I'm afraid," remarked Lulu uneasily and coloring deeply. "But I'm willing to for the sake of pleasing you, papa, and being taken everywhere with you."

"That's right, dear child," he said, giving her a smile of approval.

"And I think you will look very nice and neat, Lu," said Violet. "My dear, mamma and I are going into the city this morning for a little shopping, and if you trust our taste and judgment we will willing purchase the goods for Lulu's dresses. Then I will set Alma to work upon them at once and try to get Susan Allen to help her, for I think it will take both to finish them in season."

"An excellent plan, my dear," the captain replied. "And I shall be exceedingly obliged if you undertake it, for I should sooner trust your and mother's taste and judgment in such things than my own."

"Can't I go along and help choose my own dresses, papa," pleaded Lulu.

"If it didn't involve neglect of lessons, you might, daughter," the captain answered in a very kind tone. "But as that is the case, we must leave the selection to your mamma and Grandma Elsie."

A slight cloud gathered on Lulu's brow, but it cleared again when Max said, "You know, Lu, our school days together are almost over, and you don't want to miss any of them—at least I don't, for I shall never have another teacher so good at explaining, so kind and so fond of his pupils as papa."

The lad's voice trembled a little with the concluding words in spite of himself.

"I'm sure you won't, Max, and I'm sorry for you," returned Lulu with a slight sigh. "For myself, too, that I'm not to have your company in the schoolroom after this week."

"Please, don't talk about it," begged Gracie, hastily wiping away a tear. "I'll just have to try not to think of it, or I'll be crying all the time."

"Which would not be at all good for your eyes," added her father. "So you had better take your mamma's advice and turn your thoughts upon pleasant subjects. I have something to suggest. Make out a list of all the toys, books, and other presents you would like to have—supposing some little angel should come and offer to supply them," he interpolated with playful look and tone. "Tell me the places you would like to visit and all the agreeable ways of spending your time this summer that you can manage to contrive. And when your list is done, let me see it."

Gracie knew her father well enough to feel quite certain that the making out of such a list at his suggestion would not be a labor lost.

"I will, papa," she said, smiling through her tears. "I think I'll begin this afternoon, as soon as my lessons are learned."

Lulu found no small difficulty in fixing her attention upon her tasks that morning. Her thoughts would fly off, now to the Naval Academy, where her brother was likely to be domiciled in the fall, now to the far West, with the fresh pleasures there awaiting her father, Max, and herself.

Glancing toward her, the captain saw that, though a book lay open on her desk before her, her eyes were fixed on vacancy. He called her to come to him. She started, coloring deeply, rose, and obeyed.

"You are not studying," he said in a grave, though not unkindly tone.

"No, sir, I meant to, but—oh, papa, I just can't study when I have so much else to think about."

"Can't is a lazy word, my daughter," he replied. "You have a strong will—which is not altogether a bad thing, though it has given both you and me a good deal of pain and trouble in past days. I want you to exert it now and force your truant thoughts to fix themselves upon the business at hand. Will you not, because it is your duty and to please your father who loves you so dearly?"

"Indeed, I will at once, papa. And perhaps I shall succeed if I try with all my might," she answered, holding up her face for a fatherly kiss, which he gave very heartily.

Returning to her seat, she set to work with such earnestness and determination that when summoned to recite she was able to do so to the entire satisfaction of both her father and herself.

Max and Gracie did equally well, and tutor and scholars withdrew from the schoolroom in a happy frame of mind.

A carriage was coming up the drive, bringing Grandma Elsie and Mrs. Raymond on their return from the proposed shopping expedition, and at once Lulu was all excitement to see what they had bought for her.

"May I see my dresses, Mamma Vi?" she asked, following Violet and her mother through the hall and up the wide stairway.

"Yes, Lu, certainly," replied Violet. "Though I'm afraid you will not think them very pretty to look at," she added with a deprecatory smile. "You know I could only try to carry out your father's wishes and directions."

"And I am sure is just what a little girl who loves her father so dearly and has such confidence in his judgment would wish to have done," Grandma Elsie remarked in a pleasant tone. "I think the goods we have selected will make up into very neat dresses, entirely suitable for the occasions on which you expect to wear them, Lulu, my dear child."

"Yes, Grandma Elsie, and I mean to be satisfied, even if they don't look pretty to me, because I know that you and papa and Mamma Vi are much wiser than I. And if papa is satisfied with my appearance, I suppose it really doesn't make any difference what other folks think," returned Lulu, seating herself on a sofa in her mamma's boudoir and undoing the package handed her by a servant.

"Three flannel dresses—a dark brown, a dark blue, and a dark green—all beautiful shades and nice, fine material," she commented. "I like them better that I expected to, but—"

"Well, dear?" inquired Violet, as the little girl paused without finishing her sentence.

"They are very pretty shades," repeated Lulu. "But I think red—a dark shade, 'most black in some lights—would be more becoming to my complexion. Don't you, papa?" looking up into his face as he came and stood by her side.

"Possibly," he answered, sitting down and drawing her to his knee. "But there might be times when it would prove dangerous. Some animals have a great hatred for that color and with a red dress on you might be chased by a turkey gobbler or some large animal," he concluded laughingly, hugging her up in his arms and kissing her first on one cheek, then on the other.

"Oh, yes! I didn't think of that!" she exclaimed with a merry laugh.

"Besides," he continued in the same sportive tone, "so thoroughly patriotic a young American as my Lulu surely does not want to be a redcoat?"

"No, papa; no, indeed! That would never do for a blue-jacket's daughter, would it? Blue's the right color, after all, and I'm glad that it was the color chosen for one of the dresses."

"And now the next thing is to go up to the sewing room and have them cut and fitted," said Violet. "Alma is there and will attend to it at once."

"We are going to have Mrs. Allen and Susan here to help, too, aren't we, papa?" queried Lulu, leaving her father's knee and gathering up the new purchases.

"There will be some parts they can work on at home," said Violet.

"You and I will drive over with some work for them this afternoon, Lulu," said the captain. "And we will call at Fairview and Ion on our way home, so you can have the pleasure of telling your little friends, Evelyn and Rosie, about the trip you are to take. Here, give me that bundle. It is a trifle heavy for you to carry. I'll go with you to the sewing room."

"Oh, you're just the goodest papa!" she returned merrily, yielding up the package, putting her hand into his, and dancing along by his side as he led her to the sewing room. "You're always contriving something to give me pleasure. It'll be fun to tell the girls. I'm in ever such a hurry to have a chance."

"Yes, my daughter Lulu is very apt to be in a hurry," he said, smiling down indulgently upon her. "And it is well not to dillydally when there is anything to be done, yet sometimes wisest to make haste slowly."

"Papa, don't tell Alma or Susan that, please," she whispered in a merry aside, for they were nearing the open door of the sewing room. "Because I want them to make haste fast this time."

"No, only that they must be deliberate enough to make sure of doing the work right, for otherwise it would but be the 'more haste the less speed.'"

"Yes, sir, I remember that old saw, and how I've sometimes found it true."

❦ ❦ ❦ ❦ ❦

In the neat living room of their cottage home, Mrs. Allen and Susan sat that bright June afternoon, the mother busily plying her needle, the daughter running a sewing machine.

The little garden was bright with flowers, and the vines over the porch were in full bloom. The drowsy hum of the bees came pleasantly in at the open door and window, accompanied by the sweet scents of the flowers, and now and then from an adjacent field or wood the cheery bird call, "Bob White! Bob White!"

"How delightful it is here," remarked Susan, stopping her machine for a moment to readjust her work. "The air is so sweet. The sounds are, too. I like to hear that bird calling out so cheerily."

"Yes," rejoined her mother, "it is a very agreeable change from the old sounds of scolding, quarrelling, screaming, and crying that used to assail our ears in our former abode."

"In Rose Alley? Yes, I was just thinking of that and how hot and stifling the air must be there today. Oh, mother, I do believe I should have been left alone in the world before now if we had had to stay on there! When I think of that I feel that I owe a debt of gratitude to Mrs. Travilla and Captain Raymond that I can never, never pay."

"To them and to Him who put in into their hearts to do such great kindness and gave them the ability," responded her mother. "I feel like another woman—find it a pleasure to busy myself with this beautiful napery. See, I am at the last dozen napkins, and I will be ready to begin on those linen sheets presently. Yes, this is easy and pleasant employment, yet I should prefer something that would keep me out of doors most of the day. Dr. Conly says it would be the best thing for my health, and I have a plan in my head that perhaps I may be able to carry out if our kind friends approve, and they will give me a little assistance at the start."

"What is that, mother?" asked Susan. Then, glancing from the door, "Oh, there is the Woodburn carriage now!"

She sprang up and ran down the path to open the gate for its occupants and bid them welcome.

They were Grandma Elsie, the captain, and Lulu. They greeted her with a pleasant "Good afternoon" and kindly inquiries about her mother. Then Lulu, handing out a bundle, said, "I've brought you some more work, Susan—parts of dresses for me. Alma says they are all cut and basted, so that you won't need any directions about them, and Mamma Vi says you may please lay aside other work and do this as promptly as you can."

"Yes, Miss Lulu, but won't you all 'light and come in? A bit of chat with you and the captain does mother so much good, Mrs. Travilla."

They had not intended doing so, but that plea was powerful to Grandma Elsie's kind heart.

"Yes, I can spare a few minutes," she said in reply to the captain's inquiring look.

He at once alighted, assisted her to do so, and then Lulu.

They only made a short call, yet it was long enough for Grandma Elsie's sympathetic listening and questioning to draw from Mrs. Allen the secret of her desire for outdoor employment of a kind not too laborious for her slender strength, and her idea that she might find it in bee raising, had she the means to buy a hive, a swarm of the insects, and a book of instructions.

"You shall have them all," Grandma Elsie said. "Everything that is necessary to enable you to give the business a fair trial."

"Many thanks, dear Mrs. Travilla," returned the poor woman, tears of gratitude springing to her eyes. "And if you will kindly consider whatever you may advance me as a loan, I accept your kind offer most gladly."

"It shall be as you wish," Mrs. Travilla replied. "But with the distinct understanding that the loan is not to be repaid till you can do it with perfect ease."

"And I should be glad to have a share in the good work," remarked the captain. "Let it be my part to gather information on bee culture for you and help in raising flowers for them to gather honey from. Doubtless they fly long distances in search of such, but it must be an advantage to have plenty near at hand."

"Ah, sir," returned Mrs. Allen, "you, too, are always ready to do every kindness in your power. I hope God, our heavenly Father, will abundantly repay you both. I always think of you when reading the words of the psalmist, 'Blessed is he that considereth the poor,' for you give not only money, but time and thought and sympathy, considering their needs and how best to supply them."

While this talk went on in the parlor, Lulu was telling Susan, out in the living room, what the dresses were needed for and going into ecstasies of delight over the prospect of her journey to the far West with her father and Max.

Susan sympathized in her pleasure and promised to do her very best toward getting her dresses done in season.

"To Fairview," was the captain's order to the coachman when again they were all seated in the family carriage.

It was but a few minutes drive, and on their arrival, Lulu was pleased to find Rosie there with Evelyn, so that she could have the satisfaction of telling her news to both together, and enjoying their surprise. It was quite as great as she had expected.

"How splendid!" cried Rosie. "You are a fortunate girl, Lu. I wonder if I couldn't persuade mamma and grandpa to get up some such expedition and take me along!"

"I'm very glad for you, Lu, and I hope it will be one long pleasure from beginning to end," Eva said. "You couldn't have a more delightful caretaker than your father, and Max will be good company, too. But, oh, dear, how I shall miss you!" she concluded with a sigh, putting her arms round Lulu and holding her in a close embrace.

"And I you," said Lulu. "But when we talk that way at home papa says we should not think about that, but about the joy of reunion when we get home again."

❧ ❧ ❧ ❧ ❧

"Well, my dear, little Gracie, what progress have you made with that list? Is it ready for papa's inspection, yet?" the captain asked as the children clustered about him on the veranda after tea that evening.

"I've put down some things, papa, but maybe I can think up some more before long, if I may have a little more time," she answered with an arch smile up into his face.

"You can have all the time you want, darling," he said, caressing her. "But suppose you let me see what you have already set down."

At that she drew a half sheet of notepaper from her pocket and put it into his hand.

He glanced over it and a look of amusement stole over his face. "A spade, rake, and hoe! I thought you had garden tools," he said.

"Yes, papa, but these are to be big ones for Sam Hill to make his mother's garden with. He says he always has to borrow now, and the neighbors get tired lending to him."

"Ah, very well, you shall have money to buy them for him. But what do you want with twenty yards of calico and a piece of muslin?"

"Sam also needs shirts, and his mother some dresses, papa."

"And the slates and books are for the younger children, Gracie?"

"Yes, sir. And those things are for the Jones children. You know their father doesn't buy them anything to wear, and sometimes he takes the clothes other folks give them and sells them to buy liquor."

"Yes, it is very sad, and we must do the best we can for them. But you have not put down anything for my little Gracie. Is there nothing she would like to have?"

"I don't need anything at all, papa. I have so many, many nice things already."

"But I want to give you something to help to keep you from being lonely while Lulu is enjoying herself in the far West. Ah, I see there is something? What is it?"

"A canary bird, papa, that will sing beautifully."

"Dear child," he said holding her close, "you shall have the finest that money can buy. You shall have a pair of them and the handsomest cage we can find. I shall take you to the city tomorrow and let you choose them for yourself."

"Oh, how nice, papa!" she cried, clapping her hands in delight. "Then they will have a pretty home and be company for each other. I was afraid one would be so lonesome all by itself. I was thinking, too, that I'd be ever so lonely, at night especially, without Lu. But mamma said she will take me in with her while you are gone."

"Very kind and thoughtful of mamma," was the captain's comment.

"You'll take me to buy them tomorrow afternoon, will you papa?" she asked.

"Yes, if nothing happens to prevent."

"And mayn't Lu and Max go along?"

"Certainly, if they want to."

"Thank you, papa. I'll be very much pleased to go," Lulu said. Max added, "I, too. So there'll be four of us to choose your two birds, Gracie."

"Perhaps we may be able to persuade your mamma to go, too," the captain said, as at that moment Violet joined them. "And then there'll be five of us."

"Go where, my dear?" asked Violet, seating herself by his side.

He explained, and she accepted the invitation with the remark that she did not want to lose his company for a moment of the week he would be with her before starting on his journey to the West.

CHAPTER NINTH

THEY ALL ENJOYED their trip to the city the next day, Gracie perhaps more than any of the others. She was allowed to buy everything on her list, and some others she thought of while on the way or in the stores, selecting them herself.

But the first business attended to was the purchase of the canaries. They succeeded in getting a beautiful pair, fine singers, and a very handsome cage. Gracie was full of delight, and her father pleased himself with the hope that the new pets would save her from the loneliness Lulu's absence would otherwise have caused her.

They left her all drowned in tears when they set out upon their long journey, but, as Violet reported to the captain in a letter written on the evening of the same day, the canaries set up a song so melodious and full of joy that she presently dried her eyes and hushed her sobs to listen.

Violet herself indulged in a few tears over the parting of half of her little family, but for the sake of Gracie and the little ones soon forced herself to assume an air of cheerfulness.

Max and Lulu were sorry for those left behind, yet so delighted with their own good fortune in being permitted to accompany their father that they speedily recovered from the sadness of leave-taking and were never in better spirits.

It was on Saturday morning they began their journey. The Lord's day was spent in a strange city, very much as they would have spent it at home, and on Monday they started on again, taking a through train that would carry them to their destination, and on which they spent several days and nights, finding excellent accommodations for both eating and sleeping.

The captain watched over his children with the tenderest care—Lulu especially, as being the younger and of the weaker sex—and Max was constantly on the alert to wait upon both her and his father.

The journey, the longest the children had ever taken, was without accident. There was no detention, and the luxurious appointments of the cars prevented it from being very fatiguing.

They made some pleasant acquaintances—among them an English gentleman and his son, a lad about Max's age.

Mr. Austin, a man of wealth and refinement, was travelling for his health and to see the country and had brought his son with him as a companion—thinking, too, as he explained it to Captain Raymond, after they had arrived at terms of comparative intimacy, that travel in a foreign land would be improving to the boy in an educational way.

The acquaintance began with the children. Albert had been watching Lulu admiringly for a day or so from the opposite side of the car.

"That's a pretty little girl over there, papa," he at length remarked in an undertone. "I fancy she's English, too."

"I think you are mistaken," returned his father. "The gentleman is assuredly American, and from his manner toward the children, I fancy they are his own. There is a strong resemblance also, between the three."

"But she has quite an English complexion, sir, so rosy."

"Yes, but such complexions are not so very unusual among the American women and girls."

"No, sir, perhaps not. The boy's a nice-looking fellow and has very gentlemanly manners. Don't you think so, sir?"

"Yes, they are evidently people of education and refinement. But what is the train stopping for?" glancing from the window. "Ah, I see. They are taking on a fresh supply of fuel for the engine."

The same question had just been asked by Lulu and answered by her father in the same way, as he rose and took his hat from the rack overhead.

"You are going out, papa?" Lulu said inquiringly. "Oh, don't get left, please!"

"I certainly do not intend to," he answered with a look of amusement. "I only want to stretch my limbs for a moment and shall not go any distance from the train."

"Oh, can't we go, too?" she asked.

"Max may, but you, I think, had better content yourself with moving about the car."

"May I go out on the platform?"

"No, decidedly not," he answered in a firm though kind tone, then hurried out, Max following.

Lulu rose and stood at the window, watching for their appearance outside. They were there in a moment, right below it.

"Papa," she called softly.

He looked up with a smile. "Dear child," he said, "move about the car. It will rest you. I know you are tired of sitting to long."

He walked on, and she stepped out into the aisle and promenaded it up and down several times, stopping occasionally, now at one window, now at another, to gaze out over the landscape. There was a seemingly boundless prairie on one side with a great herd of cattle grazing in the distance. On the other were woods and low-lying hills. There was no sign of human occupancy anywhere to be seen, except the little coaling station before which the train was standing.

The car was nearly empty now, almost all the passengers, excepting a few children and those in charge of them, having, like her father and Max, taken advantage of the halting of the train to get a little outdoor exercise—Mr. Austin and Albert among the rest.

The latter, however, returned almost immediately. As he stepped in at the car door, his eyes fell upon a dainty white pocket handkerchief lying on the floor. He stooped and picked it up, glancing around the car in search of its owner.

Lulu, standing at the window near by with her back toward him, seemed most likely to be the one, and he approached her at once, asking in a polite tone, "Is not this your property, Miss? Excuse the liberty, but I found it lying on the floor and it seemed likely to belong to you," holding out the article as he spoke.

Lulu turned round at the first sound of his voice. "Thank you," she said. "Yes, it is mine, for there is my name in the corner, in papa's own handwriting."

"I'm glad to have had the happiness of restoring it to you." He said. "How extremely warm it is today. Do you not think so?"

"Yes, especially now that the train is standing still, but when it is in motion there's a nice breeze."

"There are some things I like vastly about America," he went on. "But the climate does not suit me so well as that of old England. It's so hot and dry, you know; at least, don't you think so?"

She gave him a slightly puzzled look. "I—I believe I've heard that the weather in England is rather cooler in summer, and that it rains very often, but I never was there."

"Why, aren't you a little English girl?"

"English?" she exclaimed, opening her eyes wide in surprise. "No, indeed, I'm American, every inch of me!" she exclaimed with a flash of joy in her dark eyes and little exultant laugh, as though to be able to call him or herself an American were the proudest boast anyone could make.

"I meant it as a compliment, most assuredly," he said, coloring with a sense of mingled annoyance and mortification. "I'm very proud of being English."

"And that's quite right," she said. "Papa says each one should love his own native land above all others."

"Certainly. But surely you are of English descent."

"I really don't know," laughed Lulu. "I know that my parents, grandparents, and great-grandparents were all born in America, and I never thought of asking about my ancestors any farther back than that."

"We think a great deal of family in England. It's a grand thing—a thing to be proud of—if one can boast of a long line of noble ancestors."

"Yes, papa says the knowledge that we're descended from honest, upright, pious people is something to be very thankful for. He says it's easier for such folks to be good—I mean honest and truthful and all that—than it is for the descendants of wicked people."

"Perhaps so, though I never thought of it before," and with a slight bow, he withdrew to his own seat, for the passengers were flocking in again as the call, "All aboard!" warned them that the train was about to start.

Captain Raymond was among the first, and just in time to perceive that the English lad had been making acquaintance with his little girl. He was not altogether pleased. His countenance was unusually grave as he took Lulu's hand and led her back to her seat. But there was too much noise and confusion at the moment for anything like conversation, and he made no remark.

Lulu felt that he was displeased, and several times her eyes were lifted to his face for an instant with a timid, imploring glance.

At length as the train began to move more quietly, he bent down and spoke close to her ear. "I do not want a daughter of mine to be too forward in making acquaintance with strangers, especially men and boys. I would have her always modest and retiring. But I will not blame you unheard, dear child. Tell me about it."

"I didn't make the first advances, papa," she said, putting her arm round his neck, her lips close to his ear. "Please don't think I could be so bold. I had dropped my handkerchief and didn't know it till the boy picked it up and handed it to me. He behaved in a very gentlemanly way, and when I thanked him, he began to talk about the weather. Presently he asked me if I wasn't an English girl. Just think of it, papa!" she added with a gleeful laugh.

"And what did you say to that?" he asked with an amused look. "That you were not, but wished you were?"

"Oh, papa, no, indeed!! Wish I was English? Or anything else but American? I'm sure you must know I don't."

"Yes," he returned, putting his arm about her waist and giving her a hug. "I am happy in the knowledge that all my darlings are intensely patriotic."

"Because you've taught us to be so—to love our dear native land and the beautiful old flag, the emblem of our nation's glory!" she responded, her cheeks flushing and her eyes sparkling.

Max sitting directly in front of them had caught the last two sentences of their colloquy.

"Yes, papa," he said, "everyone of us is that. Even baby Ned laughs and crows and claps his hands when he looks up at the flag waving in the breeze. I noticed it at Ion on Grandma Elsie's semi-centennial, where they had so many floating from the veranda and tree tops.

"Ah!" laughed the captain. "That was doubtless an evidence of good taste, but hardly of patriotism in so young a child."

Mr. Austin was beginning to share his son's interest in the Raymonds, and the two had been furtively watching the little scene, attracted by the animated expression of the faces of the captain, Max, and Lulu, as they talked.

"They seem a happy and affectionate trio," Mr. Austin remarked to Albert.

"Yes, sir, and you were right about their being Americans. I asked the little girl if she wasn't English, and to my astonishment she seemed almost indignant at the bare idea."

"Ah, indeed! Then I fancy she has never seen England."

"No, sir, she said she never had, but if you had seen the look in her eyes when she told me she was every inch an American, you would hardly expect even a sight of old England to make her change her mind."

"It's a great country, certainly—immensely larger than our favored isle, and had it been our birthplace, it is quite possible we might have shared her feeling. But, as it is, we assuredly look upon Great Britain as the most favored land the sun shines on."

"And he shines always upon some part of the empire," responded Albert with eyes proudly beaming their patriotic love.

It was not until in the afternoon of the next day the Raymonds reached their destination—Minersville, a town not yet three years old, that had sprung up within that period of time upon a tract of land owned by the captain and grown with rapidity that might well remind one of Jonah's gourd, "which came up in a night." It was all the result of discovery of gold in the immediate vicinity. The mine—a very productive one—was still largely owned by Captain Raymond, also the greater part of the town, and a coal mine at no great distance from the place.

The two yielded him a large income—augmented by the fortunate investment of very considerable sums realized on the sales of stock and town lots, so that he was indeed a wealthy man.

He and Mr. Austin had made acquaintance by this time and were mutually pleased. The same thing had happened with their sons, and the Englishman, after learning from the captain what was his destination, the history of Minersville, and something of the opportunities and facilities for hunting bears, deer, and other game in that region, had decided to make a halt there for a few days or weeks. Captain Raymond had given him a cordial invitation to inspect the mines and join him in hunting expeditions.

The town already boasted several thousand inhabitants, two churches, a bank, post office, a fine public school building, dry goods and grocery stores, mills, factories, and two hotels.

To one of these last went Mr. Austin and Albert, but Captain Raymond—particularly on account of having his children with him—preferred a private boarding house. Through his business agent and mine superintendent, Mr. John Short, he had already engaged rooms with a Scotch lady, Mrs. McAlpine by name, whom Short had recommended as a good housekeeper and one who kept an excellent table.

The party had scarcely left the train when a rather gentlemanly looking man approached, and lifting his hat, said, "My name is Short. Do I address Captain Raymond?"

"That is my name, sir," rejoined the captain, offering his hand, which the other took and shook quite heartily.

"Glad to meet you, sir, very glad. I have often wished you would come out and see your property here for yourself. It's well worth looking after, I assure you."

"I am quite convinced of that," the captain said with a smile. "Also, I do not doubt that it has been well looked after by my agent, Mr. Short."

"Thanks, sir," returned Short, bowing and smiling in acknowledgment. "And these are the son and daughter you wrote me you would bring with you?" he remarked with an inquiring glance at the children.

"Yes," replied the captain, looking down at the two with fatherly pride and affection. "Max and Lulu are their names. I am so domestic a man that I could not persuade myself to leave all my family behind when expecting to be absent so long from home."

"Yes, sir, I'm not surprised at that. Well, sir, I think Mrs. McAlpine will make you comfortable. She has two sets of boarders, mill operatives and miners, who eat in the kitchen, and a few gentlemen and a lady or two who take their meals in the dining room. But she has agreed to give up her own private sitting room at meal times to you and your family, as you stated in your letter of instruction you wished a private table for yourself and the children, for a consideration, of course," he added with a laugh. "But knowing you could well afford it and were not disposed to be close, I did not hesitate to accept her terms."

"Quite right," replied the captain. "And as to sleeping accommodations?"

"She can let you have a room of pretty good size for yourself and son with a small one opening into it for the little girl—or perhaps I should rather say the young lady—your daughter."

"She is only a little girl—her father's little girl, as she likes to call herself," returned the captain, smiling down at Lulu and affectionately pressing the hand she had slipped into his while they stood talking.

"Yes," she said laughing and blushing. "I do like it. I'm not in a bit of a hurry to be a young lady."

"No, Miss, I wouldn't if I were you," laughed Mr. Short. "Those changes come to us all only too fast. Shall I show you the way to your quarters, captain? I did not order a carriage, as it is hardly more than a step, and judging by my own past experience, I thought you'd be glad of a chance to use your limbs after being cramped up in the cars for so long."

"You are not mistaken in that. I think we all feel it rather a relief," the captain made answer, as they moved on together.

A very short walk brought them to the door of the boarding house. They were admitted by a rather comely girl, apparently about fifteen years of age, whom their conductor addressed as "Miss Marian," and introduced as the daughter of Mrs. Alpine. She invited them into the parlor and went in search of her mother, returning with her almost immediately. She was a middle-aged woman with a gentle, lady-like manner that was very pleasing, and the remains of considerable beauty, but had, Captain Raymond thought, one of the saddest faces he had ever seen. There were depths of woe in the gray eyes that touched him to the heart, yet the prevailing expression of her countenance was that of patient resignation.

"She is evidently a great sufferer from some cause," he said to himself. "Probably an inconsolable widow, as I have heard no mention of a Mr. Alpine."

She bade them welcome and inquired what they would have for their evening meal and how soon they would like it served.

The captain answered those questions, then requested to be shown to the sleeping room set apart for their use during their stay.

"I fear sir, they will seem poor and mean after such as you and the young folks have no doubt been accustomed to," she said, leading the way. "But they are the best I can provide, and I trust you will find them clean and comfortable.

"Our nights are cool, even when the days are very warm, and you will get the mountain breeze here, which is a thing to be thankful for, to my way of thinking," she added, drawing back the curtain from an open window of the room into which she had conducted them.

The captain stepped to it and looked out. "Yes," he said, "and a fine view of the mountains themselves with a pretty flower garden and orchard in the foreground, a river and a wooded hills between—a beautiful prospect—another cause for thankfulness, I think. The room, too, is of fair size," turning from the window and glancing about him. "That open door I presume leads into the one my little girl is to occupy?"

"Yes, sir. It is not very large, but I have no other communicating bedrooms, and Mr. Short said you wrote particularly that they must be such, or yours large enough for a corner to be curtained off for her."

"Yes, so I did, and she, I know, would prefer a small room with a door open into mine to a large and better one with a separating wall between," smiling down into Lulu's eager, interested face at that instant upturned to his.

"Indeed, I should, papa," she responded, slipping a hand confidently into his and returning his smile with one of ardent, filial affection.

Tears sprang to the sad eyes of Mrs. McAlpine at the sight, and it was a moment before she could command her voice to speak. When able to do so, excusing herself upon the plea that domestic duties required her attention, she left them.

"I would like to see my room," said Lulu, hurrying toward the open door. Then, as she gained a view of the whole interior, "I should say it is small! There is one window, one chair, a single bed, a little bit of a washstand and just barely room to move back and forth beside the bed. How different from my lovely rooms at home!" she ended with a pout and frown.

"I am sorry it is not more to your liking, my dear child," the captain remarked in a kindly, sympathetic tone. "But it cannot be helped now. Does my little girl begin to wish her father had left her at home?" he asked, laying his hand tenderly on her head, for he had followed her and now stood close at her side.

"Oh, no, no, dear papa! And I'm quite ashamed of my grumbling," she returned, taking his hand in both of hers and laying her cheek affectionately against it.

"You wouldn't do to go into the navy, Lu, if you can't put up with narrow quarters sometimes," remarked Max sportively. "So it's a good thing you're not a boy."

"Of course it is," she answered in a sprightly tone. "Who that might be a girl would ever want to be a boy? Not I, I'm sure."

"Not even for the sake of being able to grow up into such a man as papa?"

"No, I couldn't have any hope of that anyhow, for there's nobody in all the world like papa—so dear and good and kind and handsome and—"

"There, that will do," laughed the captain, bending down and stopping the next word with a kiss full upon her lips. "It is enough and more than enough, and we must be getting rid of the dust of travel and making ourselves neat for the tea table," he added.

"Yes, sir, I'm glad to be out of the cars for a while after being in them so long. And these rooms are neat as wax, even if the furniture is scanty and plain. I shan't mind that a bit, as it's only for a short time, and I wouldn't have been left behind for anything. I hope I'll not complain anymore, papa. I don't intend to. But," in sudden dismay, "oh, where am I to put my trunk?"

Her father and brother both laughed at her quite perplexed, woebegone countenance.

"You'll have to decide that question soon, for here they come," said Max, glancing from the window.

"Don't be troubled, dear child. We will find a place for it in this outer room," added her father cheerily, glancing about in search of one. "Ah, it can stand in this corner close by your door. Does that suit your ideas and wishes, daughter?"

"Yes, sir, it will be the most convenient place for me," she answered in a bright, cheery tone, quite restored to good humor.

The trunks had already been brought in and deposited according to directions.

"Will you have anything out of this, daughter?" the captain asked, unstrapping Lulu's.

"Another dress, papa, if you are willing to let me change. This traveling one feels hot and dusty."

"My dear child, can you suppose I would want you to be uncomfortable?" he asked. "Give me your key, and we will have the dress out immediately.

"Thank you, papa," she said, taking the key from her travelling bag and handing it to him. "Please choose for me the one you think most suitable."

"Do you feel inclined for a stroll about the town with your father and Max after tea?" he asked.

"Oh, yes, sir. Yes, indeed!"

"You are not too tired?" he questioned, smiling at her eager, joyous tone.

"Oh, no, sir, not at all. I think I shall feel as fresh as a lark after I have washed and dressed and had my supper."

"Then this will be quite suitable," he said, lifting out a cream-colored serge with collar and cuffs of red velvet and a bordering of Indian embroidery in which the same shade was quite prominent.

"The very dress I'd have chosen myself, papa," she remarked with a pleasant laugh. "And when we take our walk I must wear the hat that matches. I do like to wear things that match or contrast prettily and suit my complexion."

"Well, daughter, since our kind heavenly Father has made so many things beautiful to our eyes—the sunset clouds with their gorgeous hues, the myriads of lovely flowers and fruits, to mention only a few—I think it cannot be wrong for us to enjoy pretty things. Still, my dear little girl must be on her guard against vanity and pride, because of being well and tastefully attired, and careful not to give too much of her time and thoughts to dress."

CHAPTER TENTH

"WELL, IT IS NICE to eat in a house again with no strangers by," remarked Lulu when they had seated themselves at the table in Mrs. McAlpine's sitting room and the captain had asked a blessing on their food.

"So it is," responded Max. "It would almost seem something like home if we had Mamma Vi, Gracie, and the little ones here with us."

"Yes," assented their father with a slight sigh. "They make the best part of home. We must look for the post office when we are out. I hope we shall find letters there from home, and I have one to mail to your mamma."

"Why, when did you write it, papa?" asked Lulu.

"While you were dressing."

"Was I so very slow?"

"No, but you see I had the advantage of you in not needing to change my dress."

With that Marian, who had just brought in a plate of hot cakes, glanced admiringly at Lulu's costume.

"What a pretty girl that little Miss Raymond is, and so beautifully dressed!" she remarked to her mother on going back to the kitchen. "It must be a grand thing to be the daughter—"

"Don't allow yourself to envy her, my child," interrupted the mother. "'Tis God appoints our lot, and we must strive to be submissive and content."

"Mother," cried the girl almost fiercely, "ye need-na tell me God appointed this lot for you and me. I'll never believe it, never! 'Twas the father o' lies brought us here an' keeps us here, and oh, but I wad we had never left bonny Scotland!"

"Hush, hush, child!! Bairn, your wild words but add to the weight o' the cross already almost too heavy for your mother to bear," returned Mrs. McAlpine, catching her breath with a half sob. "Here, carry this to the guests in the sitting room," giving her another plate of cakes just taken from the griddle.

"Can you tell me where to find the post office, Miss Marian?" Captain Raymond asked as she again stood at his side, offering her cakes.

"Yes, sir, 'tis just around the corner, on the way to the mine. If you want to send there, sir, Sandy, my brother, will go for you willingly. They must be making up the mail for the East now, and it will close presently."

"Then I accept your kind offer of your brother's services with thanks," he said, taking a letter from his pocket and giving it to her. "Please ask him to carry this one to the post office and see that it gets into the mail. Then, inquire for letters for Captain L., Master Max, and Miss Lulu Raymond."

"I will, sir," she replied, taking the letter and hurrying from the room with it.

A few minutes later a boy who looked to be two or three years younger than Marian came briskly in, and laying a handful of letters on the table beside the captain, said, "Several for you, sir, and one apiece for Master and Miss. And the one I took for you is gone with the rest o' the mail for the East."

"I am much obliged," the captain said, putting a dime into his hand.

The boy glanced down at it. "That's too much, sir, by half. The errand wasn't worth a nickel, and in fact I didn't expect any pay for doing it."

"Then take the dime as a gift, my boy. I like your honesty," returned the captain.

"Thank you, sir," responded the lad quite heartily, and with a grin of satisfaction, he turned and hastened away.

"Papa, is there one for me?" asked Lulu, as her father took up the letters and glanced at each of the superscriptions.

"Yes, daughter, and one for Max. And as we have all finished eating, we will go immediately to our room to read them."

The letters brought only good news. The dear ones left behind were all well and, though missing the absentees, content and happy, at least so far as could be gathered from the cheerful tone of their epistles.

Lulu's was the joint production of Eva and Gracie and gave an interesting account of the doings and sayings of the babies and the parrot.

The last named, they said, was continually calling, "Lu, Lu, what you 'bout? Where you been?"

The letter told, too, of the beautiful singing of Gracie's canaries, the doings of her kitten, and of Max's dog Prince. There was more about the last named in Max's own letter, which was from Violet with a postscript by Gracie.

The captain read his letter from Violet, first to himself, then portions of it aloud to the children. Then, they offered theirs, and he read them aloud in turn and chatted pleasantly with them about the contents of all three.

"Well," he said at length, "if we are going to take that walk, it is about time we were setting out. Lulu, you may put on your hat, while I glance over these other letters."

That was a welcome order to the little girl, and it did not take her many minutes to obey it. They found Mr. Short on the pavement before the front gate as they went out.

"Ah, captain," he said, "I was just coming to ask you if you did not feel inclined for a stroll about the town. May I have the pleasure of acting as your guide?"

"It will be conferring a favor, sir, if you will do so," replied the person addressed, and the two walked on, leaving Max and Lulu to follow.

"I wish he hadn't come," she muttered. "I thought I was going to have the pleasure of walking beside papa with my hand in his."

"That's very pleasant for you," said Max. "But I think you might care almost as much to walk with me, considering that you'll probably not have many more such opportunities to do so."

"Oh, I forgot that! Oh, I wish you weren't going away from home, Max!" she exclaimed. "I seem to grow fonder of you than ever when I think of that!"

"Yes, blessings brighten as they take their flight," he returned with a little laugh that actually sounded rather forced.

The new home made by his father for him and the others and especially the being taken by that father into a close intimacy, friendship, and confidence, such as are seldom given by a parent to a son of his age, had been so delightful that the thought of going away among strangers, leaving all the dear ones behind, and having communication with his father only by letter instead of the pleasant daily and hourly familiar exchanges could not fail to cause the boyish heart a pang.

Yet, on the other hand, there was great joy and exultation in the thought that he was about to enter upon special preparation for his chosen profession — the work that he was going to do as a man. It seemed to him the beginning of the putting away of childish things, the putting on of the armor, and the gathering up of the weapons for the great battle of life, and at times he was eager for the day when he should appear before the examiners at Annapolis.

"Yes, and you are a blessing to me, Maxie. You always have been," Lulu said in reply. "And I am sure papa thinks you a very great one to him."

The captain's quick ear caught the words, and he glanced smilingly around at the two without pausing in his talk with his agent.

Mr. Short gave the names of the streets as they passed along and pointed out the public buildings and the prettiest private residences, telling to whom each one belonged and sometimes adding a little character sketch in a humorous way or slightly satirical vein. He seemed a good natured, jovial sort of man, anxious to entertain and amuse.

It did not take long to traverse the town, and having presently reached the outskirts, they ascended an eminence from whence might be obtained a bird's eye view of the whole place and its surroundings of valley and wooded hills.

They paused here to gaze upon the landscape spread out at their feet, and Lulu, stepping to her father's side, quietly slipped her hand into his. His fingers closed affectionately over it, and he gave her a pleased, loving look, though he seemed to be listening attentively to something Mr. Short was saying about the mine.

"I must visit it tomorrow if the weather is at all favorable," the captain said in reply. "I want to take my children with me, and as I expect to be in the vicinity for several weeks, there is no special haste—no need of hurrying out there through a storm."

"Oh, I do hope the weather will be good!" exclaimed Lulu, while she and Max exchanged glances of delight.

"I think there is every indication of pleasant weather for some days to come," remarked Mr. Short.

"Is it far to the mine?" asked Lulu. "Will we have to ride or drive?"

"No, Miss, I think even you could easily walk it," replied Mr. Short. "The distance is not over a mile."

"Then I can," she said. "I've walked more than two miles many a time."

"No doubt of it," said her father. "But you must have a pony for longer excursions. Have you succeeded in securing a suitable one, Mr. Short? Horses for myself and my son, also?"

Short replied to the effect that he had succeeded in procuring a steed for each of them, which, though probably by no means equal to those they were accustomed to at home, would, he hoped, answer their purposes quite well.

"Are you accustomed to riding horseback, Miss?" he asked.

"Oh, yes," Lulu said. "Papa gave me a pony of my own more than a year ago, and before that I used to ride one belonging to somebody else."

"Here come Mr. Austin and Albert up the hill," said Max, and the next moment the English gentleman and his son had joined themselves to the little group.

The Raymonds and Mr. Short had already made acquaintance. Polite greetings were exchanged, and then all stood together watching the sun as he sank behind the western hills.

It was a grand sunset, the whole western horizon ablaze with gold, orange, and flame color, shading off here and there into the more delicate shades— rose, pale green, and amber.

They lingered for many minutes, silently gazing upon the ever-changing panorama until most of its glories had at last faded away. They then slowly descended the hill and wended their way back to their temporary abodes.

It was growing dark, the stars coming out one by one overhead, and a young moon showing herself above the hilltops, when the captain and his children reentered Mrs. McAlpine's gate and walked up the path leading to the front porch.

There were several persons sitting there, among them the lady of the house. She rose, said "Good evening," and turning to a gentleman who had risen also, introduced him as the Reverend Green.

He and Captain Raymond shook hands cordially, each expressing pleasure at the meeting, and when Max and Lulu had also been introduced and all were seated, the two gentlemen fell into earnest discourse—the mission work and its interests and needs in that region of country being their principal theme.

The children listened in silence and presently learned from the remarks of the minister, what was news to them—that their father had given town lots for church, parsonage, and schoolhouse, and nearly the whole amount of money their erection had cost.

"Papa must be rich. Very rich, Max," whispered Lulu in her brother's ear.

"Yes, and generous, too—far more generous and liberal than most folks," Max whispered back. "I'm proud as can be of being his son."

"And I of being his daughter," she returned.

They gave open expression to these sentiments in talking with their father when, a little later, they found themselves alone with him in his room.

"My dears," he said, "as I have often told you, the money is the Lord's, and I am only his steward. How, then, could I do otherwise than use it for the advancement of His cause and kingdom?"

"Yes, papa, and you did it for the good of our dear country, too, didn't you?" asked Lulu, taking a seat upon his knee and putting her arm affectionately about his neck.

"Yes, daughter, for if we would ensure her safety, we must do all battle earnestly against the threatening evils of ignorance, error, and superstition. The only way to preserve the liberties of this land and make her a power for good to the rest of the world is to instruct and evangelize all classes, whether native or foreign born."

"Now," he continued, opening a Bible which he had taken from his trunk and laid upon a table before going out, "we will close the day with reading and prayer as we do at home. Then we shall go to our rest, for we are all in need of it, I think."

He kept Lulu on his knee while he read, one arm about her waist, and Max's chair was drawn close up on the other side. Then they all knelt together while the father gave thanks for all the blessings of the past day, made confession of sins, and implored the protecting care of their heavenly Father through the silent watches of the night — for themselves and the dear ones far away.

The captain had always been careful not to make family worship seem long and tedious to his children. Tonight it was shorter than usual in consideration for their weariness, consequent upon the long journey but just completed.

When they had risen from their knees he took Lulu in his arms and kissed her tenderly two or three times, saying, "Now you may go to your own room, my darling, and when you are quite ready for bed, set the door wide open so that you can feel that papa is near enough to hear you speak, should you want anything in the night."

"Max, too," said her brother laughingly, giving her a kiss in his turn. "So that if any danger threatens you there'll be knights to fly to the rescue."

"Thank you," she returned merrily. "But if anything frightens me I shall run right to papa," giving him another hug as she spoke.

"It was a very warm evening and the windows of the room were wide open to admit air. Through one of them, looking upon the garden, Marian McAlpine witnessed the little scene. The words spoken did not reach her ear, but she saw the expression of the countenance of the captain and his children and the caresses given and received.

"What a good father! And what happy children!" she murmured aloud, as she turned away with a sigh that seemed to say her own lot was not so blessed.

Passing round the house and onto the porch, she found her mother, now sitting there alone.

Taking a chair close by her side, she said, "Mother, I think that Captain Raymond must be a very good man."

"I dare say he is, child. Certainly he has been very liberal to the mission cause in this town."

"And he looks so good and kind and seems so fond of his children," Marian went on. "I saw him reading to them tonight—the little girl sitting on his knee and the boy as close as he could well get by his side. The Bible I suppose it was, for when he closed it they all three knelt down together, and I could hear his voice as if he was praying, though not the words. Then they got up and hugged and kissed each other goodnight. They're the happiest-looking people I ever saw."

"So I think. But, Marian, you shouldn't be spying out what they are doing in the privacy of their own room."

"I didn't mean to, mother, but I happened to look up at their window—the light was so bright, you know—and I saw the girl help herself to a seat on her father's knee, just as if she was sure he'd like her to, and put her arm round his neck, and it was such a pretty scene I couldn't help standing there and watching them a bit. They don't have to share their father with a lot of other children that are not their mother's, too," she added in a suppressed and bitter tone.

"Marian, Marian, please hush!" exclaimed Mrs. McAlpine in a low voice quivering with pain. "Is your end of the cross heavier than mine?"

"No, mother, dear, not half so heavy. The cruelest part of it is seeing you suffer—you, who are as good and pure as an angel!" returned the girl passionately.

"Then for my sake, lass, try to suffer and be still. I've hard enough fight with my own rebellious heart. At times I feel I shall never be able to bring it into meek submission to His will Who doeth all things well."

"But it isn't His will! It isn't His doing! I'll never believe it, no, never!" cried the girl, clinching hands and teeth in impotent fury. "It's the will and the doings of the adversary of souls, the father o' lies, him that the Bible tells us was a murderer from the beginning and abode not in the truth, because there is no truth in him."

"Marian, Marian, ye're tempting your mother to the sin she maun ficht against nicht and day," groaned Mrs. McAlpine, relapsing into Scotch, as they were both apt to do under strong excitement. "An' oh, beware, lassie, that you dinna wrest Scripture to ye'r ain destruction and to mine."

"Wrest Scripture! 'Tis they wrest it," cried the girl in tones of fierce indignation. But before the words had fairly left her lips her mother had risen from her chair and fled her presence, as one would fly from temptation.

Marian, too, rose, closed the house, and went to bed. Alone in her own apartment, the mother spent a long time upon her knees wrestling in prayer for submission and strength to endure the cross she mistakenly deemed that He, her loving Lord and Master, had laid upon her.

CHAPTER ELEVENTH

MARIAN MCALPINE was setting the breakfast table for the Raymonds when Lulu came into the room looking bright and fresh in one of the new dresses her father had directed to be made for such excursions as that proposed for the day.

"Good morning," she said in her usual pleasant, sprightly tone.

Marian returned the salutation, and Lulu went on, "We are going to visit the mine today, and papa sent me to ask if you would like to go with us."

"Thank you, Miss. It's very kind of your father and yourself to invite me, and I should be blithe to go if mother could spare me, but I'm afraid she can't. Good help is very scarce about here, and we have to do a great deal of the cooking and other work ourselves."

"I'm sorry," said Lulu. "I'd like very much to have you go, for my own sake as well as yours, for there will be no lady in the party and no girl but me, if you don't go."

"But you'll not mind that with such a kind, tender father as yours," Marian said, a little tremulously and with a wistful glance into Lulu's bright and happy face.

"No, I'd not mind going to the world's end with papa and nobody else," returned Lulu, her cheeks flushing and her eyes shining with joy and filial love. "But how did you find out what a dear, kind father I have?"

"Surely, Miss, just the way he looks at you — as if to his mind there was nothing else so sweet and fair in all the world — is enough to tell the tale to anyone but the dullest of the dull."

The girl sighed involuntarily as she spoke and turned away, busying herself at the china closet, to hide her emotion.

"And you have none, I suppose? Oh, I am sorry for you!" Lulu said in a gentle, pitying tone.

Marian turned toward her a pale, set face, opening her lips to speak but closing them again as her mother entered the room.

"Good day, lassie, you look bright and blithe as the morning," Mrs. McAlpine said, addressing Lulu with a smile that was sadder than tears, and the little girl noticed that her face was paler than on the previous day, her countenance fuller of grief and woe, though she was evidently striving to be cheerful.

"Did you find you bed comfortable last night?" she asked.

"Oh, yes, ma'am, but I hardly touched it before I went fast asleep, and I never moved, I believe, till the sun was up."

"It must have seemed a short night to you. Sound sleep is a very great blessing," responded the lady. Then asked, "And what are your plans for the day? I fear you will find little to interest you in this small town."

"Papa is going to take us to look at the mine," said Lulu. "And we would be pleased to take your daughter with us if you can spare her."

"Certainly. Marian gets few holidays, and I would be glad to have her go. Tell your papa I thank him for the invitation, and she will be ready in good season."

Marian's eyes sparkled, and her face wore a glad, eager look for a moment. Then it changed, and she said, "No, mother, I can't go and leave you everything to do."

"There is not so much today, lass; not more than I can easily do myself," returned the mother kindly. "And I shall enjoy hearing your report when you get back."

Thus kindly urged, Marian gladly accepted the invitation. Few of what young folks are wont to call "good times" came into her life, and a visit to the mine had never been one of them.

They set out shortly after breakfast, the party consisting of Captain Raymond with his children and Marian, Mr. Austin and Albert, and Mr. Short, who acted as guide.

The two girls walked together, but Lulu managed to keep very near her father. That pleased him, both as an evidence of her ardent affection and because, knowing so little what sort of companion Marian would prove, he wanted to be near enough to over-hear their talk, that he might be able to judge what influence she was likely to exert over his child. Mindful of the declaration of Holy Writ that "evil communications corrupt good manners," he was very careful in regard to the choice of his children's associates. Poverty, if not united to viciousness or vulgarity, was considered no ground of objection, while wealth, fine dress, or fine manners could not atone for lack of moral purity and refinement.

Marian's appearance and manners had pleased him, and nothing that he saw or heard during the walk had any tendency to lower her in his estimation.

It was a pleasant walk, much of the way being shaded by forest trees, and a refreshing breeze tempered the heat of the weather. The girls were almost sorry when it came to an end.

But they found much to interest them in and around the mine. When they had seen all that was to be seen and were about to return to the town, Mr. Short proposed their doing so by a different route from that by which they had come. It was a little longer, he said, circling around among the hills, but it would give them some fine views and an opportunity to gather a variety of beautiful wild flowers.

"Oh, then do please, let us go that way, papa!" exclaimed Lulu, looking up at him with a very bright, eager face.

"If it suits the wishes of all the party, we will," he answered in an indulgent tone. "What do you say to it, Mr. Austin?"

"That it suits my inclination exactly," returned the English gentleman.

"Mine also," added Albert, as the captain looked inquiringly at him.

"It's just what I'd like to do, papa," said Max.

"Then I offer my services as guide," said Mr. Short.

"Then the question is settled in the affirmative," Captain Raymond said. "Mr. Short, will you lead the way?"

It was just dinner time when they reached home, the girls bright-eyed and rosy cheeked and with hands full of flowers.

"Are you tired, daughter?" the captain asked, as Lulu was taking off her hat.

"Oh, no, indeed, papa, not a bit!" she answered. "What a delightful morning we have had! Now what are we going to do this afternoon?"

"The first thing is to eat dinner," he said, smiling and pinching her cheek then stooping to give her a hearty kiss.

"Yes, sir, I feel ready to do it justice," she returned, putting her hand into his that he might lead her to the table.

"I, too," said Max, following them. "I don't know when I've been so hungry."

The captain had asked the blessing, and Marian began passing the plate of bread, when a voice, apparently that of a boy speaking from the garden, said, "Please, Miss, gimme a piece. I'm awful hungry! Didn't have a mouthful o' anything to eat today."

Marian started in surprise, then went toward the window saying, "A beggar. We don't often have them about here. Why," glancing out, "where is he?"

A loud barking, that seemed to come from round the corner of the house, then a shrill cry, "Oh, oh, call him off! He's got me by the leg! He'll tear me to pieces!"

"Towser, Towser!" called Marian, putting her head out of the window. "Let him go, I tell you! Come here; come here, and let that fellow alone!"

Then she rushed out to the porch to look for the boy and dog, but she was back again in a moment all breathless with bewilderment and exertion.

"I can't find either of them," she panted. "Where they could go so quickly I canna conjecture."

Lulu was casting mirthful glances at Max, but he avoided her eye and went on with his dinner as if much too hungry to think of anything else.

"Both boys and dogs can move very rapidly sometimes," remarked the captain in reply to the girl. "But don't be alarmed, Miss Marian, I dare say the beggar has come to no worse harm than a fright sufficient to send him off to get a meal elsewhere. And now, if you please, will you replenish the bread plate? Max is emptying it very fast."

"Oh, yes, sir, and I hope you will excuse me for neglecting my business," she answered, smilingly, taking up the plate and leaving the room.

"Now, Max, own up that that was you," said Lulu laughing.

"That what was?" he asked, lifting his eyebrows in mock astonishment. "Do you mean to insinuate that I'm either a beggar or a dog?"

"No," laughed Lulu merrily. "But you needn't pretend ignorance. You know well enough what I mean. Well, I shan't let Marian into the secret if I can help it, for I hope we'll have some more fun out of it. Papa, it was right good of you not to explain."

"Was it?" he asked.

But Marian's entrance with a fresh supply of bread put an end to talk on that subject for the time.

"Papa," said Lulu, "you haven't told me yet what we are going to do this afternoon."

"How would you like to try the pony Mr. Short has engaged for your use while we are here?" he asked in return.

"Oh, very much, if you will go with me!"

"I shall most certainly not allow you to go without me," he answered with a tender, loving look into the bright eyes she had lifted to his.

"You couldn't trust her alone, could you, papa?" Max said teasingly.

"No, nor with you, nor you alone," answered his father with sportive look and tone.

"There now, Maxie, don't you wish you'd kept quiet?" laughed Lulu. "You see papa doesn't consider you so very much older or wiser than I am."

"I don't hope I'll ever be too old or wise to be the better and happier of papa's company," Max answered, bestowing upon his father a look of deepest respect and affection.

"I'm glad to hear that, my boy," the captain responded, his eyes shining with pleasure.

"Well, then, I think we are all satisfied that the arrangement is for the three of us to ride out together."

"And Mr. Short to go along to show us the way?" queried Lulu.

"Yes. He has kindly offered to do so."

"I do think he has the wrong name altogether," she said laughingly. "He ought to be Mr. Long."

"People hardly ever get a name that fits," remarked Max sagely. "Mr. Carpenter will be a shoemaker, like as not, or a merchant, and Mr. Shoemaker, a hotel keeper, and so on."

"Yes, that is rather apt to be the case," assented the father. "But occasionally a man does follow the trade that fits his name. For instance, I used to know a Mr. Cobbler who made, and doubtless mended, shoes."

"Max, don't you remember the Browns that lived next door to Aunt Beulah?" asked Lulu.

"Yes, they were all very fair and had light hair and eyes. And Tom White, who went to the same school I did, was dark-complexioned and had eyes as black as sloes."

"Papa," asked Lulu, "will the horses and ponies be here soon? Will we take our ride as soon as we are finished eating?"

"No, not quite. 'After dinner rest awhile' is the rule, don't you know? You may do that for fully half an hour while I write to your mamma."

"Oh, mayn't I write, too? I'm not tired."

"Certainly, if you wish to. You and Max are both at liberty to amuse yourselves during the interval before our ride. Well, what is it, daughter?" noticing a slight expression of trouble and perplexity in her speaking countenance.

"Only that sometimes I forget how to spell a word, papa, and what am I to do about it? At home you always tell me to look in the dictionary, but we haven't any here."

"How will your father answer for one?" he asked with sportive look and tone.

"Oh, nicely, if you'll let me use you," she returned, laughing.

"I will when there's no printed one at hand."

"Thank you, sir. It will be a great deal less trouble than hunting for the word in the dictionary. But why don't you let me use you always when you're with me?"

"Because I think the spelling will be more likely to be impressed upon your memory by the trouble of having to search out the word. Beside, I want my children to learn the lesson of self-help. We should never trouble others to do for us what we can do for ourselves."

"I'll try always to remember and act upon that, papa," said Max. "Isn't it the people that help themselves all they can who are most apt to succeed in life?"

"Most assuredly, my boy," replied the captain, as they presently left the table and retired to their own apartments.

"My letter is going to be to Gracie," Max remarked, as he took out his writing materials.

"Mine, too," said Lulu. "I'm going to tell her about our walk this morning, and all about our visit to the mine."

"Just what I intended doing," Max said.

"Suppose you both carry out your intentions and then compare accounts to see how they differ," suggested their father. "Very likely each of you will tell something that the other will omit, and between the two letters Gracie will get a better idea of the little excursion than she could from either one alone."

"And shall we show them to you, papa, when completed?" asked Lulu.

"You may do exactly as you please in regard to that," he answered.

All three pens were presently scratching away, the captain's more rapidly and with fewer pauses than the other two. Presently he laid it down and began folding his sheet.

Then Max did the same, remarking to Lulu a trifle triumphantly, "I'm done first."

"Why!" she exclaimed. "I haven't finished telling about the mine, and I have all the story about the walk home to tell yet."

"Probably you are going more into detail than Max did," their father said. "And that is just what Gracie will enjoy."

At that instant Sandy appeared at the open door with the announcement that the horses had come and Mr. Short was waiting.

"My letter isn't finished!" exclaimed Lulu in dismay.

"No matter, daughter. It is not one requiring special haste, and you can finish it at your leisure, tonight or tomorrow. No, on Monday; tomorrow is

Sunday," the captain said. "Lay it in your writing desk and put on your hat. We will not keep Mr. Short waiting any longer than necessary."

She obeyed with cheerful alacrity, wondering aloud the while what her new pony would be like.

"Better tie that hat on tight, Lu," Max said in sportive tone. "He may rear and make it fall off, if he doesn't throw you."

"I'll fasten it as tight as I can," she said. "Oh, I wish I had Gracie or somebody to tie my veil on for me!"

"You have two somebodies. Isn't that enough?" asked her father, stepping up behind her where she stood in front of the mirror and tying it for her as deftly as if he had been a woman. "You will always find your father, and doubtless your brother also, ready to perform any such little service for you. As for the danger of your pony throwing you, I think you may dismiss any such fear. Mr. Short told me he had secured a safe one for you."

"Oh, I'm glad of that, papa! I thought you wouldn't let me try a dangerous one. And thank you for tying my veil. I'm quite ready now," drawing on her gloves as she spoke.

"Well, captain, what do you think of them?" Mr. Short asked with a look and tone that spoke his confidence of a favorable judgment.

The captain and his children stood on the sidewalk in front of the boarding house ready to mount the steeds the agent had provided.

"They are far better in appearance, at least, than I had expected to see," replied Captain Raymond pleasantly. "That horse is a Spanish, is it not?"

"Yes, sir. A grand piece of horseflesh for such work as you are likely to put them to. He'll stand a longer, harder gallop than any other horse I have ever ridden.

"And those Indian ponies for the use of the young folks are hardy, strong, and well broken, and though not the handsomest steeds that ever were seen, will, I think, give good satisfaction to their riders."

"I presume they will," the captain said, lifting Lulu to her saddle and putting the bridle into her hands, while Max mounted his pony without any assistance.

"You'll ride beside me, won't you, papa?" she asked, her tone expressing some slight timidity.

"Yes, dear child, so near that I can seize your pony's bridle at any moment," he replied. "But I think you need have no fear that he will misbehave with you on his back."

His horse was close at hand, and with the final words of his sentence, he vaulted deftly into the saddle and was off.

Away they went through the town, down through the valley, passing near the mine they had visited in the morning, over the hills, and far out on the grassy plains beyond.

Lulu found her pony manageable, so that soon she could partly forget him and give her attention to the country they were passing through and the talk of her companions.

She and Max thought they would never forget that ride. It was so full of pleasure to them. The air was delightfully fresh and pure, the motion of their steeds rapid and easy, and everything they saw was interesting, if only because of its dissimilarity to whatever they had heretofore been accustomed.

The principal topics of discourse between the two gentlemen were the natural resources of the territory, its development, the incoming tide of immigration, its character, and probable influence upon the future of that region of the country.

"You have some Mormon citizens?" the captain said, half in assertion, half inquiringly.

"Yes, sir, quite a good many, though they are decidedly in the minority. By the way, you Eastern folks may have little idea, I take it, of the aggressive character of Mormonism—its enmity to the Federal Government and far-reaching schemes to gain the balance of power in, not Utah alone, but as many territories and states as possible. Believe me, the Union has no more bitter foes and none who need to be more vigilantly watched and guarded against."

"I believe you," the captain returned with a look of grave concern. "And I think, too, that the Eastern people are at least beginning to awaken to the danger. One object I had in view in coming out here was to see for myself the extent of the evil and the best remedy to be applied, also to decide the important question of my own duty in the matter."

"They are mostly an ignorant set," remarked Mr. Short. "The foreign portion know so little about our government that they believe the lying assertions of their hierarchy that it is the worst and most despotic in the world."

"Whereas, it is the very best and most free!" exclaimed Max indignantly. "Isn't it, papa?"

"Certainly, my boy," returned the captain, smiling at the lad's heat.

Mr. Short smiled, too, and giving Max an approving look, remarked that he liked nothing better than to see boys full of patriotism.

"I wouldn't be my father's son if I didn't love my country," said Max.

"Like father, like son, eh?" laughed Short. "Well, it is very apt to be the case.

"There's a cattle ranch I must take you to see, Captain." Pointing in a southwesterly direction, where, far in the distance, might be dimly discerned a dwelling with outbuildings and a herd of cattle grazing near by. "It's too far for us to go tonight, but some time next week, perhaps, it may suit your plans to ride out there. I think you will find it pays to do so, as I understand you want to learn all about this region of country."

The captain assented to the proposal, adding that he thought it was now time to turn their horses' heads toward home.

❧❧❧❧❧❧❧❧

CHAPTER TWELFTH

TEA WAS NOT QUITE ready when they arrived at their boarding house, and they sat on the porch while waiting for it, Captain Raymond looking over the daily paper just taken from the mail.

Sandy McAlpine and a younger brother named Hugh were sitting nearby looking over a picture book together.

"Is your mother not well, boys?" asked the captain, glancing from his paper to them. "I think I have not seen her at all today."

"No, sir," replied Sandy. "She's lying down with a headache."

"She got a letter," added Hugh. "One of those letters that always makes her cry and get a bad headache. I wish they wouldn't come, ever, anymore."

"Hush, hush, Hugh!" muttered Sandy, frowning at his brother and nudging him with his elbow. "You know mother wouldn't like you talking so, especially to a stranger."

"I haven't said anything wicked," returned the little fellow. "May be you like to see mother cry and have a headache, but I don't. And I'd just thrash the man that sends her such horrid letters, if I could. And I will, too, when I'm a big, strong man."

Captain Raymond was seemingly quite occupied with his paper during this little aside between the lads, but he heard every word and was thinking to himself. "It is probably some financial trouble, and I must see what I can do for her relief. There are very special promises to widows, and as one of the Lord's stewards, it becomes me to be ready to assist them in distress."

Marian came to the door at that moment with the announcement that tea was ready.

The Raymonds at once arose and obeyed the summons, the captain with his newspaper still in his hand. He laid it aside before sitting down to his meal and forgot it on leaving the room after supper.

He presently remembered it, however, and went back in search of it. He found Mrs. McAlpine there alone, in tears, and with an open letter in her hand. He would have retreated but perceived that it was already too late. She was aware of his presence and opened her lips to speak.

"Excuse me, my dear madam," he said. "I had no thought of intruding upon your privacy, but—"

"You are entirely excused, sir," she answered gently and with an effort to recover her composure. "This room is public to you and your children, and you have a perfect right to enter it unceremoniously when you will. Will you take a seat?"

"Although I merely stepped in to get my paper, which I carelessly left here, I shall accept your invitation with pleasure, madam, if you will allow me the privilege of talking with you as a friend," he said in a deeply sympathizing tone. "I cannot be blind to the fact that you are in trouble, and if in any way I can assist you, it will give me sincere pleasure to do so."

Then with the greatest delicacy, he offered her financial assistance, if that were what she stood in need of.

"Sir, you are most kind," she said with grateful emotion. "But it is not that. It is something far worse. It is that this wicked, rebellious heart will not submit, as it ought, to the cross He — my blessed Lord and Master — has laid upon me. Oh!" clasping her hands together, while the big tears streamed down over her pale and sunken cheeks. "I fear — I very much fear — I have loved the creature more than the Creator and that is why this cross has been laid upon me — this cross, so heavy that it bears me to the earth!"

She sank sobbing into a chair.

He drew up another and seated himself beside her. "Dear madam," he said in moved tones, "'we have not a high priest who cannot be touched with the feeling of our infirmities, but was in all points tempted like as we are, yet without sin. Let us therefore come boldly unto the throne of grace, that we may obtain mercy, and find grace to help in the time of need.'

"I know not what your trouble is, but sure I am that thus you may find grace, mercy, peace, and fulfillment of the promise, 'As thy days, so shall thy strength be!'"

"Yes, yes, I know," she sobbed, covering her face with her hands. "And while I'm willing to bear whatever He sends, at times the cross seems heavier than mortal strength can endure, so that it crushes me to the very earth! Oh, Willie, my Willie, how happy we were in those early years o' our married life, when you were all the world to me and I was all the world to you! But now — I can no longer feel that you are mine. Others have come between us. They have stolen your love from me, and my heart is breaking, breaking!

"But, oh, this talk is sinful, sinful! Lord, help a poor, frail worm of the dust to be obedient and submissive to Thy will!" She seemed to have forgotten the captain's presence, but light was dawning upon him.

"I think you are accusing yourself unjustly, my dear madam," he said in pitying tones. "I think you are mistaking God-implanted feelings for the suggestions of the evil one."

"Alas, no!" she sighed. "Has not God given a new revelation to his prophet, ordaining that 'it is the duty of every woman to give other wives to her husband, even as Sara gave Hagar to Abram. And that if she refuses it shall be lawful for her husband to take them without her consent, and she shall be destroyed for her disobedience'?"

"No," returned the captain, and there was stern indignation in his tone—not against the poor, deluded woman but toward her base deceivers. "A thousand times, no! Any pretense of a new revelation, no matter by whom it may be set up, must be a base fabrication. Listen!"

"Ah, sir, you mean kindly," she said. "But I must not listen to you, for I perceive—what I had already suspected—that you are not one of the saints. You do not believe the teachings of the new gospel."

"New gospel!" he exclaimed, his eyes kindling. "Tell me, Mrs. McAlpine, were you not brought up to believe the Bible?" taking out a pocket edition constantly carried with him as he spoke.

"Surely, sir, I may say with the Psalmist, 'Unless thy law had been my delights, I should then have perished in mine affliction.'"

He opened his Bible, and turning to the first chapter of Galatians, he read aloud: "'I marvel that ye are so soon removed from him that called you into the grace of Christ, unto another gospel; which is not another; but there be some that trouble you and would pervert the gospel of Christ.

"'But though we, or an angel from heaven, preach any other gospel unto you than that which we have preached unto you, let him be accursed.'

"Could anything be plainer or stronger than that?" he asked with emphasis.

"No," she said slowly, looking like one waking from a dream. "Why have I not remembered those words before? But—there has been a new revelation. At least, they told me so."

"A new revelation!" he repeated in a tone of utter incredulity. "Listen again to God's own word, inspired and written many hundreds of years before the birth of your so-called prophets. 'False prophets, dreamers of dreams, who have spoken to turn you away from the Lord your God . . . to thrust thee out of the way which the Lord thy God commanded thee to walk in.'"

Opening to the very last page of the New Testament, he read again: "'I testify unto every man that heareth the words of the prophecy of this book, If any man shall add unto these things, God shall add unto him the plagues that are written in this book; and if any man shall take away from the words of the book of this prophecy, God shall take away his part out of the book of life, and out of the holy city, and from the things which are written in this book.'"

She gazed at him for an instant in awestruck silence. Then rousing herself, she said slowly, "But they say there are corruptions, mistranslations—" She paused, leaving her sentence unfinished.

"There is no lack of proof that the Scriptures are the revealed Word of God, that the writers were inspired by God, and that if any corruption or mistranslations have crept in they are so few and slight as to be of little account, making small difference in the meaning," he said. "The proofs of the authenticity and inspiration of Scriptures are so many that it would take a long time to state them all."

"There is no need in my case, sir," she interrupted. "I know they are divine—the internal evidence alone would be all-sufficient to me."

"And yet their teachings are directly opposed to those of Mormonism."

"Not against polygamy, surely? God knows I would be glad to think so, but how many of the prominent characters of the Old Testament had a plurality of wives? Even David, 'the man after God's own heart,' had many more than one."

"But the Bible nowhere tells us that God approved of the practice. And how often the history it gives shows that polygamy brought sin and misery on those who practiced it. God made but one wife for Adam."

"But Sarai gave Hagar to Abram."

"But God did not command it, nor are we anywhere told that He approved it. It was a sinful deed done in unbelief, and it brought forth the bitter fruits of sin."

For a moment or more she sat silent, evidently in deep thought. Then she spoke. "I believe you are right, sir. Though it has not struck me in that way before. It did bring forth 'the bitter fruits of sin,' very much the same fruits that polygamy brings forth here and in this day," she concluded with a heavy sigh.

Captain Raymond was again turning over the leaves of his Bible. "Listen to the words of the Lord Jesus Christ," he said.

"'Have ye not read, that he who made them at the beginning made them male and female, and said, "For this cause shall a man leave father and mother, and shall cleave to his wife; and the twain shall be one flesh! Wherefore they are no more twain, but one flesh."'

"That passage is from Matthew, and Mark also gives these words of the Master," the captain said. "And have you not noticed how Paul in his epistles always seems to take it for granted, when speaking of the marriage tie, that a man can lawfully have but one wife at a time?

"'For the husband is the head of the wife'—not wives, Mrs. McAlpine.

"'He that loveth his wife loveth himself.' 'Let every one of you in particular so love his wife even as himself.'

"'A bishop then must be blameless, the husband of one wife.'

"But Mormonism teaches that bishops may have, and ought to have, many wives. Polygamy is encouraged on the ground that the rank and dignity of its members is in proportion to the number of their wives and children. Is not that the fact?"

"Yes," she answered with a heavy sigh. "It is according to the revelation made to Bishop Young."

"A revelation indeed! Though, as we have seen, the record was closed in the time of the Apostle John, and a fearful curse pronounced on any who should add to it. A revelation opposed to all the teachings of God's word on that subject. It came from the father of lies, for God never contradicts

Himself; all the teachings of every part of His word are consistent with each other, which is one of the proofs of the divine inspiration of the Scriptures.

"From Genesis to Revelation the teaching, both direct and implied, is that God made of twain one flesh, and a man may have but one wife. Adam had but one, and in the book of Revelation John tells us the angel said to him, 'Come hither, and I will show thee the bride, the Lamb's wife,'—not wives, you will observe. There was but one."

"You shake my faith in Mormonism," she said with a startled, troubled look.

"I rejoice to hear it," he responded. "Would that I could shake it to its utter destruction.

"Popery has been well called 'Satan's masterpiece,' and Mormonism is another by the same hand. The points of resemblance are sufficient to prove that to my mind."

"Points of resemblance?" she repeated, inquiringly. "I have never thought there were any, and I have a heart hatred for Popery, as you may well suppose, coming as I do, from a land where she slew, in former ages, so many of God's saints. But surely in one thing the two are very different—the one forbidding to marry, the other encouraging men to take many wives."

"The difference in regard to that is not so great as may appear at first sight," he returned. "Both pander to men's lusts—for what are nunneries but 'priests' prisons for women,' as one who has left the ranks of the Popish priesthood has called them?

"Both teach children to forsake their parents, both teach lying and murder, when by such crimes they are expected to advance the cause of their church."

"Oh, sir, so bad as that?" she exclaimed with a deep shudder.

"It is computed that Popery has slain fifty million of those she calls heretics, and oftentimes she has secured her victims by the basest treachery. All that in past ages, to be sure, but she claims infallibility and denies that she has ever done wrong. Besides, to this day she shows the same persecuting spirit and actually kills, too, wherever she has the power to do so.

"As to Mormonism doing likewise, look at the Mountain Meadow massacre, the lying and perjury to prevent convictions for polygamy, and the private assassinations committed to carry out their fearful and wicked doctrine of blood atonement.

"In that doctrine also—asserting that the blood of Christ does not cleanse from all sin those who accept His offered salvation—they agree with the Church of Rome, whose teaching is that forgiveness of sins and final salvation are to be obtained by penance and good works supplementing the finished work of Christ. They teach that good works are to be done not—as the Bible teaches—because we are saved, but in order to earn salvation, thus flatly contradicting God's word which says:

"'A man is justified by faith without the deeds of the law.'

"'By grace are ye saved, through faith; and that not of yourselves; it is the gift of God.'

"'The blood of Jesus Christ His Son cleanseth us from all sin.'"

Again he opened his Bible and read: "'Ye are of your father the devil, and the lusts of your father ye will do: he was a murderer from the beginning, and abode not in the truth, because there is no truth in him; when he speaketh a lie, he speaketh of his own; for he is a liar and the father of it.'

"'He that is of God heareth God's words; ye therefore hear them not, because ye are not of God.'

"Are not those words of the Master peculiarly applicable to all those who are teaching doctrines so diametrically opposed to His?" he asked.

"They certainly are applicable to any who teach false doctrine," she replied.

"And can you call the Mormon doctrine of 'blood atonement,' by any softer name?"

"No, for I believe God's Word, 'the blood of Jesus Christ his Son cleanseth us from all sin' and its teaching that He is the one sacrifice for sin."

"And yet you call yourself one of them?"

"I have done so. I stood against it for a time in the old home in Scotland, but the man—a Mormon missionary—was very plausible and seemed very devout. He quoted Scripture and won Willie, my husband, over first, and they both kept at me till I grew fairly bewildered and half crazed. At last, when Willie told me he was bound to come over to America and join the Latter Day Saints, I gave up and agreed to do the same. For how could I part from him? No word at all had been breathed to either of us about polygamy. We had not thought it was one of their doctrines."

A spasm of pain convulsed her features, and for a moment she seemed unable to go on.

"Does that speak well for their honesty?" he asked in stern indignation.

She shook her head. "No," she said, chokingly. "The thought of that has sometimes made me grow weak in the faith till my heart would almost stand still with fright."

The words were spoken in a suppressed tone, little louder than a whisper and with a terrified glance from side to side, as if she feared they might be overheard.

"No wonder, considering their fiendish practice of 'blood atonement,'" he responded, regarding the poor woman with deep commiseration. "I presume you had not been long a dweller in Mormonism before you were more fully instructed in regard to those two important doctrines?"

"No, sir, not long," she replied. "As to polygamy at least, and when my husband declared his intention of carrying out the practice, I was broken-hearted and entreated him to forbear, remembering his solemn marriage to vow to cleave to me only so long as we both should live.

"He tried argument with me at first, coaxing and persuasion, but finding I was not to be moved by those, he grew angry and abusive. He hinted darkly at the danger of the blood atonement doctrine being carried out in my case if I continued obstinate in refusing my consent."

"And so you gave it?"

"Yes. Oh, sir, it was like consenting to have my heart torn from my bosom!" she exclaimed in a low tone tremulous with pain. "But to withhold it would do no good and would endanger my life—my life, no longer valuable save for the sake of my dear children. But for their sake I did desire to live. Ah, sir, I could not but ask myself, 'Is this what it is to live in free America?'"

"I blush for my country in view of the outrages she has allowed in the name of religion!" he exclaimed, his fine, manly countenance flushing with shame and indignation as he spoke. "And yet," he continued interrogatively, "you came to believe it right for a man thus to break his marriage vow?"

"I grew bewildered with misery," she said. "I had no choice but to submit and felt that I should go mad with the thought of my husband's wickedness if I held fast to the teaching of my childhood. I could not answer their arguments. I see now that more prayer and searching of the Scriptures might have enabled me to do so, yet the result would have been a violent death—probably by Willie's own hand, making him a murderer as well as a breaker of the seventh commandment. So I resigned myself to my fate—so far as I could—and have ever since been fighting with the anguish and rebellion in my broken heart."

She was silent for a moment, struggling with her emotion. Then, with a grateful look at him, "I don't know how it is, sir, that you have so quickly won my confidence," she said. "I have never before breathed a word of all this into any mortal ear. Even Marian knows no more than that I suffer because— other women share the affection that in former, happier days was all my own."

"It is sometimes a relief to unburden our hearts to a fellow creature," he replied. "There is healing and comfort in human sympathy, and I assure you, dear madam, that you have mine in no slight measure. The man who can so wound the heart of a loving wife must be worse than a brute.

"The government has at last come to the rescue of these oppressed wives. I trust the "Edmunds Bill" will prove the complete destruction of polygamy, and efface this bar sinister from my country's scutcheon at last."

"I cannot but desire it, if only for my daughter's sake," she returned. "Marian will soon be a woman, and, if your government does not help, may be forced into a polygamous marriage. She would never go into it of her own free will. She is no Mormon, and, young as she is, has declared intense hatred and abhorrence of both polygamy and the blood atonement doctrine—er—practice," she added after a moment's hesitation.

"Oh, sir, no small part of my suffering is now occasioned by the change in my child's feelings toward her father. She has gone from loving him with an ardent affection to hating him with a bitter hatred, as the destroyer of both her mother's peace and her happiness."

She ended with a burst of uncontrollable weeping.

Captain Raymond's kind heart was sorely pained by the sight of her distress. He felt himself powerless to give relief but spoke gently to her of the love and sympathy of Jesus, the "Friend that sticketh closer than a brother," and to whom "all power is given in heaven and in earth."

"Carry all your griefs, your fears, and anxieties to Him," he said. "There is no trouble too great for His power to remove, too small for his loving attention. His love to His people is infinite, and He never regards their sorrows with indifference.

"In all their afflictions He was afflicted, and the Angel of His presence saved them."

"It is true," she said tremulously. "I have found it is true in my own experience. 'In His love and in His pity He redeemed them, and He bare them, and carried them all the days of old.' And so He has done with me—His most unworthy and doubting servant. Ah, sir, you, I am sure, are one of God's own people, whatever may be your views with regard to the Mormon creed, and I beseech you to pray for me that my faith in God, in Jesus, and His gospel may be strengthened and increased."

CHAPTER THIRTEENTH

ON LEAVING THE TEA table Max and Lulu had seated themselves on the porch along with their father, and just as he went in search of his paper, they were joined by Albert Austin.

"Ah, good evening, Albert," said Max, making haste to place a chair for him near his own. "I'm pleased to see you."

"Thanks. I'm pleased to come," returned the English lad, accepting the offered seat. "I was bored with listening to papa and some other gentlemen talking on some subject that didn't interest me in the least, so I slipped away after telling papa where I could be found when wanted."

"He doesn't object to our society, then?" returned Max in a playfully interrogative tone.

"No, indeed! I fancy he thinks I could hardly be in better company. He's taken a strong liking to your father, and I think I may add to yourself, also," glancing admiringly at Lulu as he spoke.

"In spite of my not being an English girl?" she returned laughingly.

"Oh, assuredly, Miss Lulu! That could make no difference. In fact, I believe Englishmen are, as a class, great admirers of American ladies."

"In which they show their good taste," laughed Max. "My father says American ladies compare favorably with those of other nations. I wish you could see Mamma Vi and Grandma Elsie."

"Who are they?" asked Albert with a puzzled look.

"Mamma Vi is papa's wife, his second wife, while we are the children of the first. Her name is Violet. She isn't old enough to be our mother, so she told us to call her Mamma Vi. Grandma Elsie is her mother, and we call her that to distinguish her from an older lady whom we call grandma also."

"Ah, yes, I think I understand. That's one of your American ways, I suppose. And where are those ladies you would like to show me? Not in this state, I fancy, as you were already on the cars long before we entered it."

"Yes," replied Max with an amused look. "Our home is so far away that we crossed several states in coming here. But this is not a state."

"Isn't? What then?"

"A territory."

"Ah, excuse me, but I don't know the difference."

"I'll try to explain," said Max. "Papa has taken some pains to give us a clear understanding of our government and its workings.

"Each of the thirty-eight states has its very own constitution, elects its own governor, legislators, and judges. It elects two senators to send to Congress, too, and from one to thirty-four representatives, according to its population.

"But the territories can only send one delegate to Congress, and he has no vote. They are governed by Congress with a governor appointed by the President himself."

"Ah, yes, I see the difference, and that the states have the best of it. The territories, I presume, look forward to becoming states?"

"Yes, but they must have a certain number of inhabitants before they can hope to be admitted into the Union."

"Your father's an army officer, isn't he?"

"No, he belonged to the Navy, but he resigned not very long ago."

"The American Navy is quite small, isn't it?"

"It isn't so large as it ought to be," returned Max a little shortly.

"'*Britannia* rules the waves!'" quoted Albert in an exultant tone.

"Yes, when *Columbia* isn't there to interfere with her," retorted Max, a little mischievously.

"I'm thinking 'twill be a sorry day for *Columbia* when she attempts that," sneered Albert.

"It hasn't always been in the past," remarked Max quietly.

"When wasn't it?" asked Albert.

"When John Paul Jones in the *Bon Homme Richard* fought Captain Pearson in the *Serapis,* for instance.

"Well, yes, but that was a very close fight. Besides, you had six vessels and we only two."

"Two of ours were pilot boats and kept out of the fight altogether," said Max.

"So did the *Vengeance,* though she had been ordered to render the larger vessels any assistance in her power. She didn't even try to overhaul the band of flying merchantmen.

"Then the *Alliance,* commanded by that very bad-tempered Frenchman Landais, who was so envious of Jones, went into the battle only at the last moment. Instead of helping her allies, she fired her broadsides into the *Richard.* The fight was between the *Richard* with forty guns and the *Serapis* with forty-four; the *Pallas,* twenty-two guns, and the

Countess of Scarborough, with twenty-two. So there was no advantage on our side. If Landais had been in command of the *Richard* he wouldn't have tried to fight the *Serapis* at all."

"Why do you think that?"

"Because, as he dashed past her in the *Alliance,* pushing ahead to reconnoiter before the fight began, he cried out that if the enemy proved to be a forty-four, the only course for the Americans was immediate flight. He practiced on that idea, too, hauling off and leaving the *Richard* and the *Pallas* to do the fighting.

"Our French allies did us more harm than good in the naval battles of the Revolutionary War. If captain Landais wasn't crazy, he must have been one of the greatest scoundrels that ever trod a quarter-deck."

"Yes, indeed," said Lulu. "When I read about his firing into the *Bon Homme Richard* — when the poor fellows on it had been fighting so hard and long, so many were dreadfully wounded, and the ship almost sinking already — I felt as if I could hardly stand it to think he escaped being punished for it. He ought to have been hung, for his fire killed some of our poor fellows."

"So he ought, the miserable coward!" assented the English lad. "I'm not partial to the French anyway," he added. "Of course, my own countrymen come first in my estimation, but I hold the Americans next. We're sort of cousins, you know."

"Yes," said Max. "But wasn't it a crazy idea that this great big country should go on being ruled by that little one across the sea? Most absurd, I think."

"At the beginning of the trouble between them it must have looked like a great folly for the thirteen weak colonies to go into the fight with England," remarked Albert.

"Particularly to the English, who didn't know how in love with liberty and determined to keep her, the Americans were," said Max. "Papa says we triumphed at the last because our cause was the cause of right, and God guided our counsels and gave success to our arms."

"I don't believe I'm as well read on the subject as you are," remarked Albert. "I presume I would naturally take less interest in it than you would."

"Yes, I suppose so," replied Max. "I've studied the history of the United States, my native land, a great deal, especially in the last year or two. I've had many talks with papa about the events and especially the doings of the navy. They interested me more than any other part—first, because papa was a naval officer, and then because I'm hoping to go into the navy myself."

"And those studies didn't increase your love for us—the English, I mean?" inquired Albert.

"No, not a bit," returned Max with a slight laugh. He paused a moment, then went on more gravely.

"The treatment they gave the Americans they took as prisoners was simply barbarous, unworthy of a civilized—not to say Christian—nation."

"Yes, perfectly dreadful!" chimed in Lulu.

"Now I don't remember any such barbarity," remarked Albert, rather apologetically. "But you know the Americans were considered rebels, and I—suppose the British officers may have thought it a duty to—refrain from coddling them."

"Coddling, indeed!" exclaimed Max. "Do you remember about the *Old Jersey* prison ship?"

"Can't say that I do."

"It was a dismantled hulk—an old sixty-four gun ship moored in Wallabout Bay near New York City. She was so old and worn-out and rotten that she wasn't fit to go to sea, so they used her as a prison for Americans whom they captured. They starved them and treated them so horribly in every way that eleven thousand died in her."

"Wouldn't it be charitable to suppose the starving may have been because of an unavoidable scarcity of provisions?" queried Albert mildly.

"There was no such unavoidable scarcity," asserted Max. "Yet the poor prisoners were sometimes so hungry as to be glad to eat cockroaches and mice when they could catch them."

"On that vessel?" asked Albert.

"I think it was on that very vessel," said Max musingly. "But possibly I might be mistaken. There were other prison ships, but the *Old Jersey* was the worst. I'm certain it was American prisoners in the hands of the British near New York. A piece of wanton cruelty the jailers were guilty of was bringing in a kettle of boiling soup, or mush, and setting it down before those starving prisoners of war with never a spoon or anything to dip it up with."

"Yes," said Lulu. "Another time they marched some prisoners for four days without a mouthful to eat, then rolled out barrels of salt pork for them to eat raw. And another time, when they were exchanging prisoners with the Americans, they put pounded glass into the last meal's victuals they gave to the American soldiers before they let them go."

"Well, if they did that 'twas mean and wicked enough," admitted Albert. "But don't you think the world has grown a little better since those days, and that then other nations were quite as cruel, if not more so? That's always excepting the Americans, of course," he added with a mischievous twinkle in his eye.

"I believe that may be so," admitted Max.

"And some Americans — the Tories — were worse than the British," said Lulu. "Some of their deeds were perfectly dreadful, shockingly wicked and cruel! Besides, it was so contemptible of them to turn against their own country and ill-use — even to robbing and murdering — their own countrymen."

"Well, yes," said Albert. "But then, we must remember that the way they looked at it 'twas only being loyal to their king."

"The English king, you mean," she retorted. "But most of them — the Tories — were low, mean, wicked fellows that really cared for neither king nor country and were only glad of an excuse to rob wherever they could."

"Then please don't blame my country with what they did," said Albert.

"No, it isn't worthwhile. She has sins enough of her own to answer for," returned Lulu demurely. "But she's so little, poor thing!"

Albert looked nettled at that. "The sun never sets on the British Empire," he said, straightening himself proudly. "And, big as your country is, I don't believe either her army or navy can compare with ours."

"Yes, our regular army is small, I know," admitted Max. "But we have a great army of militia, and all so devoted to their country that they make splendid fighters when called on to defend her. Our navy's small, too, but compares better in size with yours than it did at the beginning of the

War of 1812, and it certainly came out of that with flying colors.

"Really, I don't remember just what the fight was about," acknowledged Albert modestly.

"Don't you?" asked Max in some surprise. "Well, I shouldn't either if papa hadn't turned my attention to such subjects and talked with us about them in such an interesting way. He says he wants his children to be well acquainted with history, especially that of their own country. That's how I happen to be posted on those questions.

"When the United States declared war against England in 1812, our navy consisted of twenty vessels with the largest carrying forty-four guns. Most of the others rated under thirty, while England had over a thousand ships on the rolls of her navy, 254 of them ships of the line, mounting over seventy-four guns each.

"It really wasn't much wonder the British laughed at the idea of our attempting to fight them, especially as *Britannia* had ruled the wave up to that time."

"Yes, the Americans must have been a plucky little nation to even try it," laughed Albert. "They must have been desperately angry about something."

"They were and with good reason," returned Max. "Oh, such wrongs as our poor sailors had endured for many years from British naval officers! It makes my blood boil just to read, at this late day, of their arrogance and injustice and the dreadful cruelties they were guilty of toward Americans they kidnapped from our vessels."

"Kidnapped?" repeated Albert.

"Yes, what else could you call it when a British man-of-war would stop an American merchant vessel on the high seas—in time of peace—board her, order the crew mustered aft, pick out any man they chose to say was an Englishman, and carry him off to their own vessel against his will?"

"Oh, yes, I see you refer to the right of search."

"Right of search, indeed!" exclaimed Max hotly. "There was no right about it; it was all an outrageous wrong. The British had no more right to search our ships than we had to search theirs."

"But deserters should be caught and punished," said Albert.

"Perhaps that's so," said Max. "I don't say it is or it isn't, but they often took native-born Americans, asserting without a shadow of proof that they were English. American captains said they always chose the most ship-shape sailors in the crew, and, of course, those wouldn't always be the Englishmen, supposing there were even any Englishmen among them.

"One can only imagine that it was exceedingly exasperating to be forced in that way into foreign service, especially that of a nation their own country had been having a bloody war with only a little while before and to serve under the red flag of England, too, instead of the beautiful Stars and Stripes they loved so well.

"And if one of them showed any unwillingness to serve his kidnappers, he was triced up and flogged till his back was cut to ribbons and the blood spurted at every blow.

"Of course they detested the service they had been forced into, and it was made so dreadful to them, they would desert whenever they had a chance. And if they were caught again they were speedily hung at the yard arm."

"It was hard when a mistake was made and a real American impressed," conceded Albert. "But, of course, the English government had a right to take her own men wherever she could find them."

"I have no objection to Englishmen submitting to such tyranny if they choose," sneered Max. "But Americans are made of different stuff. They are free and glory in their freedom, and they never would and never will put up with such treatment. And I say again, British officers had no right to board our ships without leave or license and forcibly rob them of part of their crew. It was an abominably cruel and tyrannical thing for them to do, even before the Revolution, and most outrageously insulting besides after the war when we were no longer colonies of Great Britain but free and independent states."

"I don't recall the occurrence you refer to," said Albert. "But surely before the war they had the same right to impress American subjects as they had to take their fellow subjects of Great Britain."

"Let me recall one incident to your memory, and you see if even an Englishman can approve of it these days," said Max.

"In 1764—eleven years before the beginning of the war, you will remember—the British man-of-war *Maidstone* lay in the harbor of Newport. It was a time of peace, and the officers had nothing to do, so they amused themselves sending out press gangs to seize any luckless American sailor who happened to be on shore and force him into his Majesty's service aboard their vessel.

"The life on board a British man-of-war was a dreadful one in those times for any sailor. The cat-o'-nine-tails was flourished often and for such slight offenses—even a boy-midshipman could order a poor fellow to the grating to have his back cut to ribbons.

"So no wonder American sailors dreaded being forced into it. They had no peace of their lives with those press gangs roaming the streets in search of them every night and breaking into taverns where a group of them might be smoking and chatting together to seize and carry them off.

"But the incident I was going to speak of was this. One day a brig came sailing up the bay into the harbor of Newport. She had been on a long voyage—to the west coast of Africa—and the poor fellows aboard her were just wild with joy to think they had reached home at last and were going ashore presently to see their mothers and wives and sweethearts and all the rest of their dear ones they had been separated from for so long. They all had crowded on the dock to watch the brig coming in.

"Oh, I can imagine how they felt! For I remember how glad we always were when papa's vessel came in from a long voyage, and we knew that he'd be with us presently. And so I know something of how terrible, how perfectly unbearable, it must have seemed to them, when, just as their ship was anchored, a couple of long boats from the man-of-war came pulling up alongside the brig. Two or three officers and a lot of sailors climbed on board, and the head one ordered the American captain to call his men aft, saying 'His Majesty has need of a few fine fellows for his service.'

"It was bad enough when they thought he was going to take some of them, each poor jackie fearing he might be the unfortunate one, yet hoping he might not. But just think of it! The officer ordered every single one of them to go below and pack up his traps.

"The American captain expressed his astonishment and indignation, saying that the poor fellows were just home from a long voyage and hadn't seen their families yet. But it did no good. Every man jack of them was carried off to the man-of-war and forced to serve aboard her.

"It was such acts of tyranny as this that drove the colonies to rebel and finally to be determined to be free and independent."

"And that drove them into the War of 1812, too," said Lulu. "Oh, the States, I mean. They were not colonies then, though the British did not seem to have found it out."

"It was a plucky little nation to declare war with England," again remarked Albert good-humoredly. "I don't know how they ever got up courage to pit twenty vessels against her thousand."

"Love of liberty, self-respect, and abhorrence of insult and tyranny nerved them to it," said Max. "Do you remember that affair of the *Chesapeake* and *Leopard*?"

"Not at all. If I ever heard of it, it must have made but little impression on my mind."

"Well, I suppose it would naturally make a deeper one upon an American boy's," said Max.

"It happened in 1807, when we were at peace with England, and it seems to me the most insulting thing ever heard of.

"The *Chesapeake,* an American man-of-war lying at the navy yard at Washington, was put in commission and ordered to the Mediterranean to relieve the *Constitution.*

"It took nearly a month to get her ready. While that was being attended to, the British minister informed our naval authorities that three deserters from his British Majesty's ship *Melampus* had joined the crew of the *Chesapeake* and asked to have them given up.

"Our government was willing to do it, but on inquiring into the matter, found that the men were really native-born Americans who had been impressed by the British and forced into their service. They were even able to prove it. So, of course, they weren't given up.

"The facts were stated to the British minister, and as he didn't protest any further, it was supposed he was satisfied.

"A few weeks after this, the *Chesapeake* left the navy yard and dropped down the river to Hampton Roads. There she stayed for some days, taking on guns and stores and adding to her crew till she had 375 men. Then she weighed anchor and started on her voyage.

"But she started before she was in really proper condition. A quantity of things, such as stores, ropes, lumber, trunks, and furniture were piled on the decks, instead of being stowed away in their proper places. Somebody was to blame for that, of course, though papa says it was not Commodore Barron, who was in command. Nobody could have dreamed of the mischief the confusion was to cause, remembering that it was in a time of peace and right on our own coast.

"But there were four English men-of-war lying quietly at anchor in Lynn Haven Bay, and as our ships passed out into the ocean, there was a stir on their decks. Then one of them weighed anchor, set her sails, and started in pursuit. The *Chesapeake* had to tack frequently on account of a stiff breeze that was blowing, and the American officers noticed that the *Leopard*—the British ship—did the same and kept right in their wake. But it never occurred to them that she had any but peaceful intentions. The ship kept on her course, and the sailors set busily to work putting the decks in order.

"Presently the *Leopard* bore down rapidly, and when she got near enough, hailed, saying that she had a dispatch for Commodore Barron. So the *Chesapeake* hove to and waited for a boat to be sent. Now the two ships were lying broadside to broadside, less than a pistol shot apart. Still the commodore did not suspect any mischief. Some of the younger officers noticed that the *Leopard* had her cannon all ready to fire, and they ought to have told the commodore, but they didn't.

"Soon a boat put off from the *Leopard,* bringing an English officer. One of the American officers received him and took him to the commodore's cabin. There he produced an order from the British Admiral Berkeley, commanding all British ships to watch for the *Chesapeake* and search her for deserters.

"Commodore Barron said he did not harbor deserters, and couldn't permit his crew to be mustered by an officer of any foreign power. Just then there was a signal from the *Leopard* recalling her officer. Then Commodore Barron came out of his cabin and was much surprised to see that the *Leopard* was quite in fighting trim."

Sandy McAlpine had drawn near the little group and was listening with profound interest to Max's story. "And did they have a fight between the two ships?" he burst out, as Max made a momentary pause in his narrative.

"A fight!" echoed Max. "No, not a fight. There was a disgraceful, insulting attack by the *Leopard*, which the Americans had not power to respond to, because, though their guns were loaded and ready to use at will, no matches, powder flasks, wads, rammers, or gun locks could be found.

"While they were hunting for them, there was a hail from the *Leopard*. Commodore Barron shouted back that he did not understand. They hailed him again.

"The commodore again answered that he didn't understand, and after another hail or two, the British fired a gun at the *Chesapeake*, then poured in a full broadside. The heavy shot crashed through the sides of the American ship, wounding a number of men."

"And they couldn't fire back?" queried Sandy.

"For want of matches and the other necessary things that were not to be found, they had to let their guns keep silence. They were filled with fury that they had no chance at all to defend themselves and show their insolent foe how American bluejackets can fight. They heated pokers red hot in the galley fire, but they cooled too much before they could get them to the guns.

"So for eighteen minutes the *Leopard* kept right on firing at a helpless, unresisting foe. Then the *Chesapeake's* flag was hauled down, two British lieutenants and some midshipmen came in a boat from the *Leopard*, boarded the *Chesapeake*, and again demanded the deserters.

"Of course, there was no choice but to give them up. Four sailors were seized and carried aboard the

Leopard in triumph. One of them they hung; one died before he could escape; but five years later the other two got back to the *Chesapeake.*"

"Max, you are forgetting that one shot was fired from the *Chesapeake,*" said Lulu.

"Yes, you tell about it."

"There was a Lieutenant Allen among the officers of the *Chesapeake* who cried out in his anger, 'I'll have one shot at those rascals, anyhow,' ran to the galley fire, picked up a live coal in his fingers, and, never caring for the pain, ran with it to one of the guns and fired it off just as the flag came fluttering down."

"He was a brave fellow," commented Sandy. "Well, I s'pose the British didn't fire any more after they got what they wanted. But hadn't their shot made some big holes in the *Chesapeake?*"

"I presume so," replied Lulu. "Anyhow, she turned and went back.

"Everybody in the whole country was furious on hearing the news, which I don't blame them for, I'm sure. But it was a great shame that the government punished Commodore Barron by suspending him from the service without pay for five years. Papa says it was very unjust, for it wasn't his fault that things were not in order on the vessel, but the fault of the fitting-out officers. And I feel perfectly certain that the commodore and everybody else on the *Chesapeake* would have fought bravely if they'd had half a chance, and they would've whipped the insolent British well. Oh, I do wish they had had a chance!"

"Well, never mind," said Max. "We whipped them well in the war that followed a few years later, anyway, Lu."

"Now, if I remember right, the Americans didn't always whip in that war either on land or on water," said Albert.

"No, not always," acknowledged Max. "But a good many times. And the war accomplished what we went into it for—putting a stop to their insolent claim to a right to search our vessels and the impressing of our seamen."

"Was that mentioned and given up in the treaty of peace?"

"No," acknowledged Max. "But they haven't tried it since, and they'd better not, as I guess they must know."

"Perhaps you mightn't have fared so well if we hadn't had another war on our hands at the same time," retorted Albert.

But just here the talk was interrupted by Captain Raymond and Mr. Austin joining them—the former coming from his interview with Mrs. McAlpine in the sitting room, the latter entering from the street.

CHAPTER
FOURTEENTH

"CAN'T WE GO TO our own rooms now, papa?" asked Lulu when their English friends had bidden them goodnight and gone.

"Yes," he said, taking her hand and leading the way. Max followed not at all unwillingly.

"I suppose you want to finish your letter now, Lulu?" the captain said, as they entered his bedroom, which they made their sitting room also when desirous of being quite to themselves.

"No, sir, I don't. I'd rather let it wait till Monday, if I may sit on your knee a little while and have you talk to me."

"Have me talk to you? Or let you talk to me?" he asked with a playful look and tone, as he sat down and drew her to the coveted place.

"Both, you dear papa," she answered, putting her arms around his neck and giving him an ardent kiss.

"Am I to do nothing but listen?" asked Max, pulling forward a chair and seating himself close beside them.

"Just as you please, young man," laughed his father. "But I doubt if you can refrain from putting in a word now and then."

"He's been talking ever so fast almost all the evening," said Lulu, "only letting me have a word now and then."

"Ah, indeed! I hope it has been good humored and sensible talk?"

"Very sensible. I was quite proud of my brother," replied Lulu, giving Max a laughing glance. "But I'm not sure about the good humored. I shouldn't wonder if Albert Austin has made up his mind by this time that Max and I are not at all very partial to the English."

"I hope you haven't been rude to Albert, my children?" the captain said with sudden gravity.

"I hope not, papa. I don't think we were, though we stated a few historical facts—perhaps a little strongly," replied Lulu.

"What were they?" he asked. "You may tell me about it if you like."

They then repeated the substance of their entire conversation with Albert, their father listening with evident interest.

At the conclusion of the story, he said, "I think from your account that Albert showed much good temper and moderation in the way he bore your strictures on his country and countrymen. You cannot be too patriotic to please me, my dears, but I want you to be careful of the feelings of others, never wounding them unnecessarily. Albert and his father may be considered to some extent our guests, as strangers visiting our country, so that we should be doubly careful to be kind and considerate toward them."

"I'll try to keep that in mind, papa," said Max. "I will stand up for my own country always but not abusing his—when I can help it. Just as we were separating tonight, he said to me in a low tone, 'We must have some more talks on the subject we were on tonight. I haven't any books at hand to consult, but I must inform myself by questioning papa, and then I'll be better prepared to stand up for old England.'"

"Did he look cross when he said it?" asked Lulu.

"No," replied Max. "He's really quite a gentleman, I think."

"As his father is," remarked the captain.

"'Like father, like son,' is an old saying, so remember, my children, that people will judge me by your behavior."

"Yes, sir," said Max. "I think I shall be the more careful to behave well on that account."

"I too," chimed in Lulu. "It would be a dreadful thing if we should disgrace our father. Wouldn't it, Max?"

"Yes, indeed!" exclaimed the lad earnestly. "I have often felt, oh, so thankful that I had a father I could respect and reverence and honor, for I've known boys whose fathers were drunken, wicked men that they couldn't help being ashamed of."

"Give all the glory and thanks to God, who has kept your father from drunkenness and crime, my boy," the captain said, laying his hand affectionately on his son's shoulder and giving him a look full of fatherly affection. "But for His restraining grace I might have been the worst of criminals."

Then, taking up his Bible and opening it, "Now, we will have our reading and prayer," he said. "And then go to our beds."

"I just know Gracie is longing for this, if she's awake," said Lulu, as her father took her in his arms after prayers to give her a goodnight kiss.

"I trust she is asleep ere this, the dear darling!" he replied. "I seem to see the dear little face lying on my pillow with the sweet blue eyes closed in sleep, an almost smile on her lips, the babies asleep in the nursery with the door open between, and Mamma Vi seated somewhere near, writing a letter to her absent husband. Ah, I should be homesick tonight if I hadn't these two of my beloved flock with me."

"And I'd be dreadfully homesick if I wasn't with my dear father," she responded, clinging lovingly to him. "You are a good deal more than half of home to me, papa. And, oh, but you were good and kind to bring me with you!"

"And me, too," added Max. "Papa, I am sure this trip to the far West will be something to remember all my life."

"I hope so, my boy," his father said. "It has been my desire to make it so enjoyable to you both that it will be to you a pleasant memory all your days.

"Tomorrow we will attend morning and evening services at the mission church—Sunday school also— and in the afternoon have our usual home exercises, going on with our regular Bible and catechism lessons exactly as if we were at Woodburn.

"On Monday I expect to take you to see the cattle ranch Mr. Short pointed out in the distance this afternoon."

Both thanked him, expressing themselves pleased with the plans he had mapped out for the two days.

"Paps, shall I dress for church when I get up in the morning?" asked Lulu.

"Yes," he answered. "Wear one of your plainer dresses. I think we should not dishonor God's house by being shabby or slovenly in our attire, nor should we dress in a way to attract attention and divert the thought of others from the service."

"Yes, sir, I know that's what you have told me at home, and that you never let me wear my brightest things to church. And I suppose it would make even more difference here, where most of the congregation must be quite poor?"

"I think so," he said. "And also that you will be less likely to be taken up with thoughts of yourself and your own appearance if you are not brightly dressed, Lulu."

Captain Raymond's arrangements for spending the holy hours of the Lord's Day were duly carried out. The hour for morning service in the church he had provided for Minersville found him and his son and daughter seated among the worshippers. The Austins were there also, and it was the same again in the evening.

They all visited the Sunday school, too, and took part in its exercises. The two gentlemen had not been acquainted many hours before discovering that they were followers of the same Saviour, and each felt it to be a closer bond of union than would have been that of the same nativity without it.

The Austins joined the Raymonds, by invitation, in Monday's excursion and indeed in almost every other one taken while they all remained in Minersville, which was for several weeks.

Captain Raymond took his children with him almost everywhere he went. To Lulu's extreme satisfaction, her days were spent in walks and rides, the latter becoming more enjoyable as she made better acquaintance with her pony and grew confident of her ability to guide and control it. Her father, however, always rode by her side and kept constant watch over her safety.

Their evenings were apt to be spent on the porch, as the weather was such as to make that the most enjoyable spot at that time. Often one or more of the McAlpine family would be there—perhaps at the farther end of the porch, so as not to seem to intrude upon the Raymonds or their guests, for Mr. Austin and Albert were apt to be with them and Mr. Short, too, not infrequently.

But occasionally the young people were there without their elders—the captain, perhaps, busied with some writing in his own room.

The lads, Albert and Max, had become very good friends in spite of an occasional tilt over the respective claims of the two countries to preeminence in one thing or another—usually in regard to the bravery and competence of her soldiers and sailors.

One evening Albert began lauding Nelson as the greatest naval hero the world had ever seen, winding up his eulogy with a challenge to Max to mention anyone to compare to him in seamanship, fighting qualities, or bravery.

"Well, I don't know of any other Englishman to compare to him," replied Max cooly. "But we've had a number of officers in our navy that I think were quite equal to him."

"Which, pray?" sneered Albert.

"There was Commodore McDonough, who whipped the British in the battle of Lake Champlain. It was so terrible a fight that one of the British sailors engaged in it—one who had also been with Nelson at Trafalgar—said that battle was a mere flea-bite in comparison."

"But in the action at Trafalgar, Lord Nelson defeated the combined navies of France and Spain."

"Yes, the British whipped them, and the Americans whipped the British," said Max. "You ought to think it is a greater feat to whip the British than to conquer in fight with Frenchmen and Spaniards," he added laughingly.

"But the odds against Nelson were very much greater. Our force in the battle of Lake Champlain was only slightly superior."

"I am not so sure about that," replied Max. "I know at least one historian says it was decidedly superior. But McDonough was a Christian, and before going into the fight, he called his officers about him, and kneeling on the quarter deck, asked the help of God in the coming battle."

"Then, if his prayer was granted, he had better help than all the navies of the world could have given him."

"That's so," said Max. "And he gave the glory of the victory where it belonged. In his dispatch to the Secretary of the Navy, he said God had granted it.

"He was gallant and generous as a conqueror. When the British officers tendered him their swords after the surrender, he put them back, saying, 'Gentlemen, your gallant conduct makes you worthy to wear your weapons. Return them to their scabbards.'

"Commodore Perry was another of our naval heroes. He won the victory in the battle of Lake Erie in the War of 1812 and wrote that famous dispatch, 'We have met the enemy, and they are ours, two ships, two brigs, one schooner, and one sloop.'

"Then there were the great naval commanders of our Civil War," Max went on. "I don't believe a greater one than Farragut ever lived, or as great a one, unless it might be Porter, who had a large share in the taking of New Orleans—helping ever so much with his mortar boats.

"Why, the undertaking was so difficult, that a number of English and French naval officers who visited Farragut while he was in the lower Mississippi completing his preparations for passing on up to take the city, told him they had carefully examined the defenses of the Confederates, and that it would be sheer madness for him to attack the forts with wooden ships such as his. He'd be sure to be defeated.

"But he was not discouraged—the brave old man! He said, 'You may be right, but I was sent here to make the attempt. I came here to reduce or pass the forts and to take New Orleans, and I shall try it on.' And so he did try it on and succeeded."

"I admire such grit," said Albert. "I've read quite a good deal about that war—a tremendous one it was—and I think there were some very plucky things done on both sides."

"Yes," returned Max. "I'm proud of the bravery shown by both the 'Yanks' and the 'Johnnies,' as they called each other."

Here Lulu, who had thus far contented herself with listening, put in a word.

"I don't believe there ever was or could be a braver or more wonderful feat than Lieutenant Cushing performed when he blew up the rebel ram *Albermarle.* He dashed up along side of it in his little vessel, through a perfect shower of bullets. Then, finding that the ram was behind a wall of logs, he sheered off and dashed over that, while standing up in the stern of his boat with the tiller ropes in one hand and the lanyard of a torpedo in the other, never flinching, though a big gun was trained right on him. But he got his torpedo just where he wanted it under the ram, gave his lanyard a jerk, and fired the thing off—so that it blew up the ram at the same instant that their great gun sent a hundred pound shot right through the bottom of his boat. Oh, such a roar as the two—the torpedo and the gun—must have made, going off together in that way!"

"It was a wonderfully brave deed!" exclaimed Albert with enthusiasm. "Did Cushing himself, or any of his crew, escape alive? I have forgotten, if ever I knew about it."

"Yes," replied Lulu. "He escaped to the Union fleet after almost incredible hardship and danger— the only one of thirteen who had set out on the expedition two days before."

"And the ram was destroyed?"

"Yes, she was a total wreck. Cushing wasn't sure of it till, while he was lying hidden in a swamp and half covered with water, two Confederate officers passing along near him said to each other that the *Albermarle* was a total wreck.

"They didn't see him, but he heard what they said. It was such good news that it gave him fresh courage to bear his sufferings and exert himself to get back to the Federal fleet."

"Your father was on the Union side, I suppose?" Albert said inquiringly.

"Yes, indeed!" replied Max and Lulu, both speaking at once. Then Max went on, "But he was only a boy, younger than I am now, when the war began."

"What was it about?" asked Albert. "I'm not sure I ever clearly understood that."

"The Confederates were trying to break up the Union, and the Federals fought to save it," replied Max. "Papa has made it very clear to me that the Revolutionary War was fought to win freedom from Great Britain's galling yoke and make ourselves a nation; the War of 1812 to convince the British that we were free, independent, and not to be maltreated with impunity. Those two wars did that for us—made the dear old Union. The Civil War saved it from being destroyed by those who ought to have been ready to defend and preserve it at the risk of their lives. I do believe they would now," he added. "Or rather the new generation, who have taken their places, would. I believe, if England or France or any other nation should attack us, the people of the Southern states would fight for the Union quite as bravely and with as much fury and determination as any men of any other part of our great big country."

"Is that so?" said Albert. "Well, I trust there will be no more wars between England and the United States, Max."

"I am sure I can echo that wish," returned Max. "It seems a dreadful thing for two Christian nations to go to war with each other."

"Very true," said Albert. "It would certainly look strangely inconsistent to the heathen peoples we are both trying to convert."

"It couldn't fail to do so," assented Max. "War is a dreadful thing. Reading descriptions of the awful scenes of bloodshed and carnage on board vessels and in land battles, too, I've sometimes thought Satan must take great and fiendish delight in it."

"Yes," said Lulu again joining in the talk. "I've heard papa make a remark like that, but he said at the same time that there were worse things than war, when it was waged to secure liberty—not only for ourselves, but for others. He said that war could never be right on both sides, but it often was on one. On the side of America in her two wars with England, for instance."

"My father surprised me by saying the same thing when I questioned him on the subject after that talk we had about it before," said Albert. "He added that, of course, England being his native land, he loved her better than any other, and always should, but for all that he couldn't shut his eyes to the fact that she had not always been in the right.

"The colonies were oppressed, and they had a right to be free if they desired separation from the mother country. And after they had been acknowledged free and independent states, they were no more under English rule than any other foreign nation. And, according to international law, the public and private vessels of every nation are subject, on the high seas, to the jurisdiction of the state they belong to, and to no other. He said that no nation has the right of visitation and search of the vessels of another nation, and so the Americans were justly indignant over the insistence upon, and the carrying out, of the so-called right of search by British men-of-war—especially as native-born Americans had no security against being impressed as Englishmen and, indeed, very often were. It must have been awfully hard on them, I'm sure."

"Yes," returned Max. "Your father must be an honorable and just man to acknowledge it."

"Just my opinion," Albert said with a frank, good-humored smile. "But if it's noble to acknowledge one's own individual faults, why not also own that your country may have sometimes been in the wrong?"

"Certainly," said Max. "I've heard papa say he thought we were aggressors in the war with Mexico, and that our government had done grievous wrong to the poor Indians."

"It's very true that a good many Americans were impressed," remarked Lulu. "Thousands of them — even while we were fighting France and so helping England, she kept on impressing our sailors and seizing our ships whenever she could find the smallest excuse for doing so. They didn't respect even the ships belonging to our government when they — the British, I mean — were enough stronger to put resistance out of the question on the part of the Americans.

"And they even impressed three of our sailors after the War of 1812 had begun. I read about it not long ago, and I remember very well how shamefully they were treated.

"They refused to serve against their country, and for that they were punished with five dozen lashes, well laid on. Still they refused, and two days later they got four dozen more. Two days after that they got two dozen more.

"But all the beating the British could give them wouldn't make them fight against their country, so they put them in irons for three months till the ship reached London.

"There they heard of the glorious victory of the *Constitution* over the *Guerriere* and were so rejoiced that they made a flag by tearing up some of their clothes into strips and sewing them together. They hung it on a gun and cheered for the Stars and

Stripes. Of course, they got another flogging for that one.

"There were twenty thousand American seamen in the British navy, five times as many as we had in our own navy and quite too many to beat into subjection, so they imprisoned thousands of them in old hulks, where they froze in winter and sweltered in summer and suffocated all the time—so crowded together they were hardly able to catch a breath of fresh air. They were eaten up by vermin, also, and only half-fed on very poor food, too.

"Of course, they grew sick and altogether had a dreadful, dreadful life—all because they wouldn't fight against their country."

"It was awfully hard on them," admitted Albert. "But, please, Miss Lulu, don't hold Englishmen of the present day responsible for what was done so many years ago."

"I'll try not to," she said with a smile. "Certainly I shall not hold you responsible, for I feel quite sure you would never be so unjust and cruel."

"Thanks," he returned with a gratified look, and she went on.

"I know there were Englishmen, even in that day, who wouldn't have had one poor sailor so treated if they could have helped it. Captain Dacres, of the *Guerriere*, for one.

"He had an American captain prisoner on his vessel at the time of his battle with the *Constitution*, and before the fight began, he politely told him, as he supposed he didn't want to fight against his country, he might go below if he chose. And he gave the same privilege to ten American sailors who had been impressed on his ship."

"Yes," said Max, "he was a fine fellow. If all his countrymen had been like him, I don't believe there would have been any war between England and America at all."

"I admire his conduct," Albert said. "I hope I should have acted as he did, had I been in his place then."

"I dare say you would," said Max.

CHAPTER FIFTEENTH

"PAPA," SAID MAX, on finding himself alone with his father and sister that evening, "we'll spend the Fourth here, won't we?"

"Probably, my son," was the reply. "I do not now expect to leave Minersville before the middle or perhaps the last of July. But why do you ask?"

"I was thinking whether we mightn't get up some sort of a celebration," said Max.

"Oh, yes. Do let us, papa!" cried Lulu. "It would be such fun."

"Would it?" he said, smiling at her eagerness. "I should think that would depend on how we celebrate. What would you two like to do to show your patriotism on the nation's birthday?"

"We shall want your help in deciding what might be done, papa," said Max.

"We might treat the mission school, couldn't we, papa?" asked Lulu.

"I like that idea," he answered, "but we must consider what sort of treat it shall be."

"Good things to eat, such as they do not get every day—nuts, candies, raisins, oranges, figs, cakes, anything nice that we can get. Could we send away somewhere for such things, papa? I'm afraid they are not to be had in the stores here—at least not many of them."

"I think I can order by telegraph and have them brought in season by express on the railroad," he answered. "We have about a week in which to make our arrangements."

"Oh, good! Then you'll do it, won't you, papa?"

"I think so," he said in an indulgent tone.

"And let's distribute some small flags among the children," said Max. "And have fireworks in the evening, too."

"Oh, yes, yes!" exclaimed Lulu, clapping her hands and jumping up and down in delight. "Mayn't we, papa?"

"I think we will," he said. "But before we quite decide the question we will talk the matter over with Mr. Short. He knows the tastes of the people here much better than we do, and he may have some good suggestions to make."

"Perhaps the minister and the teacher might give some good suggestions, too," Max said.

"Very likely," replied his father. "We will consult them as well."

The proposed consultations were held early the next morning, and the necessary orders dispatched to the nearest points where they could be filled.

Max and Lulu were very full of the subject and talked of it at the table not a little, exciting a good deal of interest and curiosity in the mind of Marian, as she overheard a remark now and again while attending to their wants.

There was a fine natural grove of forest trees on the outskirts of the village. There it had been decided the town's people were to be invited to assemble on the morning of the Fourth to listen to an oration by the foremost lawyer of the place, and the reading of the Declaration of Independence by Captain

Raymond. They were also to join in the singing of patriotic songs.

The children of the mission school would be taken to the grove in a body, marching in procession, carrying flags and banners. After the exercises were over they would be marched back to the schoolroom and treated to cakes, candies, fruits, and ices.

There were to be fireworks in the evening set off in front of Mrs. McAlpine's boarding house, which, cornering on two very wide streets, was quite a good place for the display.

"Mr. Short seemed really pleased with the idea of having a celebration, didn't he, papa?" Lulu said at the dinner table.

"I thought so" returned her father. "And it was fortunate that he knew someone capable of delivering an oration on the subject at so short a notice, and that arrangements could be made in season for a little advertisement of our plans for the Fourth in this week's issue of the county paper."

"I daresay it will be the first celebration of the Fourth of July ever seen by Albert or his father," remarked Max. "I hope everything will go off nicely, so that they maybe favorably impressed."

On leaving the table Lulu seated herself on the porch with a book. She was still sitting there alone when Marian came out with her hat on and a basket in her hand.

"Do you feel inclined for a walk, Miss Lulu?" she asked. "I am going downtown on an errand for mother, and I should be delighted to have your company if you would like to go."

"Yes, I should," returned Lulu. "I'll go if I can get permission from my papa. He is in his room writing letters. Can you wait a minute while I run and ask him, Marian?"

"Oh, yes, indeed—two minutes if you wish," replied Marian sportively, and Lulu hurried into the house.

She was back again almost immediately with hat, gloves, and a parasol.

"Papa says I may go with you to do your errand, but I must come directly home again."

"I didn't suppose you would have to ask his permission just to go downtown with me," remarked Marian in surprise, as they walked on together. Your father seems to cuddle you so that I had an idea you could do exactly as you pleased."

"Oh, no, indeed!" Lulu answered with a contented little laugh. "Papa hugs and indulges us all, but still he is very strict about some things. I must never go anywhere without asking leave—not even outside of the grounds, by myself, when I'm at home."

"I suppose that is because he's afraid something might harm you—something or somebody?" Marian said interrogatively.

"Yes, I know that's his reason, and it's because he loves me so dearly. If it wasn't for that I'd be very rebellious sometimes, I'm afraid, for I'm naturally very willful, always wanting to have my own way."

"Yes, but one would bear almost anything for the sake of being loved so," Marian said with an involuntary sigh. Then suddenly she changed the subject.

"Miss Lulu, won't you tell me more about the celebration you were talking of at breakfast and dinner today? I mean particularly why Americans should make so much of that day? I'm afraid you must think I ought to be ashamed of my ignorance. I suppose I ought, but you must remember that I've lived in America only a few years, and I have not mingled much with native-born citizens.

"It was a Mormon missionary that persuaded father and mother to come over, and most of the people I've known about here have been Mormons from foreign lands. They are all taught by the Mormon leaders to believe that the United States government is the worst and most tyrannical in the world and to hate it accordingly.

"So, of course, they haven't made anything of celebrating the Fourth of July. I do know enough to be aware that it's the patriotic people who do that."

"We keep it because it's the nation's birthday," said Lulu. "And we've good reason to be glad and thankful to God that our nation was born. For instead of our nation being the worst and most tyrannical, it is the very best and most free in the world."

"The nation's birthday? How do you mean? I don't quite understand."

"We celebrate the day of the signing of the Declaration of Independence. The Continental Congress signed it.

"You see, when the colonies began the struggle with England that we call the Revolutionary War, they had not thought of separating from her, they loved her and called her the mother country, but as the fight went on, the breach grew wider and wider, till, after a while, the people began to see that it could never be healed. They saw that the only thing to do, if they would be anything better than slaves to Great Britain, was to become a separate nation—declare themselves free and independent and fight the British till they forced them to go back where they belonged and let us alone.

"Of course, the declaration had to be made and signed by the leaders of the people, and that made us a new nation—one by ourselves—and so we call it the nation's birthday. Although most of the fighting to carry it out and make the British and other nations own that we were really what we called ourselves, had to be done afterward.

"It's quite a nice story about the signing, and if you'd like I'll tell it to you some time. Tomorrow, papa and Mr. Austin and Max and Albert are all going with a hunting party, and I shall be home alone. That will give me a good opportunity to tell the story, if you can find time to sit with me for awhile."

"Thank you, Miss Lulu," said Marian. "I shall certainly try to find the time and will be very glad to hear the story."

Here the conversation came to an end, as they were just on the threshold of the store to which Marian's errand led her.

While she attended to that, Lulu, glancing curiously about, spied a box of narrow ribbons of various colors, asked to be allowed to look at them, inquired the price, and selecting a red, a white, and a blue piece, said, "You may please wrap these up for me," and taking out her purse, paid for them.

She noticed that Marian watched the proceeding with some little surprise and curiosity, though she asked no question and made no remark.

"I suppose you are wondering what I bought these ribbons for?" Lulu said, as they left the store.

"Yes," replied Marian. "But still more that you should buy them without asking permission, when you couldn't even walk down the street with me till you had asked your father if you might."

"Oh, that was quite a different thing," said Lulu. "Papa allows me to spend my pocket money as I please—at least, within certain bounds. He wouldn't let me buy whiskey or tobacco or dime novels, of course," she added with a laugh.

"I should think not, indeed," said Marian, joining in the laugh. "Yet I dare say he would be likely to let you do it as you would want to do so."

"Yes, I can't say that I have any inclination to spend my money so, even to prove my independence. Though, now I come to think of it, I'm pretty sure I would be allowed to buy tobacco if it was as a present to some of our people who are very fond of it."

"It must be fine to have money of your own to do as you will with," remarked Marian. "I never was so fortunate, but I hope to earn for myself some day. Poor mother has always had a struggling time," she went on. "And I could never have the heart to take pocket money from her, even if she offered it, but the folk about town say your father is very, very rich, Miss Lulu."

"Just say Lulu, Marian. You needn't call me Miss," Lulu said. "I suppose it is true that papa is rich, but he never says so and always tells us he is only the Lord's steward, bound to use the money entrusted to him for the upbuilding of Christ's cause and kingdom. He also says that no one—no matter how rich—has any right to be wasteful, extravagant, or idle. And he says that not only money, but time and ability to do anything useful, are talents entrusted to us to be used and increased—that at last the Lord may say to us each, 'Well done, good and faithful servant, enter thou into the joy of thy Lord.'"

"I think your father must be a very good, Christian man," was Marian's answering remark.

"Indeed he is!" returned Lulu emphatically. "He's always Christian, always loving Jesus, and trying his very best to please and honor Him by doing exactly as the Bible says."

The captain had finished his correspondence and gone out to mail his letters, and as Max, too, was out, Lulu found no one in their rooms when she went back to them on her return from her walk with Marian.

But on the table beside which her father had been sitting lay a pile of clothes fresh from the iron—just brought in from the wash.

"There," thought Lulu to herself, "if Mamma Vi were here she would soon take papa's clothes from that pile and see if there were any buttons to sew on or stockings to darn. And if there were she'd sit right down and attend to it. She lets Christine or Alma attend to Max's clothes, but unless she is sick, no one but herself must do papa's, because, as she says, it is a great pleasure to her to care for her husband's comfort.

"I always love to do things for papa, too, and I like to be kind and helpful to Max, for he's a dear, kind brother to me. And, of course, my own mending belongs to me, so I'll just sit down to this pile of clothes and put them all in order."

She hastened to put away her hat and gloves and get out her workbasket, which was thoroughly furnished with all the needed articles and implements. When her father came in he found her seated in a low chair between table and window, busily plying her needle.

"My little busy bee," he said, regarding her with a pleased smile. Then bending down, he kissed her forehead.

She laughed and held up her rosy lips in mute invitation. He kissed them, too, then laying his hand tenderly on her head, said, "My little girl looks quite matronly. Are you playing at being Mamma Vi?"

"Yes, sir, I am like her in at least one thing."

"What is that?"

"In feeling it a pleasure to do anything for you, sir. Papa, I thought it was just dreadful when you wouldn't let me wait on you for four whole days, because I'd been disobedient and rebellious."

"Yes, I know you did. And it was very hard for me, too—hard to do without my dear little daughter's loving services."

"But you denied yourself for my sake—to make me good, because you know no one can be happy who is not good—you dear papa!" she said with a grateful loving look up into his face.

"Yes, my darling, that was exactly it," he said, repeating his caresses. "And it makes me very happy that of late I have rarely needed to punish or even reprove you. It is so much more pleasant to commend and reward my children than to punish them."

He had drawn up a chair and seated himself by her side. "I did better for myself than I was aware of in bringing my eldest daughter along," he remarked. "I had no thought of making use of you to keep my clothes and Max's in order."

"But you are pleased to have me do it, papa?"

"I am."

"Papa, I bought something when I was at the store with Marian. See!" opening a brown paper parcel, which she took from the table beside her, and displaying the ribbons.

"Ah! What use do you expect to make of your purchases?" he asked.

"Badges for the school children. They are the national colors, you see, papa."

"Yes, it is a good idea, and I presume the children will be much pleased. When do you propose to make your badges?"

"Tomorrow, papa, while you and Max are off on your hunt. But I mean to finish this mending first."

"That's right. I am glad you have found something to do to keep you from being lonely while we are away. I should like to take you along but for the exposure to danger."

"Mightn't I as well be exposed to it as Max?" she asked in a playful tone.

"Max is older and a boy," he said. "You are very fearless, I know, but women and girls are not so strong physically as our sex, and it is not to be expected that they can endure the same amount of exposure and fatigue. You could hardly be of much assistance in fighting a grizzly, for instance," he added laughingly, bending over her and softly smoothing her hair as he spoke.

"No, sir," she returned, laughing a little. "I'm not fearless enough to enjoy the idea of facing one of them. And it frightens me to think of you and Max fighting one. Oh, papa, don't try it!"

"Would you have your father a coward?" he asked.

"No, sir. Oh, no, indeed! I know you are brave, as brave can be. And it makes me very proud, but what's the use of fighting bears?"

"To rid the country of them as dangerous enemies to settlers. Also their flesh is good for food, and the skin, too, is valuable. But here comes Max, and there is the tea bell. Put up your work and let me lead you to the table."

Max met them in the hall.

"Where have you been, my son?" asked the captain.

"Out to the mine with Albert, papa. You know you gave me permission to walk with him when I chose, provided we did not go farther than that from town."

"So I did. I'm glad you went, for I should not wish you to be cooped up in the house in such weather as this."

They sat down to the table, and after the blessing had been asked, Max began telling about his walk.

"We found the sun rather hot, going," he said. "But coming back it was very pleasant indeed. There was a nice breeze from the mountains."

"Had you any adventures?" asked Lulu.

"No, hardly that," he answered with a slight laugh. "But as we were going, Albert thought he heard a child crying in the bushes and started off to hunt for it. I kept straight on. He was disgusted with what he called my heartlessness.

"I said, 'I don't believe there is any child there,' and he answered, 'There. I'm certain of it, for I heard it cry, and dare say it's some poor thing that has wandered away from home and is lost. Didn't you hear it?'

"Then I said, 'I heard something, but I'm pretty sure it wasn't a child. I've read that a panther will imitate the cry of a child so that almost anyone would be deceived, and hunting for the child might get so near the panther that it could spring on him before he could get out of its way, or even knew it was there. But if you think best, I'll go with you into the bushes and make sure whether there is a baby there or not.'"

"Oh, Max, you knew what it was all the time, didn't you?" laughed Lulu.

"I'm glad he didn't find you out," Lulu said with satisfaction. "Because I hope we'll have some more fun with him. You'll try it one of these evenings when we're all together on the porch, won't you, Max?"

"Perhaps, if I can think of something."

"Albert's very full of the bear hunt for tomorrow, papa. Says he wouldn't miss it for the world."

"Ah? And how does my boy feel about it?"

"Pretty much the same, I think, papa," Max answered with a light laugh. "I'm sorry for Lu that she's only a girl and can't have the pleasure of going along."

"I could if papa would let me," replied Lulu demurely. "But I wouldn't be a boy for the sake of being allowed to go."

"So, you think a boy's privileges are more than counterbalanced by a girl's?"

"Yes, papa takes me on his knee, while you can only sit by his side. And I shall stay at home with him, while you will have to go away to the Academy at Annapolis."

"I go of my own free will," returned Max. "I don't believe papa would compel me against my will."

"Not at all," said the captain, "and I am glad you are both so well satisfied."

CHAPTER SIXTEENTH

THE HUNTERS STARTED the next morning, shortly after an early breakfast.

"Papa, when do you expect to be back?" asked Lulu, as she helped her father with the last of his preparations, some anxiety showing itself in her tone.

"Toward evening, daughter. I can't set the hour," he answered cheerily. "Better not expect us too soon, lest it should make you feel lonely and disappointed. Your better plan will be to keep yourself busy reading, writing, sewing—as you prefer, and you may take a walk about town with Marian, if you choose, but don't go outside of it.

"Perhaps you will find letters at the post office after the mail comes. Maybe you'll have the pleasure of handing me one from your mamma when I get back. Now, good-bye, my darling."

He held her in a close embrace for a moment, kissing her tenderly two or three times, released her, and was gone.

Max was following with a hasty, "Good-bye, Lu." But she ran after him, calling, "Max, kiss me; let me kiss you. Suppose the bear should get hold of you and hug you so tight that I'd never have a chance to do it again," she added, laughing to hide an slight inclination to cry.

"Just imagine now that he has hold of you," Max said, throwing his arms round her and squeezing her so hard that she screamed out, "Oh, let me go! You're bear enough for me!"

"Bears must be allowed to hug, for 'tis their nature to," he said, with a laugh, giving her another squeeze and a resounding kiss. "Good-bye, I must be off now, to catch up with papa."

Lulu hurried out to the porch to watch them mount and ride away, her father throwing her a kiss from the saddle. She then went back, rather disconsolately, to her work of sorting over the clean clothes and giving them the needed repairs.

She had finished that and had begun upon her badges, when Marian came in with some sewing and asked if she might sit with her and hear the promised story of the signing of the Declaration.

"Yes, indeed! I'll be glad of your company and glad to tell the story, for it's one I like very much," said Lulu.

"Thank you," Marian said. "But before you begin, may I ask what those pretty badges are for? You forgot to tell me what you were going to do with the ribbons."

"Oh, so I did! These are our national colors, and I'm making badges for the mission school children to wear on the Fourth. I'm glad you think them pretty. Now for my story.

"It was in Philadelphia it all happened, on the fourth of July, 1776. But I must go back and tell of something that happened before that.

"Of course you know about the Pilgrims coming over from England and settling in the wilderness that America was then, so that they might be free to worship God as they thought right, and about the settling of the thirteen colonies, and how King George the Third and the British Parliament oppressed them, taxing them without representation, passing that hateful Stamp Act, and so on, till the people couldn't stand it any longer.

"They just wanted to make all they could off the American people and give them nothing in return. But the Americans wouldn't stand for it. They weren't the sort of stuff to be made slaves of. So when the tax was put on tea they said they wouldn't buy any. They would sooner go without drinking tea than pay that tax.

"Great shiploads were sent over, but they wouldn't let it be landed. At last they grew so angry that they boarded a ship loaded with tea lying in Boston harbor and threw the chests of tea into the water.

"That was the Boston 'tea party' that is so often spoken of in talking about the struggle between the colonies and Great Britain. That happened in 1773. Then the next year—1774—there was another tea party something like it, though not exactly, in New Jersey. It was at a small place called Greenwich on the Cohansey.

"A brig named the *Greyhound*, commanded by Captain Allen, came up the river to Greenwich on the twenty-second of November landed her load of tea there.

"It was put into a cellar not very far from the wharf, and somebody that saw it ran and told someone else.

"The news spread very fast. People were quite astonished and angry. They had never expected such a cargo to come there, and they had no notion of letting it stay, for most of them were quite as patriotic as the Boston people.

"So a party of them disguised themselves and assembled together in the dusk of the evening. They got the chests of tea out of that cellar, carried them to an old field, piled them up there and set them on fire—burned them entirely up."

"Quite as good a way to be rid of them as by throwing them into the sea, I think," commented Marian. "But wasn't anyone punished for it?"

"Not that I ever heard or read of," replied Lulu. "I suppose nobody who would have wanted to tell knew who the men were that did the deed."

"I think they had something of the spirit of our Scotch folk of early times, who would never submit to be ruled by the English," remarked Marian.

"Yes, papa has told me that a good many who did good service to their country in the Revolution were of Scotch and Scotch-Irish descent. He says it is a race that never would brook oppression.

"Well, the next spring after the burning of the tea at Greenwich—that is on the nineteenth of April, 1775—the war began with the battle of Lexington. Still, most of the Americans didn't think of anything but forcing the English government to treat them better, but the fight went on. The British had no idea of giving up their oppressive doings, and soon the wise ones among the Americans began to see that there was no way to get their rights but by separating from England and setting up for themselves. And that was what brought them to the writing and signing of the Declaration of Independence."

"But who did it? The officers of your army who were fighting the British?"

"No, oh, no! It was the Continental Congress assembled at Philadelphia. They appointed a committee to draw up the paper, and when it was read to them, everyone voted for it. Then, one after another, each of the fifty-six members present signed his name to it.

"It was a very dangerous thing to do, for the English king and his government would call it treason and put the signers to death if they could catch them. The people were quite afraid that the hearts of the congressmen would fail them when it came to the signing, and the thing be given up.

"A great crowd was gathered on the day of the signing in the street outside of the State House where Congress met, and there they waited, oh, so anxiously, to hear that the deed was done.

"There was a bell at the top of the State House, and the ringer was there ready to let the crowd know by ringing the bell when the signing was done. He was an old man, and down on the landing by the stairs leading to the belfry sat a little blue-eyed boy who was to call up the news to him.

"All was very quiet indoors and out. The crowd was listening for the news — the old man and the little boy also — and the congressmen feeling very solemn because of the great risk they were running and the necessity for taking it if they would save their country.

"There was a deathlike stillness in the room while one after another went from his seat to the table and wrote his name at the bottom of the paper. And when all had signed, oh, how still it was for a moment till Franklin broke the silence by saying, 'Now, gentlemen, we must all hang together, or we shall surely hang separately!"

"I suppose somebody had stepped to the door and spoken to the little boy. The old man in the belfry was saying sadly to himself, 'They'll never sign it! They'll never sign it! When all at once the little boy clapped his hands and shouted 'Ring! Ring!'

"The old man was all ready with the bell rope in his hands, and he did ring without waiting one instant. With the first peal the great crowd in the street below set up a wild, 'Hurrah! Hurrah!' They went almost wild with joy.

"Then people farther off heard and caught up the shout, and I suppose not many minutes had passed before everybody else in the whole city knew that the Declaration was signed."

"And everybody was glad?"

"Everybody but the Tories, I think. No doubt there were some of them even there."

"But it seems to me the rejoicing was premature, as they could not be certain of winning in the fight that was hardly more than begun."

"Perhaps so, but they had been so very patient and borne repeated wrongs till they felt that they could bear no more. They would now fight on till death if victory didn't come before that.

"Oh, I must tell you of a strange coincidence in connection with the bell that rang to tell that the deed was done! It had been cast years before, but there was a motto on it that couldn't have been made more suitable to what it did on that fourth of July if all the doings of that day had been foreseen.

"Oh, I'd forgotten that I've read that the declaration was only adopted on the fourth of July and proclaimed on the eighth."

"But what was the motto?" asked Marian.

"It was a verse from the Bible," Lulu answered. "'Proclaim Liberty throughout all the land, to all the inhabitants thereof.' Isn't that a very strange coincidence, Marian?"

"Very, I think," Marian replied. "I'd like to see that old bell. I suppose they keep it in memory of that time?"

"Yes. Oh, yes, indeed!" I've seen it. When we were in Philadelphia not very long ago, Papa took me to the State House—or Independence Hall, it gets both names—and showed me the old bell. It isn't in use now, because it has a large crack in it, but they keep it for people to see. And I saw the Declaration—the very paper those brave men signed—and the pen they wrote their names with. I saw a great many other things connected with the revolutionary and colonial times. Did you ever hear of Patrick Henry?"

"No, never. Who was he?"

"I think you will like to hear about him because, though born in America, he was the son of a Scotsman. He lived in the time we've been talking about, and he was one of our very patriotic men and greatest orators. He was a Virginian, and in 1765—ten years before the Revolutionary War began, when George the Third was oppressing the colonies so, and had the Stamp Act passed—he belonged to the House of Burgesses.

"They were debating about the Stamp Act, and Patrick Henry was wanting resolutions passed declaring that no one but the House of Burgesses and the governor had a right to lay taxes and imposts on that colony.

"Some of the other members were very much opposed to his resolutions and grew very angry and abusive toward him. But he wouldn't give up to them. He went on with his speech and said some brave words that startled even the patriots and have been famous words ever since. They were

'Caesar had his Brutus, Charles the First his Cromwell, and George the Third'—just there he was interrupted by cries of 'Treason! Treason!'—'may profit by their examples.' He added, 'If this be treason, make the most of it.'"

"That was fine indeed!" Marian exclaimed, her eyes shining. "I'm thinking he was a worthy descendant of some of our Scotch heroes. But did they pass his resolution?"

"Yes, by a majority of one."

"Ten years after that—just a few weeks before the battle of Lexington that began the war—he was talking in a convention at Richmond in Virginia. He wanted to organize the militia and make the colony ready for defense against Great Britain, but some of the others were very much opposed.

"He made a grand speech to them, trying to convince them that what he wanted done was the wisest thing they could do. In it he said some brave words that I admire so much that I learned them by heart—committed them to memory, I suppose, would be the proper expression."

"Oh, say them over to me!" entreated Marian, her eyes sparkling with enthusiasm. "I dearly love to hear brave, bold words that speak a determination to be free from the tyranny of man, whether he would lord it over soul or body, or both."

"So do I," said Lulu. "And no one was more capable of saying such words than Patrick Henry. These are the ones I spoke of.

"'There is no retreat but in submission and slavery. Our chains are already forges. Their clanking may be heard on the plains of Boston. The next gale that sweeps from the north will bring the clash of resounding arms. I know not what course others may take, but as for me, give me liberty or give me death!'

"I think the convention couldn't hold out against such brave and eloquent words, for they passed his resolution without anyone saying a word against it."

"I'm proud to know that he was a Scotsman's son," said Marian.

"And I that he was a native-born American," responded Lulu.

"And your government is really a free one though the Mormons say so much against it?" queried Marian.

"Yes, indeed! But I wish it had broken up Mormonism long ago."

"So do I," responded Marian almost fiercely. "Yes, before it had time to get well started and could send out its missionaries to deceive folks in other countries and persuade them to come over here, where women, at least, are nothing but slaves!"

Lulu looked at her in both surprise and sympathy, for she detected in her tones a bitter sense of personal wrong.

"Was that how you came to emigrate to this country, Marian?" she asked. "Are you and your mother Mormons?"

"I'm no Mormon!" exclaimed the girl through clenched teeth. "But they made one of my father and led him to break my poor mother's heart, so that I hate him. I used to love him, but now I would never set eyes on him again if I could help myself."

"Hate your own father!" cried Lulu, aghast at the very idea. "Oh, how can you?"

"He isn't like yours," Marian returned in quivering tones. "If he was I'd love the very ground he walked on. He used to be kind, but now—he's as cruel and heartless as—I'd almost said the father o' lies himself!"

"Oh, Marian, what has he done to grieve your mother so?"

"What the Mormons teach that every man ought to do if he wants a high place in heaven—taken other wives."

"Why!" exclaimed Lulu. "That's very, very wicked! They send men to the penitentiary for doing that."

"They deserve worse than that," said Marian, her eyes flashing. "I'm no Mormon, I say again. Do you know they teach the women that they can't go to heaven unless they have been married?"

"I know better than that," Lulu said emphatically. "For the Bible says, 'Believe on the Lord Jesus Christ and thou shalt be saved.' And I know some very good Christian ladies who have never been married. I don't see how anybody who believes the Bible can be a Mormon."

"No, nor I," said Marian. "For a good many things they say one must believe are directly the opposite of what the Bible says. For instance, that the blood of Christ doesn't atone for all sin, but some sins have to be atoned for by shedding the sinner's own blood. I think that, beside contradicting the Scriptures, is the same thing as saying that Jesus' blood is not of sufficient value to pay for all the wickedness men have done and buy their salvation. If only they would choose to accept it as a free gift at His hands, believe in Him, and love Him with all their hearts, so that they will be His servants forever."

"But," said Lulu, "I know that is the way the Bible tells us we may be saved, and I'll certainly believe the Bible—God's own word—though every human creature should contradict it."

"So will I," Marian said firmly. "I'll never forget the good teaching of my minister and Sunday School teacher in old Scotland. Everything they taught they proved by Scripture. And from them I learned that man's teachings are not worthy of the smallest consideration if they do not agree with the teachings of God's Word."

"And I've learned the same from papa. How good our heavenly Father was to give us His Holy Word, that we might learn from it just what He would have us believe and do! I feel sorry for the poor heathen who haven't got it, and I want to do all I can to send it to them."

"Have you ever read anything of Scotland's martyrs, who laid down their lives for the love of Jesus and His word?" asked Marian.

"Yes, indeed, and papa has told me about them, as well as of martyrs who suffered in other parts of the world. How strange it is that men should want to persecute each other so and pretend they do it to please God, who is so kind and merciful. You know the Bible says He proclaimed Himself to Moses.

"'The Lord, the Lord God, merciful and gracious, long suffering, and abundant in goodness and truth, keeping mercy for thousands, forgiving iniquity and transgression and sin, and that will by no means clear the guilty.'"

"How do you explain that?" asked Marian. "I mean the not clearing the guilty, yet forgiving iniquity, transgression, and sin?"

"For Jesus' sake, you know," returned Lulu. "Papa explained it to me, saying, 'God's law does not call him guilty for whom Christ has borne the punishment.'"

"Ah, yes, I see. Christ takes the sinner's guilt and gives him of His own righteousness. And to try to add some of our own is like fastening filthy rags on a beautiful white wedding garment. What better is it to try to pour some of the sinner's own polluted blood into that pure fountain opened for sin and uncleanness?"

"Not one bit better, and Mormonism cannot be a true religion. Indeed, there can be but one true religion, I know — that which teaches salvation through the blood and righteousness of Christ."

The dinner hour was approaching, and Marian found she must go to her mother's assistance.

Lulu spent most of the afternoon alone but amused herself with writing letters to Evelyn and Gracie. Marian went with her to the post office to mail them when finished, and to Lulu's great satisfaction, there were letters from home for her father, for Max, and for herself.

"One of these is from Mamma Vi," she said to Marian. "I'm so glad I shall have the pleasure of handing it to papa. Of course, he's always glad to get her letters."

"Your mamma, did you say?" asked Marian.

"My step-mother," explained Lulu. "She's not old enough to be my mamma. My mother had been dead two or three years when papa married again."

"It's all right, then," Marian commented with some bitterness of tone, thinking of Mormon teaching that a man may have many wives living at the same time. "I have never heard of any religion that teaches it is wrong for a man to marry again after his wife is dead."

They had entered the house and passed on into the sitting room. At that moment there was the sound of horses hooves on the street and some seemed to pause at Mrs. McAlpine's gate.

"Oh, I do believe they've come back!" cried Lulu in joyous tones. "Yes, I hear papa's voice," and she ran to meet him, Marian's eyes following her with a wistful, longing look.

The captain had just stepped across the threshold, as his little daughter came flying to him, crying, "Oh, papa, I'm so glad you're safely back again! I was so afraid you might get hurt."

He bent down, caught her in his arms, and giving her a loving kiss, said, "Yes, I have been taken care of and brought back unhurt. My little girl should have trusted me to our heavenly Father's care and not tormented herself with useless and unavailing fears."

"It was foolish and wrong," she acknowledged. Then, catching sight of her brother, "Oh, Maxie, I'm glad to see you safe, too!"

"Are you?" he returned in a sportive tone. "I was beginning to wonder if it made any particular difference to you."

"Oh, did you see any bears?" she asked, as they moved on into their own rooms.

"Yes," answered her father, and Max added, "Papa shot him right through the heart; so he fell dead instantly."

"I was almost sure papa would be the one to shoot him," Lulu exclaimed with a look of triumph. Then with a sudden change of tone, "Papa, you're very tired, aren't you?"

"Rather tired, daughter, and I have a slight headache," he answered. "Were there any letters for me?"

He was taking off his coat, preparatory to ridding himself of the dust gathered during his ride.

"Yes, sir, one of them from Mamma Vi," replied Lulu. "Papa, won't you sit down in the easy chair while you read it and let me stand beside you and brush your hair gently to see if that will help your head?"

"Yes, dear child, I shall enjoy having you do so, if you do not find it too wearisome."

"It won't tire me at all, papa," she asserted with warmth. "There's nothing else I enjoy so much as doing something to make you comfortable."

"My own dear little loving daughter," he responded, giving her a look that filled her heart with gladness.

Max, no less ready than Lulu to wait upon their father, had seized a clothes brush and the captain's coat. Carrying them to the window, he was giving the coat a vigorous shaking and brushing.

"Thank you, my dear boy," the captain said, as Max presently brought the garment to him, looking much better for what it had just gone through. "Truly I think no man was ever more fortunate in his children than I am in mine."

"If there's anything good about our conduct, papa, I think your training deserves all the credit for it," replied Max. "Your training and example, I should have said," he corrected himself.

"If so it is by God's blessing upon it all in the fulfillment of His promise, 'Train up a child in the way he should go, and when he is old he will not depart from it.' I hope, my children, you will never depart from it in youth or in later days."

"I hope not, papa," said Lulu. "Now please sit down and let me try to help your poor head. I'll brush very softly. There, how does that feel?" after passing the brush gently over his hair two or three times.

"Very soothing, darling. You may go on while I open and read my letters."

There were several home letters, and they enjoyed them together as usual, the captain reading aloud, while Lulu continued her labor of love, and Max attended to his own things—brushing his clothes and hair and washing hands and face. There was nothing of the dandy about the lad, but he liked to be neat for his own comfort and because it pleased his father to see him so.

By the time the letters were disposed of and the tea bell sounded out its summons, the captain was able to assure Lulu that his head was almost entirely relieved. He gave the credit to her efforts and rewarded her with a kiss.

CHAPTER
SEVENTEENTH

"GOOD EVENING, Cap'n. So they tell me 'twas you shot and killed that big b'ar?"

The speaker was an elderly man in his shirtsleeves and with a pipe in his mouth, who had stepped onto the porch and took a seat near Captain Raymond as he made the remark.

"I reckon now we'll have to own that yer a better marksman than most o' the fellers about these here diggin's," he added, puffing away at his pipe.

"That does not follow, by any means, Mr. Riggs," returned the captain modestly. "I happened to get the best opportunity to aim at a vital part. That was all."

"Well, now, I'll say fer you that you don't seem to be noways stuck up about it, an' I've seen fellars as proud as a peacock over a smaller streak o' luck— or maybe 'twas skill—than that. But you're a lucky man, sir. Nobody kin deny that, seein' how this ere tract o' land that they tell me ye bought for a mere trifle, has riz in value."

"Yes, I have been very fortunate in that and many other things," replied the captain with a glance at his son and daughter, seated near, that seemed to include them among the blessings that had been granted him, "though wealth has sometimes proved a curse rather than a blessing to its owner."

"It's a curse as most folks is glad to git," laughed the old man. "I tell you I was wild with joy when it fell to my lot to come upon the biggest nugget as has ever been seen in these parts. I began life poor, never had no eddication to speak of, but I've more money now than half the fellers that's rubbed their backs agin' a college."

"But education has other uses than enabling a man to accumulate wealth. Also there are things that contribute more to one's happiness than money. How many millions do you suppose would tempt me to part with my son or daughter, for instance?" And with the question the captain turned his gaze upon his children, his eyes full of fatherly pride and affection.

"Well, Cap'n, I don't s'pose you'd be for sellin' of 'em fer no price," returned the old man with a grin. "They're a likely lookin' lot, and you've plenty o' the evil fur them and yourself, too."

Lulu, mistaking the old man's meaning, shot an angry glance at him, moved nearer to her father, and slipped her hand into his.

Riggs observed it with a laugh. "I wasn't sayin' nothin' agin your dad, miss," he said. "I was only referrin' to the way folks has o' callin' money the root o' all evil, but I observe there's precious few of 'em that isn't glad to git all he kin lay his hands on."

"Yes," said the captain. "But do you know where they got that idea?"

"Well, now, they do tell me there's Scripter fer it."

"That's a mistake, my friend. The Bible says, 'The love of money is the root—or a root—of all evil.'

But it does not say it of money itself. It is a very good thing, if honestly got and put to right uses."

"And what do you call right uses?"

"'Providing things honest in the sight of all men,' relieving the wants of the destitute, helping every good cause, and especially sending the light of the gospel into all the dark places of the earth."

"Well, sir, that's purty good doctrine, and I rayther think ye're livin' up to it, too, by all I hear.

"As fer me, I've been a hard-workin' man all my days, 'cept since I come upon that thar nugget, and I 'low to take my ease fer the rest o' my days. I'm goin' ter fix up my house as fine as I know how. My gal she says 'tain't nowheres big 'nough fer rich folks, and I'm goin' to build a condition to it with a portfolio at the back."

"What's that? He! He! Never heard o' such a thing!" cried a squeaky little voice that seemed to come from behind the old man's chair.

He sprang up and turned round, asking in a startled tone, "Who's that? Who spoke? Why, why, why! Where's the feller gone to?" rolling his eyes in wild astonishment, as he perceived that no one was there.

"Where are your eyes, man? Here I am."

It was the same voice, now coming apparently from behind a large tree growing a few feet away from the porch, its spreading branches reaching to and partly resting upon its roof.

"Humph!" exclaimed Mr. Riggs, hurrying down the porch steps and round to the farther side of the tree, "What are you up to, you rascal?"

"I'm no rascal, sir. What do you call me that for?" queried the voice, sounding as if the speaker was making the circuit of the tree, keeping always on the side farthest from the old man who was pursuing him.

"You were making fun o' me, that's why I call you a rascal, sir," panted Mr. Riggs.

"Oh, no, sir, I was only wanting to know what your conditions and portfolios were—such odd things to talk of adding to a house."

"Odd, indeed! I reckon you'll sing another song when you see 'em. Where under the sun are you?"

"Here, right up here."

The voice seemed to come from among the branches overhead.

"Well, if you ain't the spryest rogue ever I see! I've a notion to climb after you and throw you down."

"Come ahead then. Who's afraid?" the sentence ended in a mocking laugh.

"I'll find a stone, and I guess that'll fetch ye," muttered Riggs, stooping and feeling about the ground for one.

"Ho, ho! Better be careful, you might happen to break a window. Good-bye. I'm off."

The voice came from the roof this time and was immediately followed by a sound as of scrambling and of shuffling footsteps—at first, near at hand, then gradually dying away in the distance.

Meanwhile the captain was fairly shaking with suppressed mirth, and Lulu nearly convulsed with her efforts to control an inclination to burst into uproarious laughter. Max laughed a little when Riggs was talking, but he was sober as a judge when the strange voice answered.

Riggs came stumbling onto the porch again and dropping into his chair, panted out, "Well, if that isn't the beatenest thing I ever hearn of! How that fellar could git away so—keepin' out o' sight all the time—is more'n I can understand. I thought I knowed everybody about these diggins, but that there voice didn't belong to none on 'em. It sounded like the voice of an oldish man, but the villain sartainly did skedaddle equal to any youngster ever I see. Did ye catch sight o' him, cap'n?"

"I saw no one but ourselves," returned Captain Raymond in a quiet tone.

The four had had the porch to themselves, the other boarders being out, the McAlpines at supper. But at this moment the gate opened and several gentlemen—Mr. Short and Mr. Austin among them—came in. Most of them had taken part in the hunt that day, one or two others were old hunters who were interested in the affair and desirous to talk it over with the captain and also to tell of past experiences of their own.

There were stories told of encounters with panthers, bears, deer, buffalos, and smaller game—all interesting, some amusing, some thrilling because of danger or death narrowly escaped.

One told by a very old man whose business had been hunting and trapping in the early days when great herds of buffalo roamed over the plains of the far West, was both thrilling and mirth provoking.

He said that on one occasion he had fallen in with a company of young army officers who were very desirous to shoot one buffalo or more. They must have a taste of the sport, however dangerous.

"And it is mighty dangerous," he went on, "mighty dangerous, as I told 'em. They're shy critters, them buffalo, but if you wound one and don't kill him, he's very apt to turn and charge head down, gore you with his big horns, toss you up, and when you come down again, stamp you to death with his heavy hoofs.

"But those young chaps wasn't to be sheared out o' the notion. Being soldiers, they was bound to show themselves afeared o' nothing, I s'pose. So I led 'em along the buffalo tracks to one o' the critters' drinkin' places, and, sure enough, we found a big herd gathered round it. They was to windward of us, but we'd hardly come up with 'em when by sight or scent some of 'em became aware of our vicinity, and off started the whole herd, we after 'em.

"One young officer—I furgit his name now—had a swifter horse than the others, and presently he got near enough the hindermost ones to send a bullet into a big bull. The critter was hurt purty bad, but not killed by a good bit, so round he wheels and charges after the feller that had hit him. He put spurs to his horse and it was a race fer life, now I tell you.

"And to make matters worse, somehow the man lost his balance, or the saddle turned, and there he was a-hangin' with one foot in the stirrup and clingin' to the horse's neck with his left arm, the pistol in his right hand, the buffalo comin' up on t'other side o' the horse, and it a runnin' like mad.

"Fer a bit it seemed the poor young chap would never come out o' that alive, but one o' his mates put another bullet into the buffalo so he staggered and fell dead just as it seemed there wasn't no escape for horse or man. And somehow the feller had got back into his saddle in another minute, the horse was still tearin' over the prairie at a thunderin' pace.

"So it all ended well, after all. He'd killed a buffalo—leastways he and the feller that fired the last shot into the critter—and 'scaped without no hurt worse'n a purty bad scare.

"But here comes the fun o' the thing. He told us he'd about give himself up fer lost when he found hisself hangin' by the stirrup and the horse's neck, and that mad buffalo bull after him, bellowing and pawin' up the ground and comin' on as if he'd a mind to gore and toss man and beast both, so he thinkin' there wasn't no earthly help for him, concluded he'd better fall to prayin', but whe he tried he couldn't fer the life o' him think of nothin' to say but the words his mother'd taught him when he was a leetle shaver, 'Now I lay me down to sleep,' and they didn't seem no ways appropriate to that particular occasion.

"No, I'm wrong thar. He did say that, finally, somethin' else come into his head, but it warn't much improvement on t'other. It was the fust words o' the blessin' his father was used to ask afore eatin'. 'Fer what we are about to receive make us truly thankful.'"

When the laugh that followed the old hunter's story had subsided, Mr. Austin remarked, "That goes to show the folly and danger of neglecting prayer on ordinary occasions—one is not prepared to employ it in emergencies."

"True as preachin', sir," replied the hunter. Then, rising, he bade goodnight, saying he was used to early hours and thought it likely the gentlemen who had been out that day would feel ready to go to bed.

At that the others followed his example and the captain and his children went to their own rooms.

"What a funny old man that Mr. Riggs is!" remarked Lulu, laughing at the remembrances of his talk that evening. "Papa, what did he mean when he said he was going to build a 'condition to his house with a portfolio at the back'?"

"An addition with a portico, I suppose."

"And he couldn't imagine who or where the fellow was that laughed at him. Max, you did that splendidly!"

"I did it?" exclaimed Max in astonishment so well feigned that for an instant she doubted the correctness of her surmise, though before it had almost amounted to a certainty.

But the next moment she laughed merrily, saying, "Oh, you needn't pretend innocence! I'm sure you were the naughty fellow. Didn't he do it so very well, papa?"

"Very, I thought," replied their father, regarding his son with a proudly affectionate smile.

"Papa, shall I call you dad?" asked Lulu merrily, taking possession of his knee and putting her arm round his neck.

"No, I shall think you very disrespectful if you do. You may say either papa or father, but I shall answer to no other titles from you — unless I should, some time when you have been very naughty, forbid you to call me anything but Captain Raymond."

"Oh, papa, dear, don't ever do that!" she pleaded, hugging him tight. "I think it would be a worse punishment than you have ever given me, for it would seem as if you were saying, 'You don't belong to me any longer. I won't have you for my own.'"

"No, my little darling," he returned, holding her close, "I shall never say that, Lulu, however ill you may behave."

"I do mean to be good—always obedient—and never in a passion again. But I can't be sure that I shall. It's sometimes so much easier to be naughty.'

"Yes, sad to relate, we all find it so," he sighed. "What a happy place heaven will be! For when we get there we shall have no more inclination to sin, but shall be always basking in the sunshine of God's love and favor."

"Yes, papa, being so happy when you are entirely pleased with me helps me to understand how happy we shall all be when we are with our heavenly Father and He smiles on us and has no fault to find with us. I like that Bible verse, 'Like as a father pitieth his children, so the Lord pitieth them that fear Him,' because I know you pity and love me when I'm in trouble, even when I've brought it on myself by being naughty."

"I do, indeed, my child, and God's love for His children is infinitely greater than that of any earthly father for his."

"It seems to me," Max remarked, "that if that officer the old hunter told about had been used to thinking of God as His kind, loving Father, and praying to Him, it would have been easy enough for him to ask for help when in such danger."

"I think you are quite right," his father said. "And now," opening the Bible, "we will read a portion of His word, then ask for His kind, protecting care while we sleep."

CHAPTER
EIGHTEENTH

Mr. Short took great interest in the planning and preparations for celebrating the fourth and was quite anxious that "the captain's young folks" should have their every wish in regard to them satisfied.

Also he thought it would be a fine thing to give them an agreeable surprise. He had a private consultation with Captain Raymond, and one result was that Max and Lulu were unexpectedly aroused from sleep at sunrise of the important day by the firing of cannon and ringing of all the church bells, while at the same moment a flag was flung to the breeze from every public building.

"Oh, it's the fourth, the glorious fourth!" cried Lulu, springing out of bed and running to her window. "It's a lovely day, too, and there are flags flying. Papa," she called, "is it too early for me to get up?"

"No," he answered, "not if you wish to. Max and I are going to rise now. You may close your door and dress yourself for the day."

She made haste with her dressing, arraying herself in white, which she considered the most suitable thing for the "glorious fourth," and adding one of her badges to her adornment.

Her father smiled approval when she came to him for the usual good morning kiss.

"My little girl looks sweet and pure in papa's partial eyes," he said.

"It's nice to have you look at me with those kind of eyes, you dear papa," she returned, giving him a vigorous hug and laughing merrily.

"I think it's with that kind of eye papa looks at all his children," remarked Max. "And I believe it is for our happiness and his, too."

"Very true, my son," rejoined the captain.

Lulu was full of pleasurable excitement. "Papa, do you know if all the things you have sent for have come?" she asked.

"I think it likely the last of them came in on the midnight train, which brings the express," he answered. "I will make inquiry after breakfast. Now try to forget those matters for a little, while we have our reading and prayer."

She sobered down at that and earnestly tried to give her thoughts to the teachings of the portion of Scripture her father read and to join with her heart in the prayer that followed.

That duty attended to, and the breakfast bell not having rung yet, they repaired to the front porch to wait for it.

There seemed an unusual stir in the town, people passing to and fro, early though it was—firecrackers going off here and there.

"You seemed to have stirred up the patriotism of the people here, Captain," Mr. Short said laughingly, as he came in at the gate and up the path to the porch steps. "Good morning, sir. Good morning, young folks. We are favored with as good weather as one could ask for, and your packages all arrived by last night's train, so that everything looks propitious for your celebration, so far. I had the things taken directly to the school house, and doubtless they will be unpacked in good season."

The captain said, "Thank you," and invited Mr. Short to walk in and take breakfast with them. The bell rang at the moment, and the invitation was promptly accepted.

"You are honoring the day, I see, Miss Lulu," remarked Mr. Short with a smiling glance at her attire.

"Oh, yes," she said, looking down at her badge. "I want everybody to know that I'm a patriotic American girl. I made this badge and a whole boxful beside for the school children to wear.

"Papa, mayn't I carry them to the schoolhouse myself after breakfast and help the teacher fasten them on?"

"You may go, and I'll go with you," he said. "If the children fancy wearing them, and the teacher will accept our services, we will do as you have proposed, daughter."

"I'll be bound the children won't object but will be delighted with the gift of the pretty bunch of ribbons, whether they have, or have not, any patriotism in their makeup," laughed Mr. Short.

"By the way, Captain, I met Riggs on the street as I came here, and he informed me that he would be present at the oration, reading of the Declaration, and so forth, and that he hopes the people would turn out 'copitiously.' He's rather original with his use of words."

"So I have discovered, Mr. Short," came the captain's quiet reply.

"Has he told you of his plans for improving his house?" asked Mr. Short with a humorous look.

"Yes, and how he obtained his wealth in spite of his entire lack of education."

"It was a lucky find, and he's one of the richest men in town. But if he had education he would get twice the satisfaction out of his wealth that he does as it is—at least, I think so."

"And I do not doubt that you are right," assented Captain Raymond.

"Well, Miss Lulu, how many pounds of firecrackers do you expect to set off today?" asked Mr. Short. "So patriotic a young lady will hardly be satisfied with less than two or three, I suppose."

"Indeed, sir, I do not expect to fire one," she returned merrily. "Papa has promised me something else in place of them. I don't know yet what it is, but as he says I will enjoy it more I'm quite sure I shall."

"Now, I shouldn't wonder if I could guess what it is," returned Mr. Short with a twinkle in his eye.

"Perhaps so, sir, but I don't want to be told till papa's time for telling me comes, or by anybody but him."

"Good girl, uncommonly loyal and obedient," he said laughingly.

"No, sir, you are mistaken in thinking me that," she said with heightened color. "I'm naturally very willful, so that papa has had any amount of trouble to teach me to obey."

"But the lesson has been pretty thoroughly learned," said her father kindly.

Mr. Short added, "I'm sure of it, and she is quite certainly honest and frank."

The school children were delighted with the badges, the teacher glad of Lulu's help in pinning them on, and of the gentlemen's assistance in forming her procession. All were on their best behavior, and everything went prosperously with the celebration.

The captain and his children, following in the wake of the procession, returned to the school-room to see and assist in the distribution of the candies, cakes, and fruits. The delight and gratitude of the recipients was a pretty and pleasant thing to behold.

By the time that was over, the Raymond's dinner hour had arrived, and they hastened back to their boarding house.

As they left the table, the captain caught an inquiring look from Lulu.

"Yes, child, you shall know now. You have waited very patiently," he said. "I am going to teach you how to handle a pistol and shoot at a mark."

"Oh, good, good!" she exclaimed, clapping her hands in delight. "I always did want to know how to shoot, but I didn't suppose you'd ever let me touch a pistol or gun, papa."

"I won't, except when I'm close beside you," he said. "At least, not for a long time to come. But I am going to teach you, because there may be a time in a woman's life when such knowledge and skill may be of great value to her."

"Max will take part, too, won't he?" she asked.

"Yes, certainly. It is even more important for him to know how to use firearms than for you. Mr. Short will join in the sport, too, and you may invite Marian to do so also, if you choose."

"Oh, thank you, papa! I will," she said, running back to the room they had just left, while her father went on to his.

Marian was clearing the table as Lulu came rushing in, half-breathless with haste and excitement.

"Oh, Marian," she said, "papa is going to teach me to use a pistol, to shoot at a mark, and he told me I might ask you if you would like to learn, too. Would you?"

"Thank you, yes. It's just what I've been longing to learn, for if the United States Government can't, or won't, protect me from the Mormons, I want to know how to protect myself," returned the girl, her eyes flashing. "Helpless women are their victims, but I don't mean to be a helpless one. I'll learn; if your father will teach me. Then I'll get a pistol of my own and use it, too, if I have occasion."

"Marian, what makes you so fierce at them?" asked Lulu in surprise. "Is it because they persuaded your father to be a Mormon and leave his own country?"

"Yes, and because they force women to marry against their will. They force them into sin, making them marry horrid creatures—calling themselves men, but not worthy of the name—that already have wives, sometimes a number of them.

"If a woman dares resist they say she is weakening the faith—supposing she is called a Mormon—and according to their wicked, fiendish, blood atonement doctrine she must be put to death. So they murder her in the name of religion.

"I know of one poor creature that ran away from her husband to escape that dreadful fate. He told her they thought she was weakening the faith and that he was to kill her. Every night he hung a dagger at the head of her bed, and he told her that some night she would hear a tap at the window at midnight and that would be a signal for him to stab her to death with the dagger.

"Now do you wonder I think it would be well for me to have a pistol and know how to use it?"

"No, indeed!" exclaimed Lulu. "I'm sure I should in your place. And I'm dreadfully ashamed that my government doesn't protect you so well that no one would dare do such things to you or to any woman or girl, or anybody. It's just awful! I shall tell papa about it and ask him if something can't be done. I think he'll find a way. And I can tell you, if he sets out to do a thing it's pretty sure to be done."

"You have great confidence in him," Marian returned with a sad sort of smile. "Ah, you're very fortunate, Miss Lu, to have such a father."

"Don't I know it?" replied Lulu exultantly. "Max and Gracie and I think he's just the best man and kindest father that ever lived. He knows all about firearms, too, and if anybody can teach us how to use them, he can."

"When do we take the lessons, Miss Lu?" inquired Marian.

"I suppose in a few minutes, but you can come just when you are ready. I must run back now and tell papa that you will join us."

She was full of what Marian had just told her of Mormon doings, and at once repeated it all to her father, winding up with, "Oh, papa, isn't it dreadful? Can't something be done to put a stop to such wicked, cruel doings? I do think it's a perfect disgrace that such deeds can be done in our country."

"And I quite agree with you," he sighed. "I am resolved to exert myself to the utmost to put a stop to the commission of such crimes in the name of false religion.

"Talk of the right of Mormon men to civil and religious liberty," he went on, rather thinking aloud than speaking to her, "what has become of the woman's right to the same, if they are to be permitted to murder her when she ceases to believe as they do, or to conform her conduct to the will of their hierarchy? Oh, it is monstrous, monstrous, that this thing called Mormonism has been allowed to grow to its present proportions!"

"Can't you put a stop to it, papa?" she asked.

"I, child? I put a stop to it?" he returned, smiling slightly with amusement. "You may well believe that if I had the power I would need no urging to exercise it."

"I'm sure I wish you had, papa," said Max. "But as you haven't, I'm afraid we may be obliged to fight one of these days to rid the country of that tyrannical Mormon hierarchy that is aiming to destroy our free institutions.

"So, Lu, you will do well to make the best of your opportunities to learn the use of firearms, for there is no knowing how much help men and boys may need from the women and girls if that tug-of-war comes," he added, suddenly dropping the serious tone in which he had begun and adopting a sportive one.

"You needn't make fun of us, Max," she retorted. "I'm sure women and girls have sometimes done good service in time of war."

"I willingly acknowledge it," he said. "History gives us a number of such instances. They have carried dispatches at the risk of their lives, concealed and befriended patriots when pursued by the enemy, taken care of the many sick and wounded soldiers, made many sacrifices for their country, and in some instances even put on men's attire and fought in the ranks. Perhaps that last is what you'd like to do," he wound up laughingly.

"No, I wouldn't," she said. "But I think I could and would do the others if there should be any need for me to."

"I believe it," her father said. "Because I know you are both courageous and patriotic. I will give you this when you have learned how to use it," he added, taking a small, silver-mounted pistol from his pocket and putting it into her hands. "It is not loaded, and you may examine it and learn all you can in that way, while we are waiting for Mr. Short to come. He will bring the target and set it up in the shade of those large trees down yonder by the river, where we can shoot at it without danger of a stray shot striking where it might harm anyone or anything."

Mr. Short came presently; the little party repaired to the designated spot; and the two girls took their first lesson in the use of the pistol.

At length they had all had enough of it, and putting up their empty pistols, they returned to the house.

They seated themselves on the shaded porch and had hardly done so when they were joined by Mr. Austin and Albert.

"I heard someone say you were target shooting," remarked Albert to Max. "And that the captain hit the center of the mark every time."

"So he did," said Max. "But shooting at a target is nothing to papa. He shoots birds on the wing. Indeed, I've seen him bring down several of a flock with one shot. He also throws up two potatoes and sends a bullet through them both before they can even hit the ground."

"I'd like very much to see him do that last," Albert said. "Though I don't in the least doubt your word—especially as all the men about here who have hunted with him say he's a capital shot."

At that Max turned to Sandy McAlpine, standing near, and asked if he could get him two potatoes.

"Cooked or raw?" asked the boy.

"Raw, of course," laughed Max. "And I'll hand them back when I'm done with them. I don't think they'll be hurt much for cooking and eating."

Sandy ran off around the house in the direction of the kitchen, and he was back again with the desired articles almost immediately.

"Papa," said Max, holding them up to view, "won't you load your pistol and show what you can do with it and these?"

"Yes, to please you, my boy," the captain replied, taking out and loading the little weapon of warfare that Lulu began already to look upon as her property. Then taking the offered potatoes, he threw them high in the air and fired. They came down each with a hole through it.

"Admirably done, Captain!" exclaimed Mr. Austin. "I am considered a very fair marksman at home, but I could not do that."

"There is nothing like trying, sir. And probably you excel me in many another thing," the captain said pleasantly, as he stepped onto the porch again and resumed his seat.

Then the gentlemen fell into discourse about the event commemorated by that day's celebration.

"Your Declaration of Independence handles King George the Third with much severity," remarked Mr. Austin, addressing Captain Raymond.

"Yes, sir, the truth is sometimes the severest thing that can be said," returned the captain, with a good-humored smile.

"You are right, sir," pursued the Englishman. "I cannot say that I altogether admire the character of that monarch, though he had some excellent traits, and in reading of the struggle of the colonies for freedom, my sympathies have always been with them.

"As you are no doubt aware, many of the English of that day sympathized with them and rejoiced over their success. Fox, Burke, and Chatham had kept the merits of their cause well before the public mind."

"For which we owe them a debt of gratitude," responded the captain. "As we do John Bright, also, for his outspoken sympathy with our federal government in its efforts to put down the rebellion—a time of sore trial to Union-loving Americans, a time 'when days were dark and friends were few,' and even such men as Gladstone and Guthrie showed themselves sympathizers with the would-be destroyers of our nation.

"It seemed passing strange to loyal Americans of that day that the English, who had for many years so constantly reproached our land for allowing the existence of Negro slavery within her borders, should, when the awful struggle was upon us, side with those whose aim and purpose it was to found an empire upon the perpetual bondage of millions of that race—their fellow-men. For, as the Bible tells us, God 'hath made of one blood all nations of men for to dwell on all the face of the earth.'"

"I acknowledge the inconsistency," returned Mr. Austin. "But do not forget that not all Englishmen were guilty of it. Mr. Bright, according to your own showing, was a notable exception, and there were many others.

"Nor is inconsistency a fault confined to Englishmen," he added with a slight mischievous smile. "The readers of your Declaration in the days when Negro slavery flourished in this country, must sometimes have felt uncomfortably conscious of the inconsistency of the two—the contradiction between creed and manner of life."

"No doubt," acknowledged Captain Raymond. "And thankful I am that the blot is removed from the scutcheon of my country."

"'Slaves cannot breathe in England!'" quoted Albert with pride and satisfaction.

"I think they were never deprived of that privilege in America," remarked Max soberly but with a mischievous twinkle in his eye.

"Ah, it is not meant in that sense, but Englishmen have never been guilty of holding men in bondage—in their own land, at least."

"Haven't they?" cried Max, pricking up his ears. "Why then did Alfred the Great make laws respecting the sale of slaves?"

"I had forgotten that for the moment," returned Albert, reddening. "But I was thinking only of Negro slavery."

"White slaves, they were to be sure," admitted Max in a slightly satirical tone. "But I can't see that it's any less cruel and wicked to enslave white men than black men."

"But those were very early times, when men were little better than savages."

"Alfred the Great among the rest?"

"Assuredly Alfred the Great was no savage," returned Albert, slightly nettled. "But then he was far ahead of his time, and I must still insist that you go very far back to fasten the reproach of slave-holding upon Great Britain."

The two fathers had paused in their discourse to listen to the talk of the lads, and they seemed to have forgotten the presence of their elders.

"Well, then, to come down to a later day," said Max, "don't you remember the statute made by Edward the Sixth, that if anybody lived idly for three days, or was a runaway, he should be taken before two justices of the peace, branded with a V with a hot iron on the chest, and given as a slave to the one who brought him for two years. And if during that time he absented himself for fourteen days he was to be branded again with a hot iron, on the cheek, with the letter S, and to be his master's slave forever! The master might put a ring of iron round his neck, leg, or arm, too, feed him poorly, and beat, chain, or otherwise abuse him.

"That white slavery in England was worse than Negro slavery was in the United States of America."

"Well, they who practiced it were the ancestors of the Americans as truly as of those of the present race of Englishmen, that have to bear the reproach of the slavery of the very early times you first spoke of," retorted Albert.

"Maybe so," said Max. "And I suppose they—the Americans—inherited their ancestors' wicked propensities—same as the Englishmen—which may account for their becoming slaveholders."

"Well," Albert said, "you can't deny that England has always been a foe to the slave trade, and—"

"Oh! Oh! Oh! How you forget!" exclaimed Max. "History says that she began in 1563 to import slaves from Africa into the West Indies. And the trade was not finally abolished till the spring of 1807. Also, that by the peace of Utrecht in 1713 England obtained a monopoly of the slave-trade and engaged to furnish Spanish America with one hundred forty-four thousand Negroes in thirty-three years, that a great slave-trading company was formed in England, and Queen Anne took one quarter of the stock, that the King of Spain took another quarter, so that the two sovereigns became the greatest slave-dealers in Christendom.

"That company brought slaves into the American colonies, and to some extent slavery was forced upon them by what they then called the mother country. Queen Anne directed New York colonial government to encourage the Royal African Company and see that the colony was furnished with plenty of merchantable Negroes at moderate rates.

"In the face of such facts, can you deny that England was largely responsible for the slavery that has proved such a curse to this country in years recently past?"

Alfred's countenance wore a discomfited expression, and instead of replying to Max's query, he turned to his father with the question, "Is he correct, sir, in the statements he has been making?"

"I am afraid he is," replied Mr. Austin. "Though some of his facts had slipped my memory till he brought them up. Europe has no right to twit America on the subject of slavery or the slave trade, especially now when Negro slavery no longer exists in any part of the Union."

"And our government abolished the act of slave trade in the same year that yours did," remarked Captain Raymond.

"Yes," acknowledged Mr. Austin. "But the act for the abolition of slavery throughout the British colonies was passed thirty years before Lincoln's Emancipation Proclamation set the last of the Negroes free in this country."

"True, but as a set-off against that, remember that the first Negroes brought to Massachusetts — the first in New England — were sent home at the public expense by the General Court of the colony.

"That was in 1640. In 1652, Roger Williams and Gorton made a decree against slavery in Rhode Island, while as late as 1672, white slaves were sold in England to be transported to Virginia."

"Not sold into perpetual slavery, however," said Mr. Austin.

"No, but for a term of years. Still, it cannot be denied that they were slaves for the time being.

"But I give England all credit for her persistent efforts to suppress the slave trade since she finally abolished it in 1807."

"By the way," said Mr. Austin, "I have been, since coming into this community, using every opportunity for studying the Mormon problem, and it strikes me as a strange thing that such a system of hierarchical tyranny and outrage has been so long permitted to exist and grow in this land of boasted freedom — civil and religious."

"It cannot seem stranger, or more inconsistent, to you than to me, sir," replied Captain Raymond, flushing with mortification. "I am exceedingly ashamed of this bar sinister on the scutcheon of my country. But I trust that vigorous measures are about to be taken for its expunging.

"Some have defended the let-alone policy on the ground that to restrain and punish them would be to abridge religious liberty, but I cannot see it so. We have, in fact, allowed a most tyrannical hierarchy to persecute even to putting to death, those who, having unfortunately fallen into its power, attempted an escape from it, or refused to submit to its dictation in regard to either belief or practice.

"Women have been forcibly detained among them — the self-styled "Latter-Day-Saints" — horribly ill-used, and when caught in an attempt to escape, foully murdered.

"The perpetrators and abettors of such deeds of darkness mistake liberty for license. Every man or woman has a right to life, liberty, and the pursuit of happiness — yet only so far as he does not interfere with the exercise of the same rights by others. The victims of Mormon tyranny and intolerance have most certainly a right to complain that they have been deprived of both civil and religious liberty."

"Very true," responded Mr. Austin. "And I have learned with mortification that the ranks of the Mormons are largely recruited from Great Britain."

"Yes, I wish your government were as anxious to keep that class of its citizens as its sailors, particularly its man-of-war's men — far off at sea," returned the captain laughingly.

A short discussion as to the comparative amount of freedom enjoyed by the citizens of the two countries and the comparative security of life and property followed, each gentleman maintaining that his own was the more favored land.

"Mormonism has for years destroyed in a great measure the personal liberty of the citizens of this part of your country where it flourishes," remarked Mr. Austin. "And certainly there is neither civil nor religious liberty to be enjoyed within the walls of the monasteries and convents scattered over the whole length and breadth of your land."

"That is true, only too true!" sighed the captain. "But, as regards monastic and conventual institutions, as true of your country as mine.

"Who can tell the suffering that may have to be endured by the hapless inmates of those prisons for innocent victims?

"Some will say they should not be interfered with, because the shutting up of men and women in that way is part of the Romish religion, and that the victims go into their confinement voluntarily. But it is certain that some do not do so voluntarily, and that others are wheedled in by false representations of the life to be led there.

"When they learn by experience what it really is, they often abhor it and long for the restoration of their freedom. But, alas, they find themselves in the hands of jailers, fastened in by bolts and bars and so forced to remain, no matter how unwillingly they are detained. Where for them is the liberty guaranteed by our Constitution to every citizen from the highest to the lowest?"

"It is a great wrong, both here and in Great Britain," Mr. Austin said. "One occasionally escapes and thrills the public mind for a time by her tale of the horrors of her prison. But they— her captors and tormentors—assert that she is insane, her tale the fabrication of an unsound mind, and presently it is all forgotten by the fickle populace, drowned out in thoughts of other more prominent matters.

"But what remedy would you propose? The abolition of monasteries and convents?"

"No, that would savor of interference with their religious liberty. But I would have them obliged to open their doors to the visits and inspection of the police at any and all times without previous warning. And the fact made certain that every grown person in the establishment was left entirely free to come and go at his or her pleasure. While that liberty is not secured to them, it cannot be said with truth that they are free citizens of a free country."

CHAPTER
NINETEENTH

THE LITTLE PARTY gathered on the porch again after tea and amused themselves with conversation while waiting till the setting of the sun and the fading away of the twilight should give a better opportunity for the display of the fireworks.

"I fancy," remarked Mr. Austin, "that our present sovereign is more appreciated in America than was her royal grandfather George the Third?"

"There is no comparison." replied Captain Raymond. "Americans highly appreciate your queen's kindly expressions of sympathy in the sad days of our poor Garfield's suffering, and she has many admirers among us."

Just then Mr. Riggs came up the path from the front gate, and greeting the company with a, "Good evenin', cap'n, Mr. Austin, and young folks," took a seat in their midst.

"Well, we've had a riglar old-time glorious Fourth," he went on, addressing no one in particular. "On'y 'tisn't done yit, thank fortin', an' I've come 'round to see them fireworks set off. The folks did turn out copitiously this mornin', and I don't mistrust that they won't do it agin tonight."

"Of course they will. Who wouldn't turn out to see fireworks?"

It was the squeaky voice again right behind his chair, as on the former occasion.

He sprang up as if he had been shot, faced about, and with a scared look asked, "Why, where is he — the old raskil?"

"Rascal, indeed! I'm no rascal, sir, but a patriotic, honest American citizen."

It was the squeaky voice again, and this time sounded a trifle farther off, as if the speaker might be descending the porch steps, but though distinctly heard, he could not be seen.

"Well, now, if it isn't the beatenest thing! I do wonder ef I'm a-gittin' crazy!" exclaimed Riggs, staring wildly round from side to side. "You all heered him, didn't ye? But has anybody seen the raskilly feller?"

The Austins and Mr. Short were dumbstruck with astonishment. The Raymonds did not speak either, but the next moment a loud, "Ha, ha, ha!" coming apparently from among the branches of the nearest tree was followed by the squeaky voice. "You can't see me? That's only because you don't look in the right place. I'm big enough to be seen by the naked eye, even at a considerable distance."

"But ye'r always playing at hide and seek," said Riggs. "And a body can't never find ye."

"Why, who is he? And where is he?" queried Albert, staring up into the tree. "His voice seems to come from among those branches, but I see nothing there."

"It is growing dark, Albert," remarked Captain Raymond in reply.

"Yes, sir, but still I could see a man or boy if he were really there."

"Come up on the porch roof, all of you," called the voice, now seeming to come from there. "It'll be the best place to see the fireworks from."

"It is time to begin setting them off, isn't it, papa?" asked Lulu.

"Yes," he said, and Max, springing down the steps and the walk to the gate had sent up a sky-rocket in another minute. As it darted skyward, the same squeaky voice cried out from the upper air, "Up I go!"

"There, did you hear that?" screamed Riggs. "He's gone up with the rocket. He must certanly be a wizard."

"Ha! There is certainly a ventriloquist among us!" exclaimed Mr. Austin.

"I agree with you," said the captain. "It is the only rational explanation of the phenomenon."

"And is it you, sir?"

"No, sir, if I have any talent in that line it remains to be discovered by myself even."

And without waiting for further embarrassing questions, the captain hurried to Max's assistance.

Mr. Short did likewise, and for the next hour or more the display of the fireworks absorbed the attention of everyone present, almost to the exclusion of thoughts on other matters.

It was quite a fine display—for the captain had been generous in his outlay for the celebration of the fourth, and many were the expressions of delight and admiration from the crowd of spectators who had gathered to witness it.

There were rockets, squibs, Roman candles, Bengal lights, Catherine wheels, and others of more complicated structure, some of which sent out figures of men and animals.

One of these Max reserved for last, and as the tiny figure of a man issued from the brilliant coruscation and darted upward, it cried out in the squeaky voice that had troubled Mr. Riggs so often, "Good-bye, I'm off!"

"There the feller is at last. I seen him this time," screamed the old man. "Now did ye ever? How did he git in there? And how did he git out?"

The faces of the crowd were full of surprise and perplexity as they first gazed upward, then turned toward each other in half-breathless astonishment.

"There is a ventriloquist among us," repeated Mr. Austin. "There must be without doubt."

"Ven—ven—what is it anyway?" asked Riggs.

"Ventriloquist. One who can speak without moving his lips and cause his voice to seem to come from somewhere outside of himself—from some person or animal, or place near at hand or farther off."

"You don't say. I never heered o' sech doins!" exclaimed Riggs, while several others standing near cried out, "A ventriloquist. Is there one here? If there is, let him give us some more of his tricks. We'd like no better fun."

"Just you keep quiet then, all of you, and perhaps he will," said Mr. Short, who, though he knew absolutely nothing in regard to the matter began to have strong suspicions that Captain Raymond could tell all about it if he would.

A short, sharp bark, that seemed to come from the coat pocket of the speaker, made him start involuntarily and thrust his hand deep into it.

He drew it out with a laugh. "Nothing there, as I might have known," he said.

But the words were hardly out of his mouth when a loud, furious barking, growling, and snarling began in the midst of the crowd, causing them to scatter pell-mell to the sidewalks—women and children screaming, men and boys shouting, bursts of laughter following, as they perceived that the cause of the fright was but another trick of the ventriloquist.

"Who is he? Who is he?" was the question bandied from one to another, but it was answered by no one.

"Hoo, hoo, hoo!" came from amid the branches of a tree in Mrs. McAlpine's yard.

It sounded like the cry of an owl, but it was soon followed by a human voice, "Goodnight, friends. We have had a glorious Fourth, and it is time to go home and to bed."

"That means the show is done for tonight, I s'pose," remarked Riggs. "And we may as well git fer home. But I just wisht I could find out who the feller is," he mumbled to himself, as he moved down the street.

The crowd dispersed, and the Raymonds retired to their own apartments.

"Oh, Max, how good it is that nobody's found you out yet!" laughed Lulu gleefully.

"I'm glad they haven't," returned Max. "Papa, did I do anything objectionable?"

"I have no fault to find with you, my boy," his father replied with a slight smile and a very affectionate look at his son.

❦❦❦❦❦❦

CHAPTER TWENTIETH

CAPTAIN RAYMOND and his children lingered some time longer in Minersville.

It was near the middle of July, and his traveling arrangements had been made for starting upon their homeward journey in a day or two, when early one morning he, Max, Mr. Short, and the Austins set out upon their final hunt together.

Lulu was, of course, left behind in the boarding house again.

As her father kissed her good-bye, he said, "I am very sorry to leave you alone, dear child, but I trust that you will be able to pass the time agreeably in reading, sewing, or letter writing—whatever employment you fancy that can be attended to at the house—for I want you to stay within doors. The day is a very warm one, and I much prefer that you should not be exposed to the heat of the sun.

"I hope to be back in season to take you for a walk or ride in the cool of the evening."

"I shall like that, if you don't come home too tired, papa," she replied, clinging about his neck for a moment. "Oh, do take care of yourself, and don't be a bit troubled lest I should be lonesome. I shall do nicely and be so glad to see you when you come back."

She followed him out to the porch with a book in her hand, and after seeing the hunting party quickly disappear down the street, took a seat in a comfortable armchair in the shade of the vines and amused herself with reading until joined by Marian with a basket of mending.

"There!" exclaimed Lulu, closing her book. "I have some stockings to darn. I'll go and get them and my workbasket, and we'll have a nice time together, Marian."

"I'd like that very much," Marian said. "But don't let me hinder you from reading your book."

"I'd rather stop reading and talk awhile. I'm remarkably fond of talking," laughed Lulu, as she hurried into the house.

She was back again almost immediately, and as she resumed her seat, Marian said, "I was glad to hear you say you were fond of talking, because I wish very much you would tell me about your home and your brothers and sisters—if you have any beside the one that is here."

Lulu willingly complied with quite a glowing description of Woodburn, Mamma Vi, Gracie, and the babies, ending with a fond description of the happy life led there by the whole family.

Marian listened with a deep interest, tears sometimes starting to her eyes as she was struck by the contrast between that life and her own—most of all in the tender fatherly love and care in which the Woodburn children rejoiced, that which had been so sadly lacking in her experience since the blighting curse of Mormonism had fallen upon the McAlpine household.

Lulu noticed her emotion, guessed at the cause, and made an effort to divert the poor girl's thoughts from the sorrows of her lot, telling very amusing anecdotes of little Elsie's sayings and doings.

"Of course," she said, "Mamma Vi began as soon as Elsie was able to talk to teach her to say the little prayer, 'Now I lay me.' She soon said it nicely, but whenever she came to the part, 'If I should die,' she would put in, 'but I won't die!'

"Not long ago Mamma Vi told her she thought she was old enough now to learn the Lord's Prayer. 'It is a good deal longer than the other,' she said. 'Do you think you can remember it?' 'Yes'm,' Elsie said. 'I'll set it down.'

"Then Mamma Vi began teaching it to her, but she has never succeeded in getting her to say it all right yet, for she always will ask for daily corn bread. We have corn bread on the table at least once every day, and Elsie likes it much better than wheat.

"She often says things that make us all laugh. Once Mamma Vi had just finished a very pretty dress for the little darling and put it on her for the first time. Then she took her to Grandma Elsie, who was visiting us, to ask what she thought of it.

"'See, gamma,' little Elsie said, walking up to her.

"Grandma Elsie said, 'Ah! Just from Paris?' and little Elsie nodded her head, saying, 'Yes'm, gamma, just from parasol.'"

"She must be a dear, amusing little thing," said Marian. "Is she pretty?"

"She is a beauty!" replied Lulu with enthusiasm.

"Ah, now here comes Edith Kingsley!" Marian exclaimed, as the gate opened and a girl a year or two younger than herself, a neighbor and intimate friend of hers, came tripping up the path.

Lulu had met Edith several times and liked her, for she was a pleasant, sunny-tempered child— innocent and artless.

"Good morning, girls," she said. "I just ran over for a minute to tell you that a party of us are going berrying this afternoon and to ask you both to go along."

"I'd like to if mother can spare me," said Marian. "But isn't it very warm?"

"Not so warm as it was," replied Edith. "There are floating clouds now, so that the sun doesn't shine so hot, and a nice breeze has sprung up. You'll go, won't you, Lulu?" turning to the latter.

"Thank you. I feel a strong inclination to go, but I can't, as papa is not here to give me leave."

"Oh, I'm sure he'd say you might go," returned Edith with eager entreaty in her tones. "The place we are going to is only a little beyond the edge of town, and the berries are so thick we shall fill our baskets directly and be back long, long before dark. So what objection could he find?"

"He said he wanted me to stay in the house till he came back," replied Lulu. "He didn't want me exposed to the heat of the sun, and he hoped to be back in time to take me for a walk or ride in the cool of the evening."

"Oh, if that was all, I'm sure he would say you could go, because the sun isn't hot any longer. And he didn't positively forbid you, did he?"

"No," Lulu said slowly, as if striving to recall his exact words. "He only said he wanted me to stay within doors and gave that reason for it. But I'm pretty sure if he were here he would give me permission to go."

"Then you will, won't you?"

Lulu considered a moment. The temptation to yield was very strong, but the more she reflected, the deeper her conviction that to do so would be disobedience—disobedience to the kindest, dearest, most indulgent of fathers, one who never denied her any pleasure that he deemed good for her.

"Come now, do say you will," urged Edith, coaxingly. "Even if your father should be a little vexed at first, he will soon forgive you."

"Perhaps so, but it would be long time before I could forgive myself," Lulu said, and then she added firmly, "No, Edith, I thank you very much for the invitation, but I can't go. I am quite sure it would be disobedience, and how could I be so ungrateful as to so grieve such a father as mine? I couldn't bear to see the sorry look that would come into his eyes when he heard of it."

"Oh, we won't tell on you," Edith said laughingly.

Lulu looked indignant at that. "I should tell on myself," she said. "I could never be happy while concealing anything from papa."

Marian had left them to consult with her mother in regard to her own acceptance of the invitation, and now she came back to report a favorable reply. She was much disappointed to hear that Lulu would not go and joined her entreaties to Edith's that she would reconsider and accept.

But Lulu was firm, both then and later, when, ready to start on their little expedition, they again urged her to accompany them.

"I think we'll have a nice time," Edith said. "It's just a pleasant walk, winding about a little way among the hills, and there are lovely wild flowers to gather as well as berries. Oh, do change your mind and come along with us!"

"I do wish you would, Lulu," put in Marian. "I shan't half enjoy myself without you, thinking how lonely you'll be here by yourself."

"Please don't urge me any more," returned Lulu. "I think you wouldn't if you knew how very much I'd like to go with you if I could have papa's permission. But I know I couldn't enjoy myself going without that. My conscience wouldn't give me any peace at all."

So they left her. She sat on the porch watching them go out of sight, then opened her book, and presently forgot her disappointment in the interest of the story.

She read on and on, taking no note of the lapse of time, though two full hours had passed since the berry gatherers disappeared round the corner. Suddenly she became conscious that some unusual excitement was abroad in the streets of the town. Men armed with muskets, revolvers, and other weapons were rushing past in the direction the girls had taken. Women and children were running hither and thither, calling wildly to each other, some crying, all seeming full of anxiety and fright.

"Oh, what is it? What's the matter, Sandy?" asked Lulu, dropping her book and springing to her feet, as the lad came tearing in at the gate—his face white with terror and distress.

"A bear!" he gasped. "A big grizzly got after the girls, and they all had to run for their lives, and he—he caught Edith—they say, and—and he's hugging her to death."

"Oh! Oh!" cried Lulu, bursting into tears and sobs. "Can't anybody save her? Oh, I wish papa was there with his gun to shoot the bear. He'd do it, I know he would. And, oh, where's Marian?"

"She's safe now. They all got away from the beast but Edith. But Marian was so out of breath with fright and running and crying because she couldn't save Edith, that she had to stop farther down the street."

Mrs. McAlpine had heard enough of the bustle in the streets to alarm her, and now she came hurrying out, asking, "What's happened, Sandy? Where's your sister?"

The boy repeated his story and had scarce finished it when Marian came in at the gate, her form drooping, her head bowed, sobs shaking her whole frame.

"Have they got her?" asked Sandy.

"Marian, my poor child, is Edith much hurt?" questioned her mother, drawing the weeping girl into the house.

Marian did not lift her head. She seemed unable to speak.

But Hugh came running in from the street, tears rolling down his cheeks. "Oh, oh, Edith's killed! She's dead! I heard a man say so. They've killed the bear, but he'd already squeezed Edith to death and tore her awful with his big claws and teeth."

"Oh, don't! Don't! Don't tell it!" shrieked Marian, covering her ears with her hands. "Oh, if we only hadn't gone there!"

"Her poor mother. Her poor, poor mother! How will she ever bear it?" sobbed Mrs. McAlpine, dropping into a chair and hiding her face with her apron.

Lulu, too, was weeping bitterly.

"What have they done with her, Hugh?" asked Sandy in a loud whisper.

"Who? Edith or the bear?"

"Edith, I meant, of course, stupid," returned the elder brother contemptuously.

"They're going to bring her home. I guess they're doing it now," as a sound as of the trampling of many feet smote upon their ears.

The body was being carried past on a hastily improvised litter, and in another moment, as it crossed the threshold of the home she had left two hours before in the heyday of life and health, a woman's wail of heart breaking anguish rent the air.

"It's her mother. Her poor mother!" sobbed Mrs. McAlpine. "Wae's me for the puir heart broken thing! But oh, thank God my lassie has come safe home to me!"

Marian burst into wild weeping, and Lulu, unable to bear any more, ran swiftly from the room to that of her father, where falling on her knees by the bedside, she buried her face in the clothes and cried as if her heart would break.

She seemed to see Edith standing before her, bright and beautiful, full of life and health, as she had seen her — oh, such a little while ago! — then in the cruel embrace of the ferocious wild beast, crushed, bitten, torn, bleeding, and dying — dead. Then the poor body, at last rescued from the clutches of the bear, but with no life left in it, carried along the highroad on its rude litter, borne into the house over the way — the happy home of the morning now darkened and made desolate by that sudden, fearful stroke of doom — the mother, bereaved in a manner so fearful of her only child, bending over it in an agony of woe unutterable.

"I might have been the one the bear attacked if I had gone with them, papa mourning over his dead daughter, his heart breaking with the thought that she'd been killed in the very act of disobeying him," thought Lulu. "I can never, never be thankful enough that I didn't do it, and that God helped me resist the temptation."

A hand rested lightly, tenderly on her head, and she started up to find her father standing by her side.

She threw herself into his arms, and as he folded her close to his heart, hid her face on his shoulder, sobbing convulsively. "Oh, papa, it is so, so very dreadful! So terrible!"

"Yes," he said in tone tremulous with emotion. "My heart aches for the bereaved parents. Oh, thank the Lord that I have my darling safe in my arms!" he said, caressing her with exceeding tenderness as he sat down, still holding her fast as a treasure he would suffer no earthly power to snatch from his grasp. "You were not with them?"

"No, papa. You bade me stay within doors—at least, you said you wanted me to—and how could I disobey such a dear, kind father? Oh, I couldn't, though I wanted to go very badly! And if I had—oh, I might have been the one to be killed in that dreadful way!"

"And your own father the broken-hearted parent weeping over his lost treasure. My dear child, I think you will never regret resisting the temptation to disobey the father who loves you as his life."

"Oh, no, I'm sure I shall not! Papa, what a good thing for me that you have trained me to obedience, for otherwise I should have gone with them, and I might have been killed—killed in that horrible way! You didn't say I must stay in the house—only that you wanted me to—but I suppose it would have been disobedience if I'd gone, wouldn't it?"

"Yes, a truly obedient child will not go against the known wishes of a parent. I trusted my daughter loved me enough to obey my slightest wish, so I did not think it necessary to put my injunction in the form of a command. We all prefer to be requested rather than ordered."

"But I have really learned to love even to be ordered by you, my own, own dearest father!" she said, creeping closer in his embrace.

"Had I been quite sure of that it would have saved me some moments of great alarm and anxiety," he said quietly.

She looked up inquiringly, and he went on. "As our party came into town on the side opposite to that where the dreadful accident occurred, a man hailed us with the news that some little girl, out gathering berries, had been attacked by a bear — one of them killed and others badly hurt.

"That last was a mistake, as we presently learned, but, oh, the pang that shot through my heart with the sudden fear that my dear little daughter might be among the injured, perhaps even the slain one. How I wished that I had positively forbidden you to leave the house at all in my absence!"

"But even then you couldn't have been sure that I wasn't with those girls, because there have been times when I've disobeyed your most positive commands," she said, in a remorseful tone.

Her heart leaped with joy at his answering words. "But you have been so perfectly obedient for a long time now, that I have come to have great confidence in your careful observance of any order from me to do or not to do."

Max, who had been lingering in the street trying to learn the particulars of the sad occurrence, which was the absorbing subject of thought and speech with every one for the time being, now came quietly in, looking thoughtful and distressed.

"They say she's terribly crushed and mangled," he said chokingly. "Oh, Lu, what a fright papa and I had, thinking it might be you!"

"But I could have been spared much better than poor Edith," she said. "She was an only child, and papa would have four still left if he lost only me."

"I should not know how to spare you or any one of my darlings," responded her father in moved tones, smoothing her hair with tender, caressing hand and kissing her on cheek and lip and brow.

"I'm glad we're almost ready to go away from here," remarked Max. "We've been having a merry, happy time, but it will seem sad after this."

"When do we go, papa?" asked Lulu.

"I have set day after tomorrow," he answered. "But while we are here, let us strive to sympathize in the grief and suffering of those so sorely bereaved than to be thinking of ourselves and our own enjoyment. The Bible bids us weep with those that weep, as well as to rejoice with those that do rejoice!"

The captain earnestly strove to carry out that teaching, and nothing was omitted or neglected that he could do to show his sympathy with Edith's heart-broken parents, or with Marian, who grieved sorely over the loss of her friend—snatched from her in so sad a manner—and the news that Lulu, to whom she had become warmly attached, was soon to leave Minersville, probably never to return.

Lulu had been seized with a longing for the dear ones at home—especially Gracie—and expected to feel only joy in turning her back upon the little western town in which she had sojourned so pleasantly for the past four weeks, but, when the time came, found she was a sharer to extent in the grief at parting that set Marian to weeping bitterly.

"Don't cry, Marian," Lulu said with emotion. "I didn't think you cared so much for me."

"Oh, I love you almost as if you were my sister!" sobbed Marian. "It nearly breaks my heart to think I shall never, never see you again."

"But perhaps you may. Isn't it possible, papa?" Lulu turned inquiringly to her father.

"Yes," he said. "I may be visiting my property here again one of these days, and in that case will be very likely to bring my eldest daughter along.

"And Marian, my good girl, if ever you should be in need of a friend, remember that Captain Raymond will be glad to do you any kindness in his power."

Marian and her mother both thanked him with earnest gratitude. Both felt that the day might not be far distant when they would stand in sore need of his friendly offices, and with the knowledge they had gained of his character in the last few weeks of daily exchanges, they could not doubt the sincerity of his offer.

The train that was to carry the Raymonds on their eastward journey was nearly due. The rest of the good-byes were hastily said, and in a few moments they were seated in the cars and speeding onward.

It was a beautiful summer morning, and the spirits of the children soon rose to such a height that they must find vent in chatter and laughter.

"Papa," exclaimed Lulu, "you actually haven't told us where we are going next!"

"To the seashore at the end of this journey."

"But that's very indefinite, for the seashore of our country is a long, long strip," she said laughingly.

"So it is, but can't you trust me to take you to a pleasant part of it?"

"Oh, yes, sir. Yes, indeed! And I'm always glad to go anywhere with you," resting her cheek affectionately against his shoulder and squeezing his hand in both of hers.

"We are perfectly willing to wait for the information till you are ready to give it, sir," added Max.

"Good children," the captain said, smiling approvingly upon them. "I had thought of giving you a surprise, but I have no objection to telling you now that we have taken again the cottages we occupied the first summer after my marriage to your Mamma Vi, and that she and Gracie and the babies—the Ion and Fairview people, too—are already there waiting for us to join them. Are you satisfied with the arrangements, my dears?"

"I am perfectly, papa," Max replied.

"And I, too," said Lulu. "Oh, I do think it will be pleasant to spend a while there again! And I hope I'll be a great deal better child to you than I was before, dear papa," she whispered in his ear, her arm about his neck.

"Dear child!" was all he said in reply, but the accompanying look and smile spoke volumes of fatherly love and confidence.

The End